"Poor child," Shirley murmured. "Poor desperate, unhappy child. Do you suppose she saw something . . . something she wasn't supposed to see? Heard something? Or . . . stole something?"

"Possible, I suppose."

"What's Xanthy doing?"

"She called April's grandmother. Grandmother evidently had some way to reach her daughter, April's mother, because she gave Xanthy an overseas number. At any rate, mother and father are flying in. I'm not sure when."

"I wonder," said Shirley, feeling the familiar soft darkness welling up around her once again. "I wonder."

"What do you wonder, old love?"

"I wonder if they'll care."

Also by B.J. Oliphant
Published by Fawcett Books:

DEAD IN THE SCRUB
THE UNEXPECTED CORPSE
DESERVEDLY DEAD

DEATH AND THE DELINQUENT

B.J. Oliphant

FAWCETT GOLD MEDAL • NEW YORK

A Fawcett Gold Medal Book
Published by Ballantine Books
Copyright © 1992 by B.J. Oliphant

All rights reserved under International and Pan-American Copyright Conventions. Published in the United States by Ballantine Books, a division of Random House, Inc., New York, and simultaneously in Canada by Random House of Canada Limited, Toronto.

Library of Congress Catalog Card Number: 92-97063

ISBN 0-449-14718-5

Manufactured in the United States of America

First Edition: February 1993

Author's Note

New Mexico is wonderfully and surprisingly real, from its marvelous scenery to its multicultural settlements, all included in what is aptly called the land of enchantment.

Enchantment notwithstanding, the persons and events in this book are fictional, as is El Rancho del Valle, the San Pedro Pueblo, and the town of Los Arboles, all of which lie a short, though imaginary, distance north of Santa Fe.

1

THE MORNING SOUNDS were not home sounds. A strange voice called out words she didn't understand, and another stranger answered. A peacock screamed its primordial question, "Where? Where?" or perhaps, "Here! Here!" Unfamiliar leaves applauded outside an open window, which was on the wrong wall to be Shirley McClintock's own window, all these sounds overlying a persistent, chuckling *baa* that could only be sheep. Altogether an exotic euphony—where, for the moment, undefined.

If she focused on where she was, she would wake up. If she woke up, she'd hurt, and that would make her angry. She didn't want either the pain or the anger; she'd had enough of both! It was clear she wasn't at home in Colorado; why not just accept she was somewhere else and let the rest go?

Because, despite the foreign sounds, the smell . . . the smell was definitely coffee.

She opened one eye far enough to see her foster daughter,

Allison, standing silently beside the bed, holding a steaming mug almost under Shirley's nose.

"What a good idea!" Shirley yawned, heaving herself against the headboard while her sore, stiff muscles protested violently. Well, she'd expected as much, and a hot shower would no doubt help. "To what do I owe all this attention?"

Allison made a little moue, pushing back her dark hair with her free hand. She'd been wearing it in braids during most of the trip; now it flowed free in a charming early morning tousle. At least so Shirley thought, being fondly charmed by Allison in most of her configurations.

Allison held out the cup. "It's for being nice and not yelling about Ape."

Shirley accepted the offering and stared through the window at the Sunday morning she'd been hearing for the past half hour. They were in New Mexico, at El Rancho del Valle, in a guest house Allison, J.Q., and she were sharing. Until yesterday, she'd shared it with Allison, Xanthippe Minging, and several other twelve- and thirteen-year-old girls— including Allison's quasi friend, April Shaour. And while it was true that Shirley wanted badly to yell about April, it was extremely unlikely that yelling would help. In fact, short of murder, Shirley had been unable to think of anything that would help. April was as April was: an adolescent elemental, a basically disruptive force.

"Why would I yell at *you* about Ape?" she asked.

Allison plumped herself down on the foot of the bed. "Because I asked you to let her come with us on the rest of our vacation. If I hadn't asked, she'd have gone home with the other kids instead of staying here and falling down a cliff and breaking her arm."

Shirley made a face. Hindsight was twenty-twenty, as usual. Yesterday, however, neither she nor J.Q. nor Xanthippe Minging had had the least compunction about leaving Allison and April ensconced by the guest ranch swimming pool while they drove the other five young people to Española to catch the bus home. The total trip, including a brief stop for groceries, had taken only slightly over an hour, and when they returned, Allison was still reading by the pool. Ape, however, had vanished. Not a word. Not a note.

"I thought she'd gone to the toilet," Allison had cried. "She didn't say anything!"

All Allison could come up with was an insubstantial memory of Ape's having said something a few days before about wanting to explore Blue Mesa. Shirley needed no mental review of the subsequent panic, the lengthy search, and the eventual rescue. The protesting muscles in her thighs and arms were sufficient reminders.

Now she shook her head and reached out to pat Allison's hand. "Allison, I never for a moment thought of you as being responsible for her."

"I thought I was, sort of," said Allison, flushing. "I thought she'd do things for me."

Shirley drank deeply before setting the cup on the bedside table and rearranging her pillows to make a more comfortable support. "Things like what?"

"Like, you know, keeping her word. And listening to people." The girl drummed her heels against the box spring. "I don't know what to do, Shirley. All the other kids at school leave her out. She said she really wanted me to be her friend. I thought she meant it. And I know how that feels, you know? Not having any friends."

Shirley felt a wave of sympathy. Allison had had her own hard times, and she wasn't the kind of person who would forget how it felt.

Allison went on: "That time we went into Columbine together, to the movie, you remember?"

Shirley remembered.

"Afterward, we went to the pet shop, so I could get some fish food. Well, she stole some stuff."

"Shoplifted?" Shirley felt her eyebrows soaring and pulled them downward into a worried frown.

3

"I guess. It wasn't even stuff she could use! And then she showed it to me, kind of showing off, and she told me she got kicked out of a school in Boston for stealing. I got really mad, and I told her friends don't get each other into trouble. So she *promised* me she wouldn't get me into trouble. That's why I asked if she could come along, because she'd promised. So then last night when I asked her why she went off like that, she said she didn't get *me* in trouble, because it wasn't me who told her to stay put."

"Wasn't I," corrected Shirley.

"It wasn't I. She called me names. She said I act like a wus. She said I'm a baby. She teased me about that boy who's staying here, and all I ever did was be polite to him!"

Shirley sipped thoughtfully. "If you want my honest opinion, Allison, I don't think anything you can say or do will outweigh thirteen years of whatever April's got festering. From what Xanthippe Minging says, it's a strange situation."

Allison brooded over this. "Her mom is American, but her dad is Arab or something, and he's all the time going back to his country on business or to see his family and stuff, and they're always fighting about Ape. His mother, Ape's grandmother, back in wherever, doesn't approve of Ape's clothes or how she acts, anything! And her mother, Ape's other grandmother, thinks Ape's dad is . . . like, you know, a foreigner, like—how do you say somebody that's the wrong religion?"

"A heretic?" Shirley offered. "A pagan? An apostate, nonbeliever, heathen?"

"I don't know. One of those, I guess. Anyhow, her folks go off and leave her with the housekeeper, and she's some kind of cousin of her father's. And her parents whisper about stuff all the time, and they don't tell her anything. She says the only way she can find out what's going on is by listening on the phone and opening their mail. And the only time they pay any attention to her is when she's in trouble."

4

"And she doesn't have any friends," said Shirley, both worried and angered by all this.

"Not any," Allison agreed. "It's hard to be her friend. I don't even like her all that much, Shirley. It's just . . . you know. I feel sorry for her."

"I know the feeling!"

"Anyhow, if you decide not to take her with us, I'd be just as glad. That's the other reason I brought your coffee, because I just want you to know that." Allison wiped angrily at her eyes. "When Ms. Minging took Ape over to the other house last night, we weren't speaking."

"Bummer," Shirley offered sympathetically. "Aside from that, Mrs. Lincoln, how've you been enjoying your vacation?"

Allison assayed a tremulous smile. "Aside from that, it's been okay, but I'd have learned a lot more if I'd been with the other kids instead of with Ape." She sighed deeply. "I mean, that's what coming to New Mexico was all supposed to be about, wasn't it? Learning more Spanish?"

"That was the ostensible idea." Shirley picked up her cup again and sipped at the cooling liquid. That had been the idea. Two weeks in New Mexico for those students at Crepmier School who had worked hard at their Spanish lessons and acquired some fluency in the language. Xanthippe Minging was along as teacher and in loco parentis; Shirley and J.Q., for reasons of their own, had consented to join the group as drivers-cum-chaperones-cum-tour guides, with the intention of stretching the two weeks into four for themselves and Allison. Plus April, who was not a superior student and had only been included in the first place because her mother had pleaded with Xanthippe Minging to take her along. Poor April, who would otherwise have been at home, alone and friendless, instead of being here, mostly alone and friendless!

Shirley drew herself up, resolving not to let the matter ruin the day. "Let's do something fun. Pack a lunch and go riding. We don't need to make any long-term decisions today."

"What shall I tell her? About, you know?"

"If April asks, tell her that nothing is being decided today."

"She'll nag at me."

"Not unless she can get you off alone. So just stay with us. We'll all stick together."

Sticking together was not something April Shaour much enjoyed. When Shirley came into the kitchen, the girl was huddled over the cast on her arm, her face in its usual scowl, while J.Q. and Xanthippe Minging busied themselves preparing breakfast. J.Q. always fixed sausages on Sunday.

"Does anyone have any objection to our going riding this morning if I can arrange it?" Shirley asked, leaning in the doorway and avoiding April's baleful glare. Poor kid. She was a wiry little thing with an unruly mop of curly dark hair, a pale but freckled face with a tilted nose and wide, surprisingly pretty hazel eyes. She could be attractive if it weren't for her habitually ugly expression.

"Sounds fine to me," J.Q. muttered around his pipe stem. "You, Xanthy?"

"A good idea." Xanthippe nodded, busily chopping onions and peppers for an omelet.

April merely glared. Shirley ignored it as she left the small house, letting the screen door bang shut behind her. A low wall separated this casita from the graveled parking area around which the main house, the various other casitas, and the outbuildings were gathered. She went through the wide gate and took several strides toward the main house . . . where something stopped her.

She stood for a long moment, immobile, not thinking of anything at all, not even aware of herself, while the world flickered and danced around her. What had stopped her was a sound, softly floating on the gusty little wind, coming in fits and starts, now clear, now indistinct, a shattered but unmistakable evocation of long-ago times. Upwind somewhere a church bell was ringing, a whisper of bellness, an essence of Sunday morning that went through her mental clutter and pain like a runnel of swift water, dissolving everything in its path. All the recent aggravations and irritations melted, puddling away to nothing. What was left behind was only a clean emptiness, one of those rare and unpredictable moments of complete clarity. No trouble. No worry. Just here, now, whatever was at this moment.

She had become so focused on the sound, she hadn't realized her eyes were shut. She opened them to see enormous cottonwoods stretching a tent of sparkling leaves between her and the already burning sky. Before her, along the wall that separated the parking area from the patio of the sprawling main house, day lilies bloomed in painterly splotches of scarlet and gold and pale lemon yellow. Peacocks strutted across the gravel, dragging their brilliant tails behind them. Peahens and guinea hens wandered here and there, feasting on grasshoppers and flower buds alike, raising their crowned or cowled heads to peer at Shirley's hands, gargling questioningly as they decided she carried nothing edible.

Before her, between two walls, she could see across a mile of pinkish desert to the shadowed bulk of Blue Mesa. To her right, down the slope toward the river, Vincente and Alberta Lucero, resident maintenanceman and housekeeper, walked arm in arm, two brightly clad figures followed by a variegated flock of tiny sheep whose voices rose as counterpoint to the church bell.

She didn't want to move. Moving might break the surcease of the moment. Nonetheless—one could not stand like a statue all day, lost in bemusement. She took a deep breath and a step, then another, crunching her way slowly across the gravel toward the patio gates. Above them, on the heavy crossbeam, three cats lay lazily in the sun, one black, one white, one orange, barely opening their eyes as Shirley went beneath them into the sun-splashed patio.

One half of the ranch management was there, stout Sarah Fielding, moving busily about among a rainbow profusion of pot plants. She looked up, examined Shirley from feet to face, and remarked, "Good morning, Ms. McClintock. You look better. Like you slept well. Or had some good news. Or something."

"After all that annoyance and confusion yesterday, I was wallowing in Sunday morning peace and quiet," Shirley responded, with a self-conscious flush. "Something like that. There for a minute, I didn't want to move. . . ."

Sarah gave her a sympathetic smile. "It's a pity we can't bottle those times, isn't it? It'd be nice to just open the bottle and take a dose whenever things get to be too much. Did you folks need something?"

"We thought we'd like to go riding this morning, and I thought you might know about the local stables."

Sarah put down the sack of fertilizer she was carrying, unbuttoned her cuffs, and rolled her sleeves high on her chubby arms as she considered the matter.

"I'd let you take Harry's and my horses, but we only have two, and they're not really trail horses. A lot of our guests have used the stable down the highway, back toward Santa Fe, but if you just want a short ride, I think your best bet might be Alfredo Duran. The Durans live a mile down the road, west, and they've got five or six riding horses and two riding mules. I know they're gentle because I see them going by here with the Duran grandkids on them, even toddlers. He might rent them to you for a morning. It's worth a try."

She nodded to herself, happy with her suggestion. "It's not as though you're greenhorns. You ride all the time, don't you? Seems to me I heard Mr. Quentin say something to Harry about that."

"J.Q. and I ride a lot," Shirley admitted. "And Allison. But this morning we just want a short ride that won't be too hard on Ms. Minging and April."

At the mention of April's name, Sarah Fielding's helpful

expression underwent a startling metamorphosis, becoming a perfect Kabuki mask of annoyance.

"Has April done something?" asked Shirley with a sinking feeling.

"That is the curly-haired little one, isn't it? The one Harry helped you find yesterday, with her broken arm and all? Is she related to you?"

"No." Shirley shook her head firmly. "But I'm responsible for her, in a sense. What's she done?"

"Phone call woke Harry and me this morning, early. One of our other guests. Seems the girl was snooping around their house, peeking in the windows at them, making faces. She's old enough to know better than that!"

"What happened?"

"I was ready to go out and spank her bottom, but Harry said he'd go. He caught her at it. Told her he'd personally have her arrested for trespassing if she didn't stay where she belonged. Oh, was he put out! Partly because it woke us up so early, I suppose . . ."

"What time was this?"

"It was about . . . oh, six? We usually sleep in on Sundays, and it was way before we'd normally have been up."

"I'll go apologize to them," said Shirley stiffly. "And I do apologize to you!"

Sarah Fielding shrugged. "Apology accepted. But it's too late to apologize to the people she was bothering. They up and left! They were reserved for four nights; they didn't even get here until after dark last night, but they told Harry they wouldn't stay. They didn't even ask for their deposit back. We'll have to mail it, I guess. Not fair to keep it under the circumstances."

"Odd they'd have just taken off."

"Well, we get some like that. Privacy nuts. People who come here because we're small and remote, and they don't want to run into anyone they know. Sometimes married men from Denver or Albuquerque, bringing their girlfriends for a quickie weekend." She laughed. "You can always tell. They make the reservations themselves, from their business phone. They pay in cash. They go in the house with their groceries. The curtains stay closed. Smoke comes out of the chimney. You never see either one of them, except maybe on their way to go out to dinner, and two days later they leave before sunup." She grinned salaciously.

Shirley found herself grinning in return. "I'm really sorry about April. The kid's simply a problem."

"Don't worry about it. Just keep an eye on her. She's what Harry calls a loose cannon. Harry was in the marines for a while, and I guess he knows a loose cannon when he sees one."

Shirley frowned, thinking loose cannons had more to do with a historic navy than with the current marines, but Sarah didn't wait for comment as she shouldered her fertilizer sack and beckoned. "Let's use the kitchen phone to call the Durans."

The kitchen was bright with Mexican tile and polished copper pots. Sarah punched in the number and handed the phone to Shirley. A child answered and went to fetch her father, her shrill voice floating behind her over the line. "Daddy! Daddy, telephone."

"She's gone to get him," Shirley said, holding the phone away from her ear.

Sarah nodded, pushed the morning paper over where Shirley could see it, and went to wash her hands at the kitchen sink.

Banging doors and hollerings came through the phone. Shirley perched one hip on the edge of the counter and leafed through the paper while she waited. The news was not designed to make the tourist bureau proud: Two New Mexican youths were being sentenced in California for knifing a woman there. New Mexico led the nation in alcohol-related car accidents; local judges were charged with going easy on drunk drivers. A newborn baby had disappeared; the father begged for his return. Members of San Pedro Pueblo had defaced a recently erected, larger-than-life statue of a conquistador and announced their intention of repeating the offense whenever moved to do so. Hispanic spokesmen voiced their outrage at this sacrilege. So much for bicultural amity.

A deep voice in her ear interrupted Shirley's perusal.

"Bueno?"

"Mr. Duran? My name's Shirley McClintock. Sarah Fielding suggested I call you. Five of us staying at Rancho del Valle would like to take a little ride today. Three of us are experienced riders, but the other two aren't. We don't want to go far, and Sarah thought you might rent us your horses."

"Oh, hell," said the pleasantly accented voice. "I don' know what I'd rent 'em for. *Los perezosos* jus' hang aroun' out there, eatin' hay an gettin' fat." He chuckled. "Sarah or Harry give you my name, that's good enough. You want 'em for a while this mornin', I'll lend 'em to you. Saves me havin' to pay somebody to exercise 'em."

When Shirley asked about a trail, he suggested one that went past his place and into the hills to the San Pedro reservoir, some six miles away.

"It's not lonesome. Lotsa tourists aroun'. It's a nice place, though, and you got a couple people don't ride so good, you don' want to be off *en las lejanías, pues*?"

Shirley hung up, thanked Sarah, and greeted stocky Harry Fielding, who had just come in the back door.

"I apologized to Sarah, but I do to you, too, Harry."

"What?"

"For April misbehaving this morning."

His face turned slightly red, his jaw clenched, and he waved her apology away. "It's okay. Forget it. Those things happen."

"Well, April makes more of them happen than she should. And after you were so thoughtful, helping us hunt for her yesterday."

Sarah made soothing noises. Harry waved Shirley's apology away again, looking decidedly uncomfortable. Shirley decided further discussion would only make matter worse, gestured a farewell, and left via the kitchen door. Back at the little house, finding the others gathered at the breakfast table, she poured herself a second cup and announced the day's projected itinerary.

"Great," said Allison, with enthusiasm. "That sounds—"

"I can't ride with only one arm," Ape interrupted in an unequivocal I'm-in-the-mood-for-trouble tone. "Nobody asked me!"

Shirley, feeling sightly murderous, drew herself up to her full six foot three and ran her fingers through her short, graying hair. "Nobody asked you because your choices are limited, April. You can choose to go with us, sitting on a led horse, or you can stay here in the house with a sitter. There's a child-care agency listed in the phone book."

"I'm too old for—"

"Up until yesterday and this morning, I would have thought so, too."

April glared. "That fat lady, she told on me. Or he did!"

Shirley sighed, sorry to have brought the matter up. "I wouldn't call her fat; her name is Sarah Fielding."

"What?" demanded Xanthippe, her voice rising dangerously. "What did Mrs. Fielding have to tell, April?"

April was stubbornly silent.

"Shirley?" Xanthippe demanded.

"Harry had to run April off this morning. She was spying on some of the other guests. Peeking through windows."

"I wanted to know what *they* were up to. They—"

"That's enough!" Xanthippe cried, her eyes throwing sparks. "April, honestly! My patience is severely tried! It will take very little more to have me put you on the plane back to Denver today! Your mother gave me three or four numbers, and I'm sure I can reach at least one of your aunts or your grandmother."

12

Allison hurriedly excused herself from the table and disappeared into her bedroom. April glared at her plate, red-faced and furious. Xanthippe was pale, tight-lipped.

J.Q. threw a sidelong look at Shirley—who was wishing she'd kept her mouth shut—and asked casually, "Where are we riding?"

Shirley kept her voice as casual. "There's a reservoir about six miles above Duran's place. We don't need to go all the way if anyone gets tired. I thought we'd pack a lunch. . . ."

"Excellent idea," said J.Q., with a rueful look at the mostly uneaten breakfast. "Why don't you and I do that while the others get dressed or brush their teeth or whatever they have to do."

April, given the choice of riding or staying in the house with a sitter, decided upon riding. At the Durans' she was boosted onto a fat and imperturbable gelding, twin to the one J.Q. selected for Xanthippe Minging. J.Q. and Shirley chose to ride the mules, and Allison picked a small black gelding for herself.

"You can leave it pretty much up to them," Fredo Duran advised. "They've been up there so many times, they know the way goin' and comin'."

"What are their names?" Allison wanted to know.

"Well, you're on Bandito. Your grandma and grandpa are on Fredo and Frita. . . ."

J.Q. cast an amused glance at Shirley. This was the first time he'd been called Allison's grandpa. That he knew of.

". . . named after me and my wife. Sort of a family joke. Your friend's on Perezoso, that's Lazybones, and the other lady's on Azucar; Perry and Sookie for short. They'll get you there and back, but none of them are up to much, you know?"

"I know," said Allison, who did indeed know. Her own horse, Beauregard, would have sneered at these mounts, but then, Beau had a high opinion of himself.

Duran nodded and pointed. "Through that gate down

13

there, across that pasture. There's another gate on the other side; that's where you pick up the trial. Keep going west; don't turn off to the sides. If nobody's been burning the signs for campfires, it's marked pretty good.''

Shirley thanked him, waved at the four generations of Durans assembled on the front porch of the long farmhouse, and led the way toward the indicated gate. The weatherman promised less heat than the day before, and she was determined to set aside prior alarms and excursions and enjoy the ride. The pasture before them was surprisingly green for this arid land, obviously subirrigated, a long, narrow strip of grass extending from below the house all the way to the river.

Allison dismounted to open the gate, shutting it carefully behind them, as befitted an animal-conscious person. They rode across the riverine pasture—shaded beneath big cottonwoods, some old, half-dead, leaning their twiggy branches almost to the ground, others young and vigorously erect—detouring around three lounging heifers. The far fence stood at the edge of a strip of woods.

''Bosque,'' said J.Q., as he dismounted to open the gate. ''That's what they call woods down here. Tamarisks. Cottonwoods. Willows. All the water-loving trees. I'll bet some of them have roots down twenty or thirty feet.''

''Over the river and through the woods,'' remarked Xanthippe. ''Or vice versa. Not to grandmother's house, presumably. There's the trail marker.''

The painted red arrow pointed them through the narrow belt of trees, across the dry riverbed, marked with only a silver trickle, and onto the desert once more, the trail a mere hoof-marked path that curved gently around clumps of silvery chamisa on its way to the hills half a mile away. Allison encouraged her horse into a grudging canter, leaving a cloud of dust to guide the others from desert into a sparse forest of piñions and junipers, redolent as incense. After a mile or so of barely sloped trail, they began to climb more steeply among taller firs and pines.

14

"Lovely smell," Xanthippe murmured at Shirley's side. "Makes one wonder why people choose to live among the stink of traffic."

"It does," Shirley agreed, troubled by the older woman's expression and tone of voice. "Is something bothering you, Xanthy? Ever since yesterday you've seemed . . . bothered about something."

The older woman laughed ruefully, reaching up to tuck a stray wisp of hair under her wide-brimmed hat. "Oh, Shirley, it's just . . . kids. Nothing is so wonderful as young people who are full of life and eager to learn, and nothing is sadder than one like April. She's so angry and hostile and confused. She hates everyone. And there are more and more like her all the time." She sighed deeply. "It seems there's more and more ugliness, violence, sickness, drugs, guns. Less and less nature and sweet days of sun. I'm seventy, Shirley. There's no time left for me to do anything about it. Sometimes I worry there's no time for any of us, and I get depressed."

The feelings expressed were far too close to Shirley's own for her to be able to offer comfort. She felt a familiar pain, an all too familiar anxiety.

"Well, you know," Xanthippe went on unwittingly. "After what happened to the land next to you. And that developer who wants to buy your place . . ."

At a very good price. Considering the current economic situation, at a very good price indeed, and yet it was like being offered money for your right arm, or for your child! The idea of leaving the McClintock ranch made her feel sick and weak, but the idea of being surrounding by development on three sides was equally terrifying. Shirley had been purposefully avoiding the issue for months. She'd come on this trip to escape thinking about it. She couldn't handle it. Not yet.

"I know, Xanthy." She nodded, casting about for something else to talk about. "April's an extremely upsetting child. Did you find out what she was up to this morning?"

Xanthippe took a deep breath. "Oh, she had a confused story about having seen the people in one of the little houses before, and their being up to something. One of April's typical wild stories. I told her whatever they were up to, it was none of her business."

"If we don't take her with us when we go on to Carlsbad, what in heaven's name will we do with her?"

"I'm going to send her home or to one of her relatives. If the housekeeper isn't available, there's two aunts living in the Denver area, plus the grandmother, in Lakewood. Unfortunately, yesterday and this morning have established we can't trust her on a nine-hour bus ride, so I'll put her on the plane in Albuquerque and have her met in Denver. If necessary, I'll go with her myself."

"But you'd planned on staying two weeks more. . . ."

"I had indeed. I said, if necessary."

"What is the father's background? Allison said he was what, Arab?"

"Not Arab, no. He's Muslim. An Azeri, I believe. Or does one say Azerbaijani? Whichever, his family is caught up in that Azerbaijani-Armenian mix-up where everybody seems to be killing everybody else. He has to go back there every few months. April's mother begged me to include April in this trip because she didn't want to take the girl with them, and April threw a fit about staying home with the housekeeper. Mrs. Shaour said she's afraid April's father will leave April there, with his mother, because he doesn't approve of the way April is being raised here. Why on earth did he marry an American woman! These men from repressive, medieval cultures who marry women reared outside that culture and then put enormous effort into breaking their wives' spirits and raising their daughters in purdah! I don't understand it!"

"Shhh," murmured Shirley. "Here she comes."

16

J.Q. had been moseying along some distance behind, but now he had caught up to them, leading April's horse behind him. April's face was frozen into her usual expression of obdurate dissatisfaction.

"I smell water," J.Q. said as they approached. "How come we haven't seen a stream?"

"I think all the water from the reservoir is diverted for irrigation," Shirley replied. "Fredo Duran said something about that."

Around the next turn in the trail the San Pedro reservoir appeared, a surface of ruffled blue that began behind a low dam, widened into a respectable lake, then narrowed again as it curved into the valley between two rounded hills. The large steel pipe at the dam overflow explained why they had not seen any water: all of it went down the valley, to feed the irrigation ditches, the acequias.

The trail split before them, the left fork winding upward among the trees, the right leading downward, toward a sloping shore speckled with fishermen and sunbathers. When they came halfway down the slope, Allison herself came into view, perched on a fallen log and peering down into the water.

"Trout," she cried, as they came within hearing distance. "We should have brought fishing poles!"

"No license," Shirley called in response. "We'll just have to admire them in their own element today."

They let their animals drink at the edge of the water, then tethered them in the shade next to Allison's. J.Q. lifted April down from her mount and fetched their picnic lunch from the pack that had been tied behind his saddle.

"Here's food. After my Sunday breakfast, I don't suppose anyone's hungry yet."

"I am," Allison contradicted from her log. "It has to be after noon."

"Eleven fifty-five," Shirley corrected her, consulting her

watch. "Which is near enough noon if anybody wants to eat."

There were individually wrapped sandwiches in the pack, apples, cookies, and a plastic bag of carrot, celery, and green pepper strips, along with a thermos of coffee and another of fruit drink. Allison made a selection and carried it out onto the log, where she sat with her feet dangling, watching the fish.

April glared sulkily after her. She couldn't get out on the log with only one arm, a fact of which Allison was no doubt fully aware.

"Here's a good stump for you, April," Shirley suggested in a purposefully kind and patient tone. "Tell me what you'd like and I'll get it for you."

"Not hungry," muttered April.

"Suit yourself. If you get hungry, it's all right here." Shirley picked out a sandwich and went out onto the log to join Allison. "How was your horse?"

"He's got probably the worst trot I've ever ridden. But his canter isn't bad. At least I can ride it without getting my brains shaken up. How were the mules?"

"Rather deliberate about the whole thing. On the way up, I was trying to remember if I've ever ridden a mule before. I think this is a first experience. They're very surefooted."

"Aren't mules what they use in the Grand Canyon?"

"Is it? I thought donkeys. I was there years ago, with my second husband. I can't remember what it was we rode. All I can recall is the scenery!"

They sat in companionable silence while they ate. Shirley finished her sandwich, folded the wrappings, and buried them in her pocket. "You want to stay awhile or start back?"

"If we go back, could we maybe go to a movie or something? Or a museum?"

Shirley gave her a long look. "I don't see why not. We haven't seen the folk art museum yet, and I know Xanthippe wants to."

18

She made her way back to the shore and up the slope where the others were sitting.

"If we start back soon, we can visit one of the museums in Santa Fe this afternoon," she suggested. "Then I'll take everyone to dinner."

"We already went to museums," said April rebelliously.

Shirley agreed. "We went to one Indian and one Hispanic museum, yes. But there's a wonderful folk art museum we haven't seen, and I'd very much like to, wouldn't you, Xanthippe?"

"If you don't want to go, April, you can stay at the ranch with me," said J.Q. "Perhaps you'd be better off if you rested this afternoon. I've got an interesting book, so it's no trouble if you'd rather. We can meet the others for supper later."

This was not what April had in mind. She sat stubbornly mute upon her stump while the others packed up the leavings of lunch, not even speaking when J.Q. helped her onto her mount once more.

Again, Allison led the way. They went up the hill, turned left onto the trail, and ambled slowly back down the hill. This time Shirley led April's horse, leaving J.Q. and Xanthippe to chat amiably some distance behind them.

"You're not going to take me to Carlsbad with you, are you?" the girl challenged when they had gone about half a mile.

"No," said Shirley suddenly decisive. "I'm not."

"You're just like my mother and father. They promise things they don't do!"

Shirley shortened the lead rope, bringing the girl up beside her. "On the way home from the hospital last night, you said the same thing. Remember what I said?"

No response.

"I told you an invitation is not a promise. We invite people we enjoy being with. We do it for pleasure, April. But you don't enjoy being with me, or J.Q., or even with Allison.

You insult people Allison is fond of and you call her names. You do things we've asked you not to. We don't enjoy that either. Why would either we or you want to spend any more time together?''

"But it's your fault that—''

Shirley looked at her pityingly. "No. It's not my fault anything. It's not J.Q.'s fault or Ms. Minging's fault or Allison's fault. If you were five years old, it might be someone else's fault. But you're thirteen. As people grow older, fewer and fewer things are other people's fault; more and more things are our own fault. That's what our laws reflect when they let us wander around alone at a certain age, and drive at a certain age, and vote at a certain age. The law says if you're five, you can't be left alone, but if you're thirteen, you can. The law is saying that at that age, things are your fault, not someone else's.''

No reply.

Shirley took a deep breath and tried again. "All of us understand your problem, April. You're old enough to understand it, too. You want people to pay attention to you, especially your family, and they don't. You want attention so badly that you will do anything to get people to focus on you. We left you and Allison alone yesterday, so you got into trouble. You were giving us a message. You were saying, *'Look, at me! You people aren't allowed to do what you want to. You people aren't allowed to enjoy yourselves. Just pay attention to me, and if you don't, I'll make you sorry.'* That's the wrong message, April. That's not how J.Q. and Allison and I intend to spend our vacation. We don't want an April-centered vacation.''

"I hate you!''

Shirley sighed, wondering if there were any words that might get through to the angry little person being jogged along beside her. She gave a mental shrug and gave up. It would take a lot of time and a good counselor to get through to this one, and Shirley hadn't the one and wasn't the other.

"I'm sorry, April. I wish, somehow—"

"You're not my mother," the girl snarled. "You have no right to tell me what to do! I hate you all."

Shirley heard a shot. She distinctly heard a shot, for her head turned away from April at the sound, then, seeing April slump, from the corner of her eye, she turned back, seeing that redness on April's forehead where no redness should be, leaning widely to her left to grab for the girl. The mule she was riding picked that moment to go straight up, a four-footed hop that threw Shirley even farther to the side. She slipped, grabbed at nothing, felt herself falling.

Then was only a crushing agony so overwhelming, she did not even know where in her body she was feeling it.

Then darkness with the sound of J.Q.'s voice shouting in it.

Then not even that.

The last thought she had was that at least there was a horse to carry her body out. J.Q. wouldn't have to do it.

2

Hот, heavy things on her legs. Echoes from hard surfaces. A glare of light through closed eyelids, too bright, too near. More hot things on her chest, on her thighs.

"Are you warm enough?" someone asked.

"No," she mumbled, shivering. "Cold."

"You'll be warmer in a moment," said the voice. "We keep the operating rooms quite cool, but you'll be warmer in a minute."

Operating rooms? What operating rooms?

Warmth came and went, cool coverings replaced with warmer ones. Her shivering stopped. She went away somewhere else.

Then the ceiling was moving.

"Taking you down to your room," said a voice. "A nice warm room. Then you can have a little sleep."

The ceiling went on moving. Then it stopped and the floor dropped. More moving ceiling.

The light changed. Someone tucked a blanket around her, around her feet. The bed was too short.

"Damn," said a voice, not her own. "The bed's too short."

"Can you hear me?" asked someone. "This tube in your nostrils is oxygen. Feel the button? This button is your pain medication. If you feel pain, press this button. Understand?"

She felt no pain. Why would she feel pain?

She went away again. The pain sneaked up on her while she slept.

"Hurts," she murmured, outraged at the intimate agony in her leg and groin.

"Here," said J.Q. "I'll press your pain button for you." Something beeped.

A long quiet during which the pain went away.

"What happened?" she said, forcing her eyes open. "J.Q., what happened?"

"You fell." His hand stroked her cheek, patted her shoulder. "You got stepped on. Your left knee got messed up. So now you've got a new knee."

"A new knee?" The idea made no sense. They couldn't just *give* her a new knee. "I didn't give anybody permission to . . ."

"I did, Shirley. We've got each other's powers of attorney. You remember."

She did remember. Sort of. Turn-off power. That's what they'd called it. Not knee power. Turn-off power.

"It was the right thing to do," he whispered in her ear. "You'll be all right. The worst is over. Nothing to worry over."

It seemed to her there was something she should remember. Something she should ask him.

"Don't go away," she murmured.

"I won't go away," he said.

This was the Los Arboles Hospital, she told herself with

painful certainty. It was necessary to know where she was. She'd been here before, not long ago. When?

Yesterday. They'd been here yesterday, when they'd brought April in. April, whose forearm was bent at an ugly and unnatural angle . . .

Xanthippe had gone with April to the emergency room. Shirley, Allison, and J.Q. had remained in the reception area near the main doors. Shirley had prowled. J.Q. had glanced at her over his glasses with ostentatious self-control. The magazines in the rack were all ones she'd read. The minuscule gift shop, with its modest selection of paperbacks, was closed. The hospital seemed abandoned. Deserted. She could see the entire length of the smooth-floored corridor, empty except at the far end where a brown-skinned man waltzed with a floor polisher, a peripatetic silhouette against the lighted glass of the emergency room doors.

The wait had seemed interminable. Allison had yawned herself into catatonia and had gone out to the car to lie down, leaving Shirley to stare after her, across the empty expanse of the hospital parking lot. Beyond the blacktop, the world fell away into crenellated canyons, slantingly and deeply shadowed by the evening sun, mesa rearing behind mesa, butte beyond butte, the shattered rimrock and pillared walls dropping from layers of ochre and gray, past slopes of pale scree to piñon-dotted canyons lost in the shadow below. A million-dollar view, totally wasted. Who came to a hospital for the view?

As she'd watched, the sun had dropped below the horizon and the sky had turned a brilliant salmon gold, transforming the ramified canyons before her into looming presences of lavender and lapiz, horizon-to-horizon grandeur, mysterious and marvelous!

The picture hung in her mind as though painted there. It was the backdrop for this place, where she was, in the Los Arboles hospital. When . . . something. Something she should ask J.Q.

She opened her eyes. He was still there, slumped in a chair beside the bed, mouth slightly open, snoring.

"Hey," she said from a mouth full of cotton and spider-webs.

He opened his eyes, shut his mouth, blinked at her a few times. "How do you feel?"

She considered the question. How did she feel?

"I don't feel anything much," she said. "I can't move my left leg."

"You've got a thing on it. An immobilizer. You won't be able to turn over or bend your leg for a while. They had to stitch things together in there."

She tried to feel her leg, but both hands were brought up short.

J.Q. leaned over the bed and took her hands. "Don't go throwing your hands around. You've got IVs in them. You're hooked up to the pain medication, and there's an antibiotic. And one of them is there in case you need blood. I wouldn't give them permission to give you a transfusion. Not unless absolutely necessary, and it wasn't. There was some bleeding in the joint, but you didn't lose much."

"No transfusion?"

"AIDS," he said. "I wasn't going to risk it. Not unless they had to, to save your life."

"Oh." She swallowed. Her mouth was still made of cotton. "I'm thirsty."

He put a drinking tube to her lips. She sucked, swallowed. Sucked again and held the water in her mouth, letting it dissolve the dry, irritated surfaces. When it felt better, she swallowed again.

"What happened?" she asked. "I can't remember."

"Somebody was shooting. The mule you were riding got grazed. You were unbalanced, I guess. You fell off and a hoof came down on your knee. If you can believe this, it messed up the inside thoroughly, but without breaking the skin."

She tried to visualize that: a hoof coming down on her knee. She flinched at the thought, glad she'd been unconscious. "Well. This's been a real vacation, hasn't it?"

He patted her hand. She tried to pat back, but it was too much effort. She heard the beep again. Somebody had pressed the pain button. Maybe she'd done it herself.

She was back in yesterday, strolling off down the hallway to the emergency room to see for herself what was going on with April, pausing to compare her watch with the large clock on the wall, passing the waltzing floor polisher with a nod and a polite smile before slipping through one of the swinging doors into a narrow and unlighted foyer where she stood, hidden in shadow. The emergency room was large, made to seem labyrinthine by scattered equipment and partially drawn cubicle curtains. The only light was at the far end where April sat beside an examining table, arm propped upon a plastic pillow, while a layer of plaster bandage was wound neatly into place by a young physician. Xanthippe Minging was poised on a stool nearby.

"It hurts," whined Ape.

Ms. Minging said something acerbic about April being thankful she was still alive to feel pain.

Ape squeezed her eyes shut, spilling sparse tears.

"Crying will not improve matters," Ms. Minging snapped.

There were further murmured words. The doctor pulled a pen from her pocket and wrote busily on a clipboard. Ms. Minging stared out the window with an enigmatic expression.

At the room corner nearest the foyer, a laundry cart came through a door, pushed by a slender and faded blonde dressed in hospital green.

Across the room the doctor spoke over her shoulder to Ms. Minging. "She'll have to give the arm a chance to heal. No more cliff climbing . . ."

The laundry woman was distracted by the sound and

26

caught sight of Shirley barely in time to dodge around her before bumping the cart through the door into the hallway.

Across the room, April wrinkled her nose and made a rude gesture in Shirley's direction.

"April!"cautioned Ms. Minging.

". . . staring at me!" April complained.

Xanthippe said something muffled and monitory.

Assessing the treatment as virtually completed, Shirley slipped back through the doors without drawing attention to herself, almost tripping over the cord to the now-abandoned floor buffer. Suppertime for employees, no doubt. When she rejoined J.Q. she turned to see Xanthippe and April emerging at the end of the hall, hearing the tone of their conversation if not the words: Xanthippe, firm and unyielding; Ape in her usual snarl of discontent. Whatever her objection was, it got nowhere with Xanthippe, for Ape went mulishly off alone, past the abandoned floor machine toward the women's toilets.

Yesterday that had happened. Saturday. They'd stopped in Los Arboles for pizza on the way home. Allison and April had had a muttered argument in the living room before Xanthippe had summoned Ape off to the other house, to bed. Why was Shirley remembering it? Why was she thinking of Ape's angry face, angry, hostile little face. . . ?

Let it go. She couldn't think what it was. Let it go.

When she opened her eyes next, she saw morning light coming through the window. Had to be morning. Yellow, level light. Not pink enough for evening. Someone was taking blood from her right arm. She shut her eyes, willing the person to go away. The person did, only to be replaced by another.

"Vital signs," said the person with dogged cheerfulness. She thrust a plastic-cased thermometer into Shirley's mouth, bound a blood pressure cuff onto her arm. *Whuff whuff whuff.* Fingers on her wrist, taking her pulse.

Go away, go away.

27

The person went.

"Ready for some breakfast?" a male voice asked in that same dogged tone of unwarranted cheer.

She opened her eyes again. It was someone else, a stocky, mustached yellow-skinned young man carrying a tray. She shut her eyes and shook her head, tried to move her leg and couldn't, thought of screaming, felt for the pain button instead. What she felt wasn't exactly pain. It was extreme discomfort, irritation, frustration, fear. Perhaps that added up to pain. Whatever it was, the button would make it go away.

She remained stubbornly somewhere else while someone washed her face and arms. While someone changed her gown. While someone fiddled about with the nylon and Velcro monstrosity on her leg. How did she know that? She must have been watching them, without even knowing it.

Someone took her temperature, her blood pressure, her pulse again. Everyone went away.

"I brought you some coffee," said J.Q., holding a cup beneath her nose. "The hospital coffee is foul."

"Smells good," she said, trying to sit up.

"Hey, let the bed do it," he said. A motor hummed and the bed raised her. She took the cup, tasted it, made a face.

"It's the morphine," he told her. "It makes even good stuff taste weird. Drink it anyhow."

"Morphine?"

"In your IV. The nurse says patients use less pain medication if they can give themselves a microdose every fifteen or twenty minutes. Patients keep themselves comfortable so they stay quieter and get well quicker, the pain never gets unbearable, the nurses have to run around less, there's less chance of overdose."

She stared at the needle in the back of her hand. "How long will I be hooked up?"

"I don't know, old love. Not long, I should suppose. You already sound almost normally irascible."

His jovial tone was belied by the worry lines in his face.

"You look awful," she said groggily.

"You're not exactly love's young dream yourself, Shirley. Half your face is turning a lovely eggplant shade at the moment."

She fumbled at her face. It was tender, sore to the touch.

"Did they find out who was doing the shooting?" she asked.

He shook his head. "Not yet. I understand both the San Pedro Pueblo police and the Santa Fe County sheriff's office are involved."

"Were we on pueblo land?"

"Partly. The reservoir is on pueblo land, and either we were, but the shooter wasn't, or the other way around, or the trail crosses a little neck of pueblo land or something. I was more concerned about you than I was over who had jurisdiction."

Shirley forced her eyes open again. Somehow, they kept falling shut. There was something she needed to know . . . needed to ask. . . .

"See you later," she whispered, falling away into an abyss of sleep.

Lunch came and went, untouched. The idea of food was actually repellent. She could not think of anything she had ever eaten that would tempt her at the moment. She dreamed a menu of all the meals ever eaten. Steamed lobster on the beach in Maine. Chinese food in New York. Elegant French food in Washington. All negative.

People took her temperature again and again.

"Hundred and one," said an assistant.

"Fever?" Shirley murmured, alarm bells ringing.

"Joint replacement patients almost always run a fever," the person said. "It goes up for a day or two, then it goes down. Yours isn't high. Don't worry about it."

Blood pressure. Pulse. Blood again.

"Why so much blood?"

"We've got you on a blood thinner, to prevent clots, so

29

we have to check your pro time. And we have to see if your count's coming up. See if you can get by without a transfusion.''

''You keep taking it, I'll need a transfusion for sure,'' she grumbled.

She slept again, conscious that there was someone else in the room, someone breathing. When she opened her eyes and looked, there was no one there, but the breathing went on and on. It wasn't important enough to worry about. Then it was evening and she looked out her window into a darkening sky against a familiar horizon. It was the same view she had seen Saturday night, waiting for April to get her arm set. Same view, same time of day. ''This is the Los Arboles Hospital,'' she said to no one in particular.

''Where did you think you were?'' the big woman in the doorway asked. She was a dark woman, a little shorter than Shirley but at least twice Shirley's girth. Indian? Samoan? Shirley remembered her vaguely. The night nurse.

''I didn't think,'' she replied. ''I've been kind of out of it.''

''Well, there are two gentlemen out here who want to see you, and I said I'd come in first to be sure you were decent. Would you like me to comb your hair?''

Without waiting for an answer, the woman came in, burrowed in a drawer, and came up with a comb and brush Shirley recognized as her own. Dear J.Q. Maybe he'd even remembered a toothbrush.

The woman's name tag said she was a Gloria somebody. Shirley couldn't make out the last name, a long one, full of vowels.

''Thank you, Gloria,'' Shirley murmured. ''At least you've tried. J.Q. says I'm pretty bruised.''

The woman gave Shirley a calm looking over. ''I've seen worse. Some women come in here, their husbands get drunk, they get mad, they beat on 'em. Real macho. I'll go three rounds with a horse anytime.'' She stood back. ''There. You don't look gorgeous, but you look clean and neat. That's about the best we can do at this stage of the game."

She went out. Shirley heard murmuring in the hall. The two men who came in were yin and yang. One gringo-Anglo, tall, blond, dressed in tan shirt and brown trousers; one Indian-Hispanic, short, brown, wearing a blue-black uniform with a shoulder patch that identified him as a member of the San Pedro Pueblo police.

"We're sorry to bother you," said the Anglo. "I'm with the Santa Fe County sheriff's office, Deputy Bob Jensen. This is Officer Ray Apodaca from the Pueblo police. We'd like to ask you a few questions if you're up to it."

Shirley swallowed and reached for her water glass. "I'll tell you what I can. I'm afraid it won't be too helpful."

"Anything might be helpful. Firstly, did you see anyone or anything at all unusual on your way up to the reservoir yesterday morning?"

Yesterday? Had it indeed been only yesterday? It seemed a week had passed. "I don't remember seeing anyone," she said, furrowing her brow in an effort to remember. "Not until we got there. There were some people fishing. At least one person—woman, I guess—sunbathing."

"You stopped at the reservoir. What did you do then?"

"We . . . we watered our horses. We tied them in the shade. We unpacked our lunch and ate it. . . ."

"What time was this?" asked Officer Apodaca.

"How long were you there?" asked the deputy, simultaneously.

"Sorry," said the deputy, with a glance at his companion.

"My watch said five to noon when we unpacked the lunch," Shirley replied. "My watch keeps good time, within a minute or two. We didn't stay long. Twenty minutes. Half an hour at the outside. We were going into Santa Fe to the folk art museum that afternoon, so we packed up our stuff and started back."

"But you didn't look at your watch when you left?"

"Not that I remember, no."

The officer asked, "On the trail, how were you riding? I mean, who was first?"

"Allison was first. Then April and I. Then J.Q. and Xanthippe Minging."

"J.Q.?" the gringo asked, leafing through his notebook. "Oh, that's John Quentin?"

She nodded, suddenly very weary.

"Were you riding close together? Or strung out?"

"Both. I mean, Allison was a good way ahead, but April and I were riding almost abreast, and so were J.Q. and . . ." She put up a hand to rub her forehead, feeling the tube drag at the needle in the back of her hand. Something. There was something she should remember.

"And you saw nobody? Nobody at all?"

She concentrated. There hadn't *been* anyone. "I don't think I would have seen anyone. It's forest up there. Whoever it was could have been behind a tree, or even way up the slope, shooting down. I think . . . I think I heard the shot. Everything happened so fast."

The two looked at each other, the officer poker-faced, the taller man shrugging.

"Bottom line," said the deputy, putting his notebook away. "You didn't see who shot the girl."

"Shot the girl!" she cried, sitting bolt upright, reaching out, remembering that blot of red where no red should be. "Which girl? Shot who?"

The big nurse came ponderously around the corner of the door, glaring at the two men.

"Shhh," she said to Shirley. "You're pulling yourself all apart." She tugged at the IV tubes, releasing the tension, at the same time pushing Shirley back onto the bed.

"What girl?" shouted Shirley, refusing to be calmed. "Damn it, what girl?"

"I'm sorry," murmured the deputy. "I thought you knew. The girl who was riding with you. April . . ."

"I saw her," Shirley cried angrily, tears on her face. "I saw the bullet hole on her forehead. I saw her slide sideways. That's why I fell. I was reaching for her. . . ."

"Will you two get out of here," said the nurse in a firm, do-it-or-else voice. "Please. Right this minute."

"What in hell," said J.Q. from the doorway. "What in hell?"

There was momentary confusion, coming and going, raised voices, murmured apologies, and then Shirley was lying alone for the moment, her face wet, though whether with gratitude or grief, she couldn't for the moment say. It wasn't Allison who'd been shot. Thank God, not Allison. But she'd known that. Surely she'd known that. . . .

"I was going to tell you tonight," said J.Q. angrily, as he came back into the room. "As soon as you were alert enough to understand what I was saying. I told them that when I talked to them this morning. I told them you were all doped up and didn't even know she'd been shot."

"Well, I really did," she said dazedly. "I did know! I saw it. I just forgot it, somehow. Or didn't choose to remember. Is she . . . She's dead, isn't she, J.Q.?"

He bit his lip. "She's dead, Shirley. Dead before she fell. Shot in the middle of her forehead. There were two shots, one right after the other. The first one hit her, the second one grazed the mule you were riding."

"Was it . . . I mean, do they think someone did it on purpose?"

"That's evidently what they're trying to find out. They asked me if I knew of any reason anyone would want to shoot you."

"You knew of several reasons, of course," she said, half laughing, half crying.

He shook his head at her chidingly. "I told them not currently, no. Not in this venue, at least. They asked me if I knew of any reason anyone would want to shoot April. I told them to talk to Ms. Minging. She told them about April's

33

proclivities, about her running off and breaking her arm, about her sneaking and spying on people."

"Poor child," Shirley murmured. "Poor desperate, unhappy child. Do you suppose she saw something . . . something she wasn't supposed to see? Heard something? Or . . . stole something?"

"Possible, I suppose."

"What's Xanthy doing?"

"She called April's grandmother. Grandmother evidently had some way to reach her daughter, April's mother, because she gave Xanthy an overseas number. At any rate, mother and father are flying in. I'm not sure when."

"I wonder," said Shirley, feeling the familiar soft darkness welling up around her once again. "I wonder."

"What do you wonder, old love?"

"I wonder if they'll care."

Tuesday morning came with unvarnished clarity. Sunlight. Coffee that shared only two qualities with real coffee: wetness and warmness. It smelled like nothing much and tasted awful. Rubbery scrambled eggs. Limp, rancid-smelling toast. An amorphous blob in a bowl that Shirley finally identified as oatmeal. A container of orange juice that was cold and sweet. She drank the orange juice, ate half a piece of toast, one bite of the eggs. Enough.

"Still one oh one," said the vital signs person, happily waving her automatic thermometer.

"I thought you said it would go down."

"It will, in a day or two. Here, let me fix your oxygen; it's breathing up your left ear."

She fixed the oxygen and departed. A nurse arrived to remove a catheter Shirley hadn't known was there. A young woman whose name tag identified her as a physical therapist, Judy somebody, arrived, introduced herself, and announced her intention of getting Shirley out of bed and into a chair.

She began by removing two plastic sleeves from around Shirley's lower legs.

"What are those?" Shirley asked. She hadn't known they were there, either.

"They're hooked up to a compressor that applies intermittent pressure to your lower legs, to prevent blood clots."

When the machine was turned off, Shirley realized it had been the source of the breathing sounds, long, buzzing inhalations followed by lengthy silences.

The young woman got Shirley's legs over the side of the bed and put an additional gown on her, back to front to cover her exposed behind, before trotting out into the hall to return with a chrome contraption.

"That's a walker!" Shirley cried, outraged. Walkers were for little old ladies!

"You can't put much weight on your new knee yet," said Judy, her entire ninety pounds and five foot one hidden somewhere beneath Shirley's left arm.

"What will you do if I fall down?" Shirley asked, curiously. She felt like a queen ant, being tugged at by one tiny worker.

Long pause. "Curse, I suppose," said a small voice. "I didn't realize you were so . . . tall. Why don't you sit here on the side of the bed while I go get Bryan."

She returned with Bryan, six foot two and husky, short-cropped hair, tight T-shirt stretched over bulging chest and arms under a white lab coat, humorless efficiency exuding from every pore. He strapped a belt around Shirley's waist, took firm hold of it, and began barking orders.

"Take your weight on your right leg. Rest the left leg, very little weight on it."

Judy bustled about, taking charge of the IV stand.

Bryan barked, "Weight on your good leg. Move the walker forward. Put your weight on your arms. Move the good leg. Bring up the bad leg. That's right. Now again."

Shirley's arms screamed protest. She remembered they

had already been sore before the . . . accident. After she and J.Q. had found April, they'd carried her a considerable distance before Harry met them with the car. Enough to make one's arms ache.

Her oddly assorted convoy moved half a dozen steps to the door of the room and then back to the chair, passing the bathroom on the way. When Bryan departed, Shirley asked, "Am I supposed to go in there when I need to go? Without bending my leg?"

"That's right. But don't try it without the walker and without help. Somebody has to manage your IVs."

Shirley's first attempt an hour later verified what she had already suspected. The toilet seat was too low; if she kept her leg straight, there was no way to sit; much of the pee went down her leg into the immobilizer. She reported this interesting fact to the assistant who was tending her IV rack. That person went off and told someone else, who eventually came in with a plastic gadget that raised the toilet seat by about six inches.

Next time much of the pee went on the floor. Shirley supposed, from a personal comfort point of view, this was an improvement.

"You'd think they'd have a better system," she growled at J.Q. when he arrived late in the afternoon. "My God, if they can figure out how to build toilets to use in space shuttles under conditions of no gravity, how much engineering would it take to rig a unisex urinal on the side of the bed?"

"If you can get your mind off your more disgusting experiences for the moment," J.Q. interrupted her. "Xanthy and Allison will be by to see you a little later. They're picking up Mama and Papa Shaour at the Albuquerque airport and taking them wherever they want to go. Then they're coming to see you."

"God. Poor Xanthy."

"This morning you mentioned April's habit of stealing.

After Xanthy left, I decided I'd better . . . go through April's things. Before her parents got here.''

Shirley nodded slowly. "Oh, that was a good idea, J.Q. I'm glad you thought of that.''

"I found these in her fanny pack.'' He took a folded paper bag from a jacket pocket and laid it on the bed, displaying the contents one by one. A small leather bag. A golden locket with seed pearls.

"That's mine!'' Shirley breathed, outraged. Though she seldom wore the locket, she always carried it. It contained pictures of her children, the last pictures she had had of either of them before they died.

"I know it is,'' J.Q. remarked, still busy with the sack. "There's more. Here's my belt buckle, the Navajo silver and turquoise one you gave me for Christmas a few years back. I hadn't worn it on the trip; it was still in my pack. Here's some letters to Xanthy. Here's a letter to Allison, from her uncle and aunt.''

"What's the little leather bag?''

"Unless I'm very much mistaken, April must have found that Saturday, on her expedition to Blue Mesa. That wasn't in her fanny pack; it was in the pocket of the jacket she was wearing when we found her.''

He opened the little bag and displayed the contents on the sheet. Pottery shards. A bone about six inches long, inlaid with jet and turquoise. A clay pipe bowl, white with black pattern. A turquoise finger ring with a rather chunky-looking turtle carved atop it. A tiny stone carving of a bear. He said, "My immediate thought was that the bag is a religious artifact, and my instinct was to put it back where she probably found it.''

Shirley shook her head slowly, pushing the items around with her finger. The bone was a shoulder bone, she thought, from a deer. "I think not, J.Q. If the bag was old, yes, but this isn't old. Look at the leather. It isn't even very dusty. Wherever April found it, it was left there fairly recently. Why

37

don't you hang on to it for now. Maybe we'll turn it over to that pueblo policeman, what was his name? Apodaca? We've already told him she was there, so her having something from there won't come as any real surprise."

"How about this other stuff?"

"Well, the other things belong to us, and we know we didn't shoot her, so they can't possibly be evidence of anything except of her proclivity for taking what didn't belong to her. The police already know about that. Let's put each thing back where it belongs. Give Xanthy her letters. Put my locket in my purse; that's where it was. Allison's letter was probably in her pack."

J.Q. shook his head as he repacked the paper bag. "April must have gone through all our luggage, through yours and Xanthy's purses, through everyone's pockets. There's one more thing." He fished in the breast pocket of his shirt, bringing out a tissue-wrapped something which he disclosed on the palm of his hand.

Shirley picked it up and turned it over between her fingers. A tiny horse, one forefoot raised, neck arched, mane and tail flowing. Mouth open. Perfect. Tiny, but intricately detailed. She hefted it. It was remarkably heavy for its size, only a little over an inch long.

"Gold?" she asked, incredulous. "Where was this?"

"In her fanny pack, wrapped up in these same tissues. I did take note the tissues are blue. The ones at the Rancho are white. Do you think she stole this?"

"From where? Except for her jaunt Saturday, she's been with other people during the entire trip. With Allison or with one of us. Where would she have encountered something like this?"

"A museum?"

"The only ones we went to were Indian museums, and there was nothing like this! If there had been, it would have been behind glass."

J.Q. ticked off an inventory of things seen: "Pots, blankets, sand paintings, silver and turquoise jewelry. Baskets. Clothing. Kachinas. Fetishes. Weapons. Dioramas. Maps. You're right. Nothing like this.''

"You'd have to go to Mexico or Central America to find gold workmanship like this from ancient times. Aside from the fact there were no horses in Central America, the style isn't of this hemisphere at all. This looks . . . This looks Scythian!''

He laughed. "Who said it was old, and how would you know it looks Scythian?''

"When I lived in D.C. I went to exhibits all the time. The National Gallery was nearby, and I loved looking at the stuff, you know. I remember a Scythian exhibit, out of tombs. Felt wall hangings. Shields, swords, bows and arrows. Bridles. Bits. Personal ornaments. A lot of the stuff was gold! I recall thinking at the time how much they cared about horses. They decorated their horses as much as they did themselves. Some of the pieces had this same . . . I don't know. The same lines, maybe? The same stylistic exaggerations? I bought a book, guide to the exhibit, full of pictures.'' She fell silent, trying to remember where the book might be. It had been years ago.

She hefted the figure again. The bottoms of the hind feet were slightly rough, and there was another rough spot at the top of the horse's neck, just below an ear, as though the little figure might originally have been part of something else and had been broken away. The handle of a dagger, perhaps. Or the hilt of a sword.

She mused, "You don't suppose one of the other kids had this along, do you?''

"I'm sure Xanthy has their phone numbers, and it won't take long to check. Shall I turn it over to the deputy? Or the pueblo officer?''

Shirley shook her head firmly. "Not until we know whether it belongs to someone who was on the trip. If so, we'll return it. We know none of us shot at her.''

He nodded, a bit uncomfortably.

She read the signs. "I know, J.Q. Logically we should turn it over to the law, but what if we do, then find out it belongs to one of the other kids, and in the meantime it's just vanished? A little tiny thing like this? I can hear the apologies now. 'Very sorry, ma'am, we stored it as evidence, but somehow it just disappeared.' "

"I suppose one of the other kids might have picked it up somewhere," J.Q. agreed unwillingly. "And one of them might have seen something, or know something. . . ."

"One of the other kids might have had it with him or her when the trip started. We'll show it to Xanthy. It may even be hers. If not, let her make inquiries. She knows these kids, probably better than their own parents do, and she'll find out if any of them have seen it before. At least, let's try it that way first." She hefted the little horse once more, then handed it back to him.

Xanthy chose that moment to appear. She pulled the one remaining chair close to the bed while J.Q. displayed the contents of his paper bag once more. She shook her head in mixed anger and pity over the packet of letters addressed to herself.

"What on earth would April have wanted with letters from my brother?" she asked the air. "Poor Hank has been in a VA hospital for the last year, and he writes to me to pass the time—and to make sure I'll write back. His letters aren't even interesting!"

"April was nosy," Shirley replied. "You said it yourself: she wanted to know about people, even personal things that were none of her business. There's a letter there of Allison's as well."

Xanthippe took the last item from J.Q.'s fingers. The tiny horse. "What's this? April had this?"

She turned it in her fingers as Shirley had done, examined it closely, hefting it. "It's old," she said. "It's . . . what?"

"Shirley said Scythian," offered J.Q.

Xanthippe hefted it again. "It has that look, doesn't it? I suppose some art expert could tell us."

Shirley said, "J.Q. and I wondered if you could call the young people who went home Saturday, ask them if they're missing anything. Find out if, by chance, it belonged to one of them. A good luck piece, perhaps."

"A solid gold good luck piece?" Xanthippe asked, disbelieving. "It weighs several ounces!"

Shirley shrugged. "My mother left me a diamond and ruby pin my dad had given her for an anniversary present. It was pretty and too small for me and quite valuable. I used to wear it pinned to my bra, for luck. People do funny things, including us."

Xanthippe shook her head as though rejecting any such notion. "I'll call them, of course, but my guess is that it belonged to none of them. Will you keep it, J.Q.? It will be safest with you. I think you're right about returning the little bag to the pueblo police. As for the other things, including my letters, we'll just put them back where they belong."

She tucked the packet of letters in her purse and sat back, saying, "I'm glad you thought of going through her things before her parents got here. Allison and I dropped them off out at Rancho del Valle. I've moved in with Allison and J.Q., giving the Shaours the small house. Allison's outside, waiting to see you, but I asked her to give me a private moment with you. I wanted to tell you about the Shaours. . . ."

She stopped, rubbed her hands together as though trying to decide how to proceed. "There's something . . . there's something odd there, Shirley."

"What do you mean?"

"I'm not sure what I mean. They're too taciturn. Too . . . controlled."

"Some people are," J.Q. said. "Some people don't grieve publicly."

"If survivors don't grieve, at least they get angry. They want to blame someone. They want to know how it happened. But the Shaours don't show anything. They're not even curious. The only thing they're interested in is seeing you, Shirley. I told them tomorrow; is that all right?"

"What do they want to see me for?"

Xanthippe gestured, palms up; she didn't know. "If it's too much for you . . ."

"No. Tell them to come." She puzzled, trying to remember the schedule of the day she had just been through. "Tell them around noon. As I recall, nobody was poking at me around lunchtime. No therapists, vital signs, bloodletting, any of that." She mused a moment more, counting off the people she had seen during the day. Nurses. Assistants. Therapists. Cleaning women. Tray deliverer. No doctor, however.

"J.Q., who operated on this knee? Shouldn't the doctor have been around?"

"He was. Yesterday. You were asleep. He was off today, but his partner stopped by for a look at your chart. You'll meet the surgeon tomorrow. Humphrey, his name is. Claude Humphrey. I checked up on him before I gave permission for surgery. He's got a good reputation."

Xanthippe rose, patted Shirley on the arm, and left, saying, "Allison will be getting impatient. Will you bring her with you, J.Q.? I'm going to run on back to the ranch."

Allison came in bearing flowers, a brilliantly orange kalanchoe.

"Are you all right?" she asked tremulously. "J.Q. told me to wait until you were awake, but I was scared. . . ."

"I told you to wait because she looked like a road kill," said J.Q. "She was all doped up, not sure what day it was, and I didn't want you frightened. This is the first time she's been compos mentis, even though her face would still scare Frankenstein."

"You must have landed on your face," Allison murmured sympathetically. "It looks awful! Kind of violet-colored."

"I landed on my head and face. I've got a lump and my

42

cheek is sore," Shirley admitted, feeling her cheekbones.
"J.Q., show Allison the little horse."

J.Q. fished it out and unwrapped it.

"It looks like Beauregard," Allison said in a delighted
voice. "Where did you get it?"

Shirley equivocated a little. "J.Q. found it. He thinks April
had it."

"She never showed it to me."

"We were wondering if, perhaps, she . . . picked it up
somewhere."

Allison turned it over, frowning. "We haven't been anyplace where they had things like this. Is it gold?"

"We think so."

Allison handed it back to J.Q. "Well, I never saw it before. If she stole it, it was probably before this trip."

"It didn't belong to any of the other kids?"

"If it did, they didn't show it to me either."

J.Q. nodded, satisfied, and tucked it away in his pocket
once more. "I'll wait for you down the hall, Allison. Take
your time. I've got a book with me."

Allison moved over into the vacated chair. "J.Q. says
you'll be in here for a week."

"I imagine I'll be in here until my fever goes down, at
least. And until I can walk a little."

"J.Q. asked the doctor. He says you'll have to use crutches
or a walker for about six weeks. It takes that long for the
bone to grow to the parts he put in."

"Parts." Shirley laughed. "Isn't medicine great? All these
replacement parts! When my father's hip went, there weren't
any replacement parts. He was in a wheelchair for the last
few years of his life."

Allison looked at her feet, swung them, looked up and out
the window.

"What's the matter, honey?"

"Did Ms. Minging tell you about April's mother and
dad?"

43

"Did she tell me what about them?"

"How funny they are?"

"Funny? Ha ha funny?"

"Strange funny. We picked them up at the airport. Ms. Minging offered to take them to the place where April . . . where her body is. They didn't want to stop there. They didn't cry, not even her mom."

"Some people . . . some people don't show their feelings, Allison."

"But they did show their feelings, Shirley. Her mom did, at least. That's what was funny. She's scared. You can tell, just looking at her. She's scared."

Claude Humphrey, M.D., showed up at midmorning on Wednesday to tell Shirley she could be disconnected from the IVs at any time. "Your blood isn't great, but you'll get by without a transfusion. I'll order oral pain medication this morning. You have to ask for it, however, and don't be shy about doing so. You'll heal quicker if you're relaxed; you'll be more relaxed if you're not in pain."

He looked at the ceiling while he was talking to her, sometimes raising one pink hand to stroke his completely bald head, sometimes smoothing his wide, narrow upper lip, as though feeling a mustache that wasn't there. His head was widest at the jaw, narrowest at the top. He looked very familiar, but Shirley couldn't place the resemblance.

He went on, "I'd keep the oxygen for a while. You don't have any blood to spare, and extra oxygen makes it easier on your body. Normally when we're doing joint replacements, we have the patient donate at least three autologous units previous to surgery. We were lucky in keeping your blood loss to a minimum. I recommended giving you a unit or two from the blood bank, but your husband—"

"J.Q. is not my husband."

His eyebrows rose. "Your friend wouldn't give us permission."

"My friend did exactly what I'd have done."

He frowned, a fleeting expression with something in it she couldn't decipher.

"I can't argue with you," he said.

"How long will I be here?"

"Oh, until the weekend, probably. By that time your fever should be gone, you'll be able to more around with reasonable care, and the incision will be pretty much closed, though it'll be four to six weeks before it feels completely normal."

"And the knee will be as good as my other one?"

The doctor grinned at her, narrow lips stretching widely. "If you let it grow in the way it's supposed to, it'll last you longer than the other one will. When the rest of you and me is dust, that knee with still be kicking."

He was far more amused by this idea than Shirley was. She went through her morning routine with Judy, exercises for glutes, exercises for quads, bend the knee, sixty degrees now, more later. Put the immobilizer on. Summon Bryan. Walk back and forth, out into the hall and back. It was easier without the IVs.

She washed her face, which was now turning green, and combed her hair, which needed washing. The Shaours arrived along with her lunch tray.

"We can come back later," the woman offered. Her voice was faint and bloodless, as though seldom used.

"The food will wait," Shirley told them. "Quite frankly, it will taste terrible no matter when I eat it."

No flicker of smile. Just two deadpan faces with the same thick white skin, the same dark hair and brows. Her face was a bit rounder, his a bit longer, but their features were much alike, their similar expressions increasing their resemblance to each other. They could be brother and sister. Maybe they had picked each other because of the resemblance.

"I'm so sorry for your loss," Shirley said. Her voice sounded formal and uninterested, even to her. Surely she cared more than that! She cleared her throat, consciously exerting herself to be sympathetic. "We all hope the police will find whoever was responsible."

"An accident," said the man with implacable certainty. "Someone hunting. An unfortunate accident."

"An accident," the woman echoed in a zombielike voice.

"The police tell us you saw no one?" he asked, walking to the window, where he stood, staring blindly over the canyons.

Shirley shook her head. "None of us saw anyone," she corrected. "The trail goes through forest. . . ."

Man and wife glanced at each other. The man pursed his lips. "Of course, there is the possibility it was not accident. If it was not . . . not accidental, then perhaps it was some crazy person. Here in America, so many guns, so many killers of girls and young women. Women are not properly protected. Men can kill ten, a dozen, twenty, before they are caught."

The woman looked up from beneath her lashes. There were tears in her eyes. She blinked them away quickly, ducking her head once more.

Mr. Shaour went on doggedly, "If that had been the case, perhaps someone had followed her? Paid attention to her? Spoken with her? Perhaps even . . . given her something?"

Shirley felt she was caught in a bad dream. What did the man want? What was he after?

She said, "I think . . . from what I've read, serial killers of young women don't shoot them from a distance. They want closer contact than that. It's almost impossible that April met anyone like that. She was with us during the whole trip. The only time she was apart from one of us was Saturday afternoon when she ran off to Blue Mesa, and she was alone then. At least, she didn't mention seeing anyone or speaking to anyone, and we saw no one while we were searching for her. Aside from the people in our group, I never saw her speaking to anyone or saw anyone give her anything except perhaps a waitress, or a tour guide."

46

"Perhaps, if someone gave her something, she could have shown the gift to someone else. Or even passed it on. To your daughter, perhaps?"

Shirley licked her dry lips, confronting his flat, lizardlike gaze. No. Not lizardlike. Crocodilian. A cold-blooded, deliberate stare. Something in her face betrayed her discomfort, for he turned back toward the window, deflecting the accusing gaze.

Shirley cleared her throat once more. "You want to know if April gave anything to Allison?"

His hand rested on the wand that controlled the horizontal blinds, and it quivered, making the entire blind shiver, as water shivers at a dropped stone.

"Your daughter would have told you."

It was less a question than an accusation. Shirley felt a familiar heat rising within her.

"Allison certainly would have told me," she said, hearing the anger in her voice almost with relief.

"Children are not always . . . frank with their parents."

"In this case, she would have been. April told Allison that she'd been expelled from a school in the East. Allison witnessed April shoplifting. Allison told me both of these facts, quite frankly, and we made reasonable inferences from them. Believe me, Allison would have been very much aware of the implications of any gift from your daughter. You are welcome to ask her, but I believe the answer will be no. April made no gift to Allison."

Mrs. Shaour turned her head away, not quite quickly enough to hide the tears in her eyes. Shirley waited for the woman to object, to contradict, to defend her daughter's reputation.

Nothing. Shirley clamped her lips shut. She was not going to describe the items J.Q. had found among April's things. If this man was talking about anything real, he was talking about the golden horse. He wanted it. He wanted it far more than he wanted whoever killed his daughter. He cared about

47

it more than he had his daughter. Under those circumstances, better leave the little horse right where it was and bring this conversation to a conclusion.

Shaour wasn't ready to conclude, however. "This place she went alone. Is it a place I can go? To see?"

Shirley was suddenly too exhausted by her conflicting feelings to deal with them any longer. "Ask Mr. Quentin," she murmured. "Harry Fielding, the manager at Rancho del Valle, told us the mesa is sacred land, but if you can get permission from the pueblo, I'm sure J.Q. will take you there."

They turned to leave, making no farewells. At the door, the woman stopped suddenly, then returned to the bedside.

"Thank you," she said, tears spilling down her face. "Thank you for being April's friend."

"Pearl!" said her husband from the door.

"Coming," she blurted, ducking her head as she followed him into the corridor.

Shirley lowered the head of the bed slightly and put her arm across her eyes, trying to get herself back together. To pain and discomfort and anger, now add a cupful of guilt! Oh, yes, Mama Shaour, Pearl, thank me for being April's friend! That's all I need!

"The nurse says you aren't eating," said J.Q.

It was midafternoon. He'd shown up just as the husky therapist was reinserting her legs in the plastic sleeves after her afternoon stroll down the corridor and back. Thump, thump thump in one direction. Turn around. Thump, thump, thump back again. The therapist turned on the leg machine and left. The machine began its ominous breathing: buzz, stop, exhale, long silence.

"Shirley," J.Q. repeated. "What's this about not eating?"

"I ate breakfast. I didn't eat lunch because I was too . . . upset," she admitted.

"The Shaours?" he asked.

She pulled herself up onto the pillow. "I suppose they kicked it off. They made me think about April, which made me think about why we'd come along on this trip in the first place, which was, as you very well know, to get away from home. That brought up the whole business about selling the ranch, or not selling it. About all that business last year. I'm stuck, J.Q. I feel like I'm at top dead center. I'm not usually indecisive, you know that. But I can't make up my mind what to do!"

She fell silent, breathing deeply. After a moment, she continued, "Living there . . . our life there has been spoiled for me, for us. Every time I look at it, all I can think of is how it used to be before all that destruction. But selling seems . . . it seems like a betrayal. That land meant so much to my folks. . . ."

He laid a firm hand on her shoulder. "Listen, lady, you are *not* going to decide today. Or next week. You will decide when you're ready. Until then, think about something else. How did April's people upset you?"

She heaved a deep breath, trying to get clean air into her lungs. "There's something unnatural about them. About him, at any rate. She was like a robot under full control. She wanted to grieve, wanted to cry, but he wouldn't let her. God, J.Q. she thanked me for being a friend to her daughter. I was anything but!"

He sat down and took her hand, punctuating his sentences with little squeezes. "You tried to be her friend, Shirley. You would have been her good friend if she'd let you. Just as I would have been, or Allison. Deal with reality. We knew the girl for two weeks, during most of which time we were fully engaged being drivers or chaperones or cooks. We've had no time to provide therapy, and in any case, neither of us is qualified. Let's not get caught up in some self-imposed guilt trip here."

Shirley wiped her eyes. "The last thing I said to her was she was her own worst enemy."

"More or less true." He put her hand down with a final pat. "Though, having met Papa, I'd bet he was the worst one."

"You met him?"

"They're staying in the little house we had rented out at Rancho del Valle, at least for today. Shaour asked me to take him out where we found April. I told him I'd ask for permission from the pueblo, and if I got it, I'd take him. I called the pueblo police, and they said they'd call me back. Do you have any idea why he wants to go out there?"

"He's looking for something, J.Q. If you want my guess, it's something about an inch long, quite heavy, probably gold."

"The little horse?"

"Right."

"You think April stole it from him?"

"How else would he know about it? I keep thinking of something Allison said. She told me the only time April's parents paid any attention to her was when she was in trouble. So try this scenario: She finds this thing hidden at home. She takes the thing; she leaves on her field trip, which she did not earn, by the way. She was included only because her mother begged Xanthippe to do so. Her father discovers the golden horse is gone, but decides the least conspicuous thing to do is wait until she returns from the field trip to find out about it. Then, suddenly, she's not going to return, and he has to find the thing."

"Why would it necessarily have belonged to him? Why not to some other kid's parent?"

"The geography, J.Q. I mentioned that Scythian exhibit I saw in D.C., and I've been lying here, visualizing the gallery and how it was laid out. The centerpiece of the exhibit was a full-scale replica of a Scythian tomb. At the tomb entrance was one of those big simplified display maps, this one showing the locations of all the tombs that had been excavated. My recollection is they were scattered all the way from central Russia west into Germany, and down between the Black Sea and the Caspian, into where Iraq is now.''

"Including, presumably, Armenia and Azerbaijan, which are down on the Iranian border.''

She concentrated. "I think most of the stuff in the exhibit I saw was on loan from Russian museums, the Hermitage, particularly. I wish I had an atlas. Isn't the whole mess right there where Iran and Iraq and Russia and Turkey all knot up?''

J.Q. nodded slowly. "Georgia to the north.''

"Which is now independent and tearing itself apart. With everybody over there preoccupied by politics and food shortages and inflation, maybe it's the best possible time to smuggle stuff!''

"If one had a way to cross borders.''

Shirley shrugged. "So long as Shaour's got family there, who's going to question his coming and going?''

"Allison says his wife is scared.''

"I thought so too. She is scared, of him, certainly, and maybe of more than him. And it's connected to that horse, which is maybe what's being smuggled. It and other things like it. Tomb stuff. And it belongs to who? Russia? Georgia? Armenia?''

"Where's the motive for murder?''

"There may not be one. The two things aren't necessarily connected. April got shot. It could have been an accident. Daddy's showing up looking for missing treasure may be a consequence, not a cause.''

"I suppose.'' He drummed his finger on the glass. "Listen, Shirley, fascinating though it is, we have to set all that stuff aside for the moment.''

"I'd just as soon set it aside forever.''

"No, just for the moment.'' He seated himself, leaning

forward to take her hand once more. "We've got to have a consultation here."

"Nothing earthshaking, I hope?"

"Not really, no. Just necessary."

"All right. What?"

"The little houses at the guest ranch were a bargain when all the young people were with us. But for only the three of us, it's rather expensive, besides which, the Fieldings have reservations starting Saturday for both the houses we've been occupying. That's point one. Point two is, you're not going to be fit to travel for a while. Allison and I talked it over. Since we'd planned to be gone anyhow for a few more weeks, and since Will Jacobs is willing to stay on at the ranch and take care of our livestock for as long as necessary, we could rent a furnished place here in Los Arboles. There are places available, and a month won't cost us any more than a week did at the guest ranch."

"Allison will miss Beauregard," Shirley offered in a faint voice. "I . . . I'll miss . . ."

"Of course you will. She will. So will I. That's not the point."

"Stay here in New Mexico?"

"There's a two-bedroom house half a mile from here. Six hundred a month, plus deposit. It's shabby, but it's reasonably clean. The woman who owns it will even supply bed linens."

"Two bedrooms?"

"I'll rent a folding cot for Allison."

She made a face. She could visualize the house. Tiny, cramped, airless. With cast-off furniture and peeling windowsills and walls that needed painting.

J.Q. saw the expression on her face. It was exactly the reaction he'd expected.

"There's an alternative. Out at Rancho del Valle, Harry and Sarah Fielding occupy a separate suite in one wing of

the main house. The rest of the house, including three bedrooms, is empty, and the owners are willing to let us use it."

"How much?"

"Harry felt terrible about what happened. He made some
kind of a pitch to the owners. They'll let us stay there for
nothing. Just be sure it's cleaned up when we leave."

She relaxed against the pillow. The picture that came un-
bidden to her mind was of last Sunday morning: church bells;
the tent of sparkling leaves between her and the sky; the
poultry wandering about; the colorful splashes of blooming
flowers.

J.Q. said softly, "Don't forget the swimming pool. The
doctor said swimming would be the best possible exercise
for that leg."

"I'd like that," she said, surprising herself. "If we've got
to stay here, that wouldn't be bad, J.Q."

"Allison agrees with you." He grinned.

The grin told her she'd been manipulated. "All that stuff
about a two-bedroom rental house . . ."

"It's there. I looked at it. I wouldn't lie to you, Shirley."

"There's lies and then there's lies," she murmured. "It
was nice of the Fieldings."

"Sarah says she likes you, though what provoked her to
that opinion, I can't say. Also, Harry and I get on well. I
helped him with the plumbing this morning early: idiot guests
putting their disposable diapers and what have you down the
drain. He had a sewer snake, but it was a hand-cranked one,
and I lent him a little muscle." He leaned forward and patted
her hand. "They're pleasant, friendly people, and it'll be a
nice place to convalesce."

She supposed it would.

"Shirley?"

"I hear you."

"Well, talk to me, for heaven's sake. You keep going off
into these . . . muses."

She cleared her throat and said in clear, measured tones,

"I agree it sounds more pleasant at the guest ranch. I'd rather do that than live in a rented, furnished house."

"I don't hear the *but*, but it's there. What don't you agree with?"

"I don't agree with any of this," she cried in sudden pain, the emotion surging up from some lower stratum, like lava, boiling and bubbling. She gestured at the walls, the ceiling. "I don't agree with my being here. Or with April getting shot, with those people who call themselves her parents, with . . . with any of this. I don't agree with what's happening to our home. It's crazy. I don't belong here."

"Of course you don't!"

"Don't soothe me, J.Q.!"

"Somebody needs to. Calm down. It's only . . . what? This is Wednesday. By Saturday or Sunday, they'll let you go. Three more days, we'll get you out of here."

She subsided, still fuming. He was right. This whole thing was getting too much for her. She had never been able to handle frustration or delay or inactivity. "What shall we do about the little horse?"

"Hang on to it. If we're staying at the ranch, I can always 'find it' later and give it to the police."

"Or to April's father."

"Or to April's father."

"Why is it I feel that giving it to him might be a dangerous thing to do?"

J.Q. regarded her thoughtfully. "A thing that should be done publicly, perhaps, with lots of witnesses?"

She shuddered, remembering his unblinking, theropsian gaze. "I wouldn't want him to think I was the only person who knew about it, that's all."

3

"I'VE BEEN WONDERING," Shirley said to J.Q., when she saw him on Thursday morning. "How did you get me to the hospital?"

He looked vacant for a moment, remembering. "Lord, it seems like a month ago. I yelled at Allison to ride like hell for the Durans' and phone for an ambulance and for the sheriff. Xanthy and I got you over your mule. Xanthy stayed with April's body."

"You knew she was . . . ?"

"Yes. We both knew she was. We were on a straight stretch of trail, and whoever shot her was up the hillside we were moving toward. Assuming it was purposeful, they had plenty of time to get the shot off as we approached, and she died the minute the bullet hit her. There was no question about it, even at the time. If your mule hadn't jumped, you might've caught the next one."

"All that detail tells me you went back and looked."

"On Monday I went back with the Santa Fe County sheriff's deputy and we looked, yes. We figured it out together."

"So you came all the way down with me over a mule?"

"Right. Allison and the sheriff's men met me at the bosque, and one of them went on up the trail while the other one helped me get you back. The ambulance was at the Durans' when we got there. Fredo had done the calling, and he's the one who picked this hospital." He gave her a sympathetic look. "Anything else you want to know?"

She shifted uncomfortably. "Not really, no. I seem to be doing a lot of half dozing at night, not really asleep, you know? Worrying about things in general; wondering about things. Like, why didn't we see anyone? And how long was it, before anyone could go looking? And why was I unconscious all that time?"

"You landed on your head, idiot! You were concussed. I figured the shape your face was in would tell you that!"

She nodded soberly. "The lump on my head should have told me if my face didn't. Xanthy wouldn't have gone looking alone after you left, would she?"

"You know she wouldn't. When I left she was sitting with April's head in her lap. Nothing would have been further from her mind than climbing around on the mountainside. The sheriff's people searched, of course, but that was much later."

"It was a rifle shot?"

"Sheriff's office says a high-powered twenty-two, determined purely by the size of the entrance wound. They figure it was steel-jacketed ammo, because it went . . . through her. They didn't find the bullet. The shots were so close together, I thought at first it was two guns."

"Why would anyone have used two guns?"

He shrugged. "They wouldn't. But the shots were very fast. And if the shooter was aiming for her head, he was a good marksman."

"You don't think the sheriff's office or the pueblo police are going to get anywhere with this, do you?"

"Nope."

"Why?"

"Firstly, the size of the gun has them convinced it was somebody out plinking at squirrels or crows or something. I mean, a twenty-two rifle can be lethal, but it isn't exactly a choice of murder weapons, is it? They're choosing to ignore the ammunition, which is certainly overkill for squirrels. Secondly, supposing April was the target, it's not a straightforward kind of thing. It's not her folks killing her for insurance. . . ."

"J.Q.! That's terrible."

"Listen, it was the sheriff who came up with that idea. He says he's heard of such cases. However, according to him, she wasn't insured, had no inheritance coming, no nothing. Seemingly no one benefited from her death. That's what I was getting at when I said it wasn't straightforward. It isn't murder for gain, murder for revenge, murder out of anger, any of those easy things we usually think of. If there was any motive at all, it may be remote from here."

"Something she did or saw back at home?"

"Quite possibly. Something she stuck her nose into. Something she stole that she shouldn't have. And, like most lawmen, the guys down here have their hands full. They aren't likely to send anyone to Colorado to find some motive that may or may not exist." He made a face and rubbed his chin in irritation. "Hell, they could spend twenty-four hours a day running down DUIs. The populace drives like maniacs. Remember when we left here Saturday night? On the way out to the car?"

She cast her mind back. Xanthy had come out of the Admissions office; April had joined them from her trip to the toilets; then the four of them had trailed out into the parking lot, still hot from the day's sun, with a gusty little wind sending candy wrappers and cigarette boxes skittering ahead of them. An ambulance had screamed eerily behind them as it circled the building toward the emergency entrance; the headlights of three cars had moved sedately along the barricade at the canyon's edge before turning in to the parking lot, the last one barely avoiding a brown pickup that careened around the corner of the building and barreled through the driveway stop sign before racing off toward town on squealing tires.

"The pickup truck," she said now. "The brown one that almost hit the car. But that happens. It's no worse than in Boston. Or New York City."

"In Boston it's defensive: too many cars bottlenecked into too few streets. In New York City it's taxicabs: drivers to whom time is money. Here in New Mexico, it's machismo. You get behind the wheel with a couple of six-packs and go cruising, yelling at your friends, threatening your enemies, picking up girls. As soon as you finish a beer, you throw it out the window because it's against the law to have open cans in the car. Since you're already throwing cans out of the car, you throw everything else out, too. The New Mexico state bird, the Road Trasher. It's a way of life. If it doesn't end in a fight, it can end in a heap of wreckage." He smoothed his mustache and scowled.

"My, you are in a tizzy."

He grunted. "The Wagoneer's in the shop."

"What!"

"On my way home from here yesterday I was hit from behind by an idiot who was waving a beer can and looking elsewhere at the time. I actually saw him in the rearview mirror, one hand on the wheel, the other one out the window waving at some guy going the other way!"

She sighed. "How bad?"

"Not too bad, considering. He, of course, was not only DUI, he was also unlicensed and uninsured. As, no doubt, were the other two guys and three girls in the car with him.

58

All that half-soused nubility and virility, just waiting to happen.''

"You're sounding a wee smitch reactionary there, J.Q. Or is it envious?''

He sighed again. "I suppose it could be, but damn it, anybody who watches the news knows this state has the highest rate of alcohol-related accidents and deaths in the country. Largely due, no doubt, to irresponsible legislators of varying backgrounds who have relatives working for the liquor industry.''

Shirley made soothing noises, but he went on fuming at himself.

"Damn it! I could've avoided that guy last night if I'd just been a little more alert!''

"So now we both have something to feel guilty about.''

"I suppose,'' he growled, shaking himself like a dog, as though to shed his bad temper. "Since yesterday I've managed to do only one constructive thing.''

"What did you do?''

"While I was waiting at the garage, I called this guy in Santa Fe, supposed to be an art expert.''

Shirley sat up eagerly. "You did? What did he say?''

"I thought it might help you pass the time if he came here, so I brought the horse for you to show him.'' He fished it out of his pocket and handed it to her. "I told him enough to pique his curiosity.''

"What's his name?''

"Dennison McFee.''

"Good old New Mexican name.''

"Maybe he's a retired yuppie. Sarah put me on to him. He's from Philadelphia originally. Now he runs a shop in Santa Fe, kind of a weird place, according to Sarah. Furniture. Art. All kinds of stuff, old and new. But he's got a good reputation. If he says something is eighteenth-century English, he's probably right, give or take a century and a country either way. I'm quoting Sarah.''

"When's he coming?"

"Sometime this afternoon."

She looked thoughtfully out the window. "Do you still have that little leather bag?"

"It's in my jacket pocket."

"Would you leave it with me?"

"If you want it, sure. You want to show it to McFee when he comes?"

"This afternoon, you said. Damn. J.Q., I don't even have—"

"A robe, I know. Xanthy went through your clothes and picked out some stuff." He pointed to a case beside him on the floor, one Shirley hadn't noticed. "She put in some long shirts, in case you're tired of hospital gowns. She says there's a robe in there that still had the tags on it."

Of course it did. She'd bought it at the Tall Shop on a whim because it had been marked down to some ridiculous price. Heavy raw silk, with a zipper down the front and a fancy belt. The shade of green would almost match her bruises. Just the color-coordinated ensemble in which to welcome an art expert to one's hospital room!

The morning brightened somewhat with Judy's arrival, bringing crutches.

"I know you hate that walker," she offered.

"I do indeed."

"You're strong on your arms, so maybe these will be easier for you. Don't try them until Bryan's here to keep you from falling."

The crutches added novelty to an otherwise dull session of leg raises and buttock squeezes. When she returned from her quite lengthy foray down the hall, she put on the green robe and got into the room's only armchair, her immobilized leg propped on a stool. She would lunch sitting up for a change. Besides, bed was no place to confer with an art expert.

Lunch was delivered. The vital signs person made her

rounds. A nurse stuck her nose in and demanded why the room hadn't been cleaned.

Shirley disclaimed any responsibility. "I didn't send anyone away, if that's what you mean."

"Helga should have cleaned in here this morning! Lately I wonder where her head is! I'll send someone."

She sent a woman with a flashing smile and no English who energetically mopped and polished, departing just before the arrival of the much-awaited expert.

He introduced himself in a mellow voice and bowed over her proffered hand before settling his lean body onto the straight chair, triangular face tilted toward her, hands held at chest level, his large, wide-apart eyes made to appear even larger by the huge horn-rimmed glasses he wore.

"Ms. McClintock," he murmured. His mouth was small, his jaw fragile-looking, but his teeth were white and sharp as a cat's.

Shirley shook herself mentally, wondering if the man's resemblance to a huge praying mantis was accidental or purposeful. Did he know he looked like a carnivorous bug? Wordlessly she took the tiny horse from her pocket and handed it to him.

"Well," he breathed. "Isn't this interesting."

"Is there some way you can tell what it is?"

He moved his head from side to side slowly, as though to avoid frightening possible prey. "I can tell you what it looks like, but Mr. Quentin told me you already know what it looks like. I agree with you, by the way. I, too, would have said Scythian. By which we mean Greek, of course. Much Scythian goldwork was done by Greek goldsmiths, though they often used Scythian stylistic conventions. As here. The breaking up of the figure into sculptural planes. The exaggeration of the mane."

"It looks new," she offered.

He nodded. "Gold always does, which is part of its allure. It doesn't corrode or rust or change its atomic structure. This little animal could have been cast a millennium ago, or yesterday. Maybe a mold was made from something old, and the metal was poured last week. Who can tell?''

Shirley furrowed her brow, trying to remember. ''Haven't I read something . . . about inclusions? When gold isn't absolutely pure.''

He smiled, his wickedly triangular smile. ''True. Gold is never absolutely pure. There are always a few traces of other elements included. Those elements can be identified, and then the item, whatever it is, can be connected, perhaps, to other items with identical inclusions, the supposition being that both would have been cast in the same location, perhaps at the same time. However, even if this item has unique inclusions, one would have to have something to compare it to. Perhaps the torque from which it came?''

''Torque?''

He put the little horse back into her hand and bent forward to take a folder from an elegantly slender case.

''After I talked to Mr. Quentin, I pulled a few things out of my files. I'm not a dealer in Eurasian antiquities, but they fascinate me. I keep clippings and pictures.''

He laid the contents of the folder on her lap, mostly pages from magazines or catalogs, printed on both sides. He leafed through them, pulling one to the top. It showed a massive necklace made of twisted rods and hammered crescents, the crescents decorated with blossoms and leaves, the space between the elements filled by processions of tiny animals: horses, sheep, griffins, lions; the whole a mass of glistening gold.

''See how the animals are connected?'' he pointed. ''The separate elements of the necklace were joined at the clasp, at the back of the neck. The little animals were cast separately, then soldered between the elements, the feet on the bottom crescent, the necks on the top one. I note rough spots on the one you have. It may have been fastened in this same way.''

"I've seen this before," she said, tapping the picture. "I remember it. Was it ever exhibited in the U.S.?"

"It was on exhibit here twenty-five or thirty years ago. As a matter of fact, I salvaged the pictures from an old exhibit catalog."

"That's why it looks familiar. I must have seen it in Washington." She held up the horse, comparing it to the picture. Similar. Similar as to size and style. Not identical.

"What do you think?" she asked.

"Your friend said someone connected with this . . . happening was from an area near the Caspian Sea?"

"True."

"After I spoke to him, I called a colleague who's a specialist in Middle Eastern antiquities. He tells me there are Scythian tombs in that area. Not as many as farther east, but rich ones nonetheless. All such tombs and their contents have been the property of the Russian state, of course. Now, with conditions as they are, who's going to assert ownership? Do the citizens even know which state they are in? Is one Armenian or Georgian? Azeri or Russian?" He rolled his eyes and turned palms up, emphasizing confusion.

She said, "So if someone had discovered a Scythian tomb and managed to keep it quiet, now might be a good time to smuggle the stuff out?"

"The authorities are certainly much distracted with other matters. People are moving across borders in great numbers. If one wished to profit from one's discovery, one would certainly find a better market here or in Japan or in Germany than one would find currently in Russia or one of the other republics. The ruble is relatively worthless at the current time. But, as I said, with gold there's no way to determine whether a thing is a copy or not. To get a good price, one would need a provenance."

"What counts as a provenance?"

He looked up at the ceiling, fingers of his left hand stroking his tiny chin, musing. "I asked my colleague what he'd accept. He said first he'd want proof of identity from the finder, who needs to be a real person, with an address and a verifiable biography. There have been cases where unfortunate curators have purchased things from Mr. Jones only to learn later that Mr. Jones never existed. Then my colleague would want a sworn statement that this tomb had been found in a specific place. He'd want maps and photographs of the place, and of the item in situ, as it was found, along with a catalog and pictures of any other pieces found in the same place. The more detail the better. If there are living witnesses to the discovery, that makes it tighter. My colleague said with documents like that, plus whatever export documents are required by the country of origin, he could buy or sell with complete impunity. Of course, he's exceedingly careful. I personally know of museum purchases made with far less provenance than that—and no export licenses at all!''

"If someone were keeping the matter quiet, they wouldn't want too much detail, would they?''

"Not if it were to be made public. Not if they had to go back over there, no. Word might get around. Among people associated with antiquities, I can almost assure you word would get around. I murmured the word *Scythian* and my friend's little ears perked up. He was very eager to know who and where and when and what. There's an international community of curators, rather like the international communities of astronomers or physicists. Despite attempts at secrecy, it exists independent of country or language. Secrets are very hard to keep.''

He nodded solemnly to himself, thinking it over before continuing: "But, if the person in question is living in this country permanently, why not give a provenance? This country has no extradition agreement with Armenia, or Georgia, though we may eventually have one. When and if we do, it wouldn't be retroactive.''

Shirley eased her leg on its support. "If my scenario is correct, this person wouldn't want to go public until he has everything over here. He's made repeated trips over there and back. He's just returned from one such trip. If he's smuggling in the treasure, piece by piece, he certainly won't want any premature publicity."

McFee smiled his wickedly triangular smile once more, as though he were about to bite off someone's head and eat it. "Under those circumstances, true."

"In which case, have we made a mistake by showing it to you?"

He laughed and made a crisscross motion with his right hand at his chest. "Cross my heart, I won't tell. If I did, I could get dragged in, and believe me, I value my quiet life more than you can possibly imagine."

He said it with such fervor that she gave him a curious look. "Is that why you're here in New Mexico? For the quiet life?"

"It is indeed. Someday, if we get to know one another better, I'll regale you with tales of dirty deals in the art and antique world, skulduggery that will make your head swim."

"You were in the middle of it?"

"Innocently. Or so I tell myself. But then, you're a countryman. You're a McClintock. I'm a McFee. We canny Scots don't get mixed up in anything nefarious!"

"There are some who would disagree," she said soberly, handing him back his folder of pictures. "I can't thank you enough, Mr. McFee."

"Call me Dennison."

"If you like. I'm Shirley."

"I know. Mr. Quentin told me about you and your connection with all this. Please be assured that I do take the matter seriously. A child dead, he said."

Shirley shut her eyes, thinking of April. "A child dead, yes. Though the more I learn, the more unlikely it is that this artifact has anything to do with her death."

"If this is a separate matter, would it upset you if someone were to tip off the authorities in customs?"

She looked a question at him.

He said softly, "I truly believe art and antiquities are the heritage of civilization, and particularly of the countries where they are found. I don't like profiteers in antiquities. I don't like pot hunters in New Mexico taking Anasazi artifacts to Japan or Germany, either, and there's a lot of that going on as well. The market in pre-Columbian art here in the Southwest is so very good that it's tempting all kinds of people who wouldn't have thought of becoming grave robbers ten years ago. Not merely scoundrels but formerly respectable people."

She thought it over. "If customs got involved, I wouldn't mind. No. You haven't met Mr. Shaour, so you'll have to take my word for it, but he's one of the most cold-blooded men I've ever met. He wasn't the least upset at his daughter being dead. He was only concerned that she might have shown this—" she patted her pocket "—to someone. Or given it to someone. At least, so I read him."

"What are you going to do with the little horse?"

"I have two choices. One is give it to the police. The other is give it to Shaour."

"You don't intend to keep it?" He stared at her from under his scanty lashes, huge lenses flashing.

She was shocked into disclaimer. "Lord, no! It isn't mine. I keep seeing . . . seeing April's angry little face, so very . . . solitary. She wasn't a nice child, you see. Quite the contrary. But when I met her father and mother . . . I knew why. I felt . . . I felt I hadn't tried hard enough with her, hadn't been patient enough. Well. I can't do anything about that now, but it would seem a betrayal just to hand this thing over to her father. The safer course is to give it to the police."

"That would be my choice. But first it should be photographed and weighed, and someone like myself should attest to the fact it is, indeed, pure gold."

"Why?"

"Oh, for later reference. Or to prevent its disappearance.

It's a little thing. Such things do disappear. I can have it back to you by the end of the day.''

''That's very kind of you . . . Dennison.''

He held out his hand and she dropped the horse into it.

She said, ''You're going out of your way to be helpful.''

''I'm intrigued,'' he said, busily jotting at a page in his pocket notebook. ''While I may have chosen to escape to a quieter life, little puzzles and confusions still interest me.'' He handed her a handwritten receipt.

''Before you go,'' she said. ''If you have just a minute more . . .''

''Certainly.''

She took the little bag from her pocket and handed it to him. He raised his eyebrows. She gestured. He opened it and put the contents on the arms of the chair. Pot shards. Clay pipe. Animal bone. A turquoise ring. A carved bear. He sat looking at them.

She asked softly, ''If you were asked your opinion, what would you say this collection represents?''

''Not a collection of things used for a ritual purpose,'' he murmured. ''I've seen some of those, and this isn't typical.''

''I didn't think so either. Though it was an uninformed opinion.''

''Evidence, perhaps?''

''Evidence?''

''As I was saying earlier, things in situ—together with a list of other things found in the same place. Provenance. I might not have thought of that if we hadn't been discussing it.''

''You mean, these might be samples?''

They stared at each other blankly.

''Can animal bone be carbon-dated, or whatever they do?''

''I don't know,'' he replied.

''How about the carvings? Or the shards.''

''Again, I'm out of my depth. Perhaps I can find out.''

"Only if you have time."

"Not immediately. But soon. I'll see what I can do."

He put the bag into his pocket and rose to bow himself out, patting the breast pocket into which he had dropped the golden horse.

She saw him again briefly, just before suppertime, when he came in, his very eastern-establishment raincoat sheeted with moisture, to return the horse, now wrapped in tissue, taped, and carefully packed in a tiny purple box with "Mc-Fee" in golden letters. He also delivered an envelope, taking it from an inside pocket, which held a description of the horse typed on his letterhead and signed by him. When J.Q. arrived at seven, also soaking wet, Shirley gave him both items.

"According to the paper, Dennison has pictures, a complete description, and a statement that the thing is pure gold," she said.

"Dennison, is it?"

"He was very nice. He suggests you give it to the police. . . ."

"The sheriff's office," he corrected. "It was found in their jurisdiction."

"All right, to the sheriff's office. But Dennison emphasizes we must get a receipt and be sure to tell them it's been examined. He says it will be less likely to vanish that way."

J.Q. tossed the little box, catching it, tossing it up, catching it. "If they ask where I found it, I'll tell them it was stuffed down in the couch next to the fireplace where April and Allison were sitting Saturday night, after we got back from the hospital. I know it wasn't there earlier, because I looked for my pocket knife there on Saturday morning. The thing looked valuable, so we asked Dennison to look at it. How's that for harmless invention?"

"They'll ask why you waited so long. We say it only occurred to us tonight that it might have anything to do with April's death," Shirley remarked.

"Right." He gave her one of his inscrutable J.Q. looks, a look that might mean almost anything. "But you don't think it does, do you?"

"Have anything to do with her death? I'm not discounting the idea entirely, but I can't make it connect up. If her daddy thought she had it, he sure wouldn't want her dead before she could tell him where it was. Of course, there may be some third party."

"Daddy's partner in crime?" he suggested.

"If Daddy had a partner, that partner might have considered her a danger."

"In which case, we haven't a clue."

"No," Shirley murmured. "If I had to bet on it, I'd bet it was something else that got her killed, J.Q. Something she saw. Something she said to someone. Talk to Allison. . . . Where is Allison?"

"Moving your things and hers over to the main house. Making up the beds. The former occupant had a lot of little stuff standing around. Allison and Xanthy are moving it out of your way, so you won't trip over your crutches."

"Is Xanthy staying?"

"She's staying at least until you get out of the hospital. She says she may stay awhile longer. There're two beds in the master bedroom, so she and Allison are sharing."

"How about the Shaours?"

"They're still out there, in the smaller house the boys and I were using, but since it's reserved by someone else starting Saturday night, the Shaours will have to leave by then. The pueblo office called and said I could take him out to Blue Mesa. I'll do that in the morning."

"Before or after you turn in the horse?"

J.Q. frowned thoughtfully. "Since Xanthy says none of the kids recognize the thing, I'll go by the sheriff's office and drop off the horse this evening. The rain was heavy earlier, but it seemed to be letting up when I came in."

"I didn't even know it was raining until I saw Dennison's raincoat."

"Sarah tells me this is the monsoon season, late July and August. Farmers love it and the highway department hates it, because it brings down rock from the arroyo walls along the highways. Always lots of accidents. People driving too fast for road conditions. Anyhow, if I turn in the horse tonight, I can mention it to Shaour in the morning. Work it into the conversation somehow."

"J.Q., you're sneaky."

He looked uncomfortable. "It takes one to know one."

"Tomorrow's Friday."

"That's right."

"Two or three more days?"

"You're getting eager."

"Oh, God, J.Q. I suppose it's not bad as hospitals go, but I want to see the last of this place. I really do!"

On Friday morning, J.Q. knocked at the door of the house occupied by the Shaours, waiting impatiently until it was answered by Suleiman Shaour himself.

"Mr. Quentin," he murmured in his virtually accentless voice. "You have received permission from the pueblo?"

J.Q. nodded. "The man called me back late yesterday. If you're willing to ride horseback."

"I do not understand."

"After all the rain, they prefer we not drive out there in a car or truck because the wheels, particularly four-wheel drive, tear up the terrain. They prefer we either hike or ride horses. I don't have time to hike. So if you're willing to ride . . . ?"

"Of course. Where do we procure horses?"

"I'll be back here with horses in about thirty minutes. If you have any less citified clothes than those, particularly the shoes, I'd put them on." He turned on his heel and left, more than a little irritated. This was not how he wanted to spend

70

the morning, and he didn't believe for one minute this man cared where his daughter had had her accident.

Since the Wagoneer was in the shop, he had borrowed Xanthy's car for the morning. He drove to the Durans' place, saddled two horses, and returned riding one and leading the other to find Shaour waiting in the driveway for him. He was dressed in khaki trousers, a light shirt, and sensible shoes. Tomb-robbing clothes, J.Q. said to himself, taking no apparent notice. Shaour at least knew which side of a horse to get on, though he mounted without assurance and rode like a sack of grain, slumped, his face set in its usual expressionless mode.

They rode down through the river bottom and onto the desert opposite, heading northwestward over dustless terrain toward the sky-filling bulk of Blue Mesa. There was something to be said for a good rain! The air was marvelously clear.

"This is the Blue Mesa," Shaour said. "What does it mean to say it is sacred?"

"I don't know," J.Q. replied. "When we told Harry Fielding that April had probably gone there, he told us that San Pedro Pueblo lands start about halfway between here and there and that the mesa itself is sacred to the pueblo. He said they don't appreciate trespassers, but that they know him, so he'd call their tourist office to tell them what we were doing and he'd also come along in case anyone asked questions."

"Who was it who found her?"

"Shirley saw her first, up on a ledge where she'd fallen. She yelled. Harry and I came running. Harry and I got her down onto the level, then he went back for the car, and Shirley and I carried her out."

"So no one has said what it means, for this place to be sacred to the pueblo?"

J.Q. shrugged. "I suppose it means a place where worship is carried on, the dwelling place of a god, maybe?"

"Ah. But still they let us go this morning?"

J.Q. himself had wondered about that. Anticipating an argument, he'd told Ray Apodaca that April's father wanted to see where she'd fallen. There'd been no argument, however, merely a muttered approval and the request not to take a vehicle unless it was absolutely necessary. No mention of the place being sacred, or taboo, or other words to that effect.

"The place April fell is around to the east of the mesa," J.Q. said, urging his mount into a reluctant trot. The other horse followed suit, and Shaour clung for his life. Sighing, J.Q. let his fat gelding lapse into a comfortable walk once more. No point in shaking the guy off, maybe injuring him, then having to pick up the pieces.

They came to the narrow canyon April had entered, winding their way through freshly fallen stones, some of them sizable. Prudently, J.Q. kept an eye on the rock walls to either side. They came to a turning in the canyon, and J.Q. kneed his horse around to the right, up a narrower way. Near the end was a series of ledges, giant steps leading up the side of the arroyo.

"There," said J.Q., pulling his mount to a stop and leaning forward on the saddle horn. "She was on the third ledge up." He knew it was the third ledge because he'd counted them when he and Harry had brought April down, though they certainly didn't look the same now. The rockfalls had been more widespread than he noticed at first. The ledges held great chunks of it, newly split off, unstained.

Shaour dismounted awkwardly and began climbing the ledges. After a moment, J.Q. followed him, finding the new rock an uncomfortable route of ascent. Some of it teetered. Some of it let loose and went down as they climbed. He gritted his teeth, hoping Shaour would be careful. He didn't want to have to haul the guy out with a broken leg!

On the third ledge, J.Q. paused. "Here," he said.

"She fell from here, or she was found here?"

"She was found here," J.Q. answered, brow furrowed.

Shaour nodded once and began climbing again.

J.Q. shook his head and followed, snarling silently to himself. The next ledge was virtually invisible under the recently fallen stone. Some of the rocks were the size of small automobiles.

"This is new?" Shaour asked, pointing to the fall.

"Last night," J.Q. agreed. "Heavy rain usually brings new stone down from these vertical walls. Roots shove between the blocks, gradually opening cracks and pushing the blocks outward. Then when it rains, the water adds weight and lubrication, and down it comes."

"If she left something here, it is covered now," said the man, as though to himself. "And what is that?"

Following the direction of his fingers, J.Q. looked into a deep vertical crevice in the cliff, darkly shadowed, one thin beam of morning light penetrating to the very back, where it illuminated a huge painted pot. And another. He stepped forward and peered. A dozen or more.

"A discovery?" Shaour said, something almost like excitement in his voice.

J.Q. turned to leave the crevice, noticing as he did so that from this height he could see over the lower arroyo walls to the canyon beyond. A pickup truck was parked in the canyon mouth. Two men lounged near it, staring toward J.Q. and Shaour.

"Can we take them?" Shaour asked eagerly, more emotion in his voice than J.Q. had heard during the entire trip. "One, at least."

J.Q. muttered. "I said this was pueblo land. Everything on it belongs to the pueblo. And there are two men in a truck down there, watching us. I suggest you leave everything here very much alone."

Shaour looked out across the arroyo, as J.Q. had done, then turned, his face expressionless once more, and slowly, carefully, examined the floor of the crevice before shrugging slightly and climbing down as he had come. They mounted, turned the animals, and rode out once more. The truck was gone from the canyon mouth when they emerged, but J.Q. smelled cigarette smoke and knew they were parked not far away.

The discovery of the pots had been unexpected, but at least it provided a perfect lead-in for the subject J.Q. had intended to raise.

"That back there was almost a buried treasure, wasn't it?" he said garrulously. "I've been finding a lot of treasure lately."

"What?" the man said alertly. "What have you found?"

"In the couch, in the house we were living in. We found this little golden horse." He sneaked a glance at his companion, seeing the man's face for the first time colored by emotion. "I was real sorry to turn it over to the sheriff," J.Q. went on. "It was a pretty little thing."

"What sheriff is that?"

"Santa Fe County," said J.Q. It was the last thing he said during the trip. Shaour asked nothing more. When J.Q. dropped him off at the house, he handed his reins to J.Q. and went inside without a thank you or a backward look.

"Why am I entitled to a private room?" Shirley asked the vital signs person on Friday morning. The subject of what April might or might not have seen had occupied her during part of the night, making her resolve to discuss the hospital with anyone who would talk about it. "I didn't know there were private rooms anymore."

"I guess it's just the way the place was built," the woman said. "It's not like a city hospital where you have to cram people in. Los Arboles is sort of a support community for Santa Fe, with some scientific labs and a few high-tech computer firms, and we're not very big, even though we serve the surrounding rural areas as well. The hospital only has twenty-one beds, not counting maternity. Half the rooms are private, half semiprivate, but even in semiprivate, it's almost always only one person to a room. Unless we get really busy. Ski season, sometimes we fill up. Everybody breaking their arms and legs and collarbones all at once.''

''A quiet little hospital,'' Shirley commented, leading toward the point she wished to explore.

''Except now.'' She *whuffed* up the blood pressure cuff and listened intently, nodding as she let the air escape and put the cuff away in its cubicle at the head of the bed.

''Except now?'' Shirley asked.

''Now, with all the feds all over the place. You heard about our losing a baby.''

''Losing . . .''

''Well, somebody took it. Him. I'm surprised you hadn't heard. We've got the FBI all over the place.''

''When did this happen?''

''Saturday evening.''

Shirley reflected. ''I guess . . . was there something in the paper on Sunday?''

''On Sunday, and Monday, and every day since. It was the Franklins' baby, Stephanie Franklin; this was her first boy, the only male grandchild, *very* important baby. Normally she'd have had him home by Saturday, but she had a cesarean, so she wasn't going home until Tuesday or Wednesday.''

''You say the name as though I should recognize it.''

''Oh, that's right, you're not from around here. Well, she's a somebody. Maybe I should say, her husband's a somebody. No, his folks are somebodies. They own about a quarter of the state. His daddy was rich, and he married a Lujan, and she was an only child, so she inherited a hundred thousand acres or so to add to his.''

''So it was a kidnapping!''

''That's what the FBI thinks. So I hear.''

''Has anybody asked for ransom?''

''Hey, nobody's telling us anything. And they're not telling the papers, either. Since Sunday, there hasn't been anything new. Haven't you noticed?''

75

"I haven't seen a paper," Shirley confessed.

"Well, hey, there's a paper box right outside the front door. Tell your visitors to pick up one for you." She departed cheerily, waving her automatic thermometer.

Already dressed in her green robe and poised on her crutches, when the therapists arrived, Shirley announced she intended to walk to the maternity section.

"I want to see where the baby disappeared from," she said, watching Bryan's face with interest as it turned slowly cerise.

"I wish everybody would shut up about that baby!" he snarled.

Judy hurriedly interposed herself between Shirley and the husky therapist. "We've all been questioned until we're sick of it, including Bryan. The FBI has been after us. The city police. County police. Everyone who was in the hospital Saturday night has been questioned over and over."

"They didn't question me," said Shirley unthinkingly. "I was here."

Too late she noted Bryan's narrowed eyes. Oh, hell. Now she was in for it.

"Come on, Bryan," Judy said, shaking her head at her colleague. "She has to walk anyhow, and curiosity's no crime."

They thump-thumped their way down the corridor, Judy at her side, Bryan behind her, holding the fiber belt buckled around her waist while Shirley ostentatiously ignored him, much as a dog walker ignores a defecating dog. He's not mine, she said to herself, staring at some point far ahead of herself. He doesn't belong to me. He merely followed me home. Bryan, his face closed and angry, seemed equally intent upon ignoring her.

They stopped at the obligatory viewing window to look at twelve little baskets, two rows of six. There were five occupants that Shirley could see, three pink blankets and two blue. Someone seemed intent upon sexual distinctions even at this early age!

"How many babies were here Saturday night?" she asked.

Judy answered. "We had a rush! Six. But only three of them were in the nursery at the time. Two little girls and the Franklin boy."

"Where were the other three?"

"With their mothers. Being nursed or shown off to daddies or to grandparents or maybe rooming in."

"That's the new thing, isn't it?" said Shirley, suddenly overwhelmed with melancholy. When her babies had been born, there'd been no rooming in. There'd been damned little encouragement for breast feeding, either.

"Is it?" asked Judy, looking up at her. "It's the way they've always done it here."

Shirley snorted. How old was Judy? Twenty-two? Twenty-three? For her, it would be the way it had always been done. Bonding. Letting parents cuddle children. Letting fathers be in the delivery room. Childbirth classes. Probably some women of Shirley's age had partaken of those advantages, if they'd known about them.

Shirley said: "When I was first pregnant, thirty-five years ago, I'd never heard about childbirth without anesthesia, and my doctor didn't enlighten me. He was an older man, one who had his own way of doing things. His way was to wait until labor started, then send you to the hospital, where they knocked you out with drugs and delivered your baby, often using forceps that weren't strictly necessary. Then they gave you medication to stop your milk. They didn't even ask, as I recall, whether you wanted it or not. Breast feeding a baby was considered uncivilized. Two days later, they wheeled you down the hall where a nurse gave a class on bathing the baby and making formula. Four days later, they handed you a screaming bundle and discharged you. From then on, you were on your own."

"You're kidding." Her eyes were wide, as though she'd just been informed of some atrocity.

"No." Shirley sighed again. "I'm not kidding. All the obstetricians were male, and they knew what was good for us, which was whatever was most profitable or easiest for them. I can even remember a particular obstetrician telling me a diaphragm could give me blood clots."

"Why would he say such a thing?"

"He was in the business of delivering babies. He couldn't make money out of my using birth control."

Bryan tugged on her belt. "If you ladies are through with your female talk . . ."

"Oh, Bryan, get off it," Judy snapped. "Just because you're not into human reproduction, you don't need to be so superior."

"Let's just say I'm not particularly interested in the subject," he said stiffly. "Past or present."

He hurried them back to the room and left them abruptly when Shirley was safely seated on the side of her bed.

"Don't pay any attention to him," said Judy, busy reattaching the plastic balloons to Shirley's legs. "He broke up with his significant other last weekend, and he's been snarly with everybody ever since. All the questioning just makes him madder, because he and his friend had their big fight here, and Bryan has had to tell about ten people about it, in detail. The FBI guys are all right, in fact, they're almost human, but some of the local police . . . you know. They're so macho that if you're gay, it's equivalent to being an enemy of the state or something, and if you're lesbian, look out. Being lesbian is like being a servant of the devil. They'd burn you at the stake if they could."

"Bryan's gay?" Shirley asked, not really surprised. "This is an odd place to break up with one's lover."

"Not if your lover's a doctor," Judy replied, turning on the machine and checking the plastic tubing that connected

78

it to the balloons. "Humpty Dumpty was here checking on one of his patients."

"Humpty Dumpty?" murmured Shirley.

"Dr. Humphrey. Claude Humphrey," the therapist murmured. "He did your leg."

At Shirley's request—made calmly and with no visible anger—she was visited by the hospital administrator, a wraith-thin, elegantly coiffed woman named Dolores Stark.

Shirley explained her concern, concluding in the coolest tones she could manage, "I am normally not at a loss for words. But in this case, I don't even know what I'm entitled to ask. Or demand. I'm concerned about AIDS."

Was that what she was concerned about? Or was that merely an excuse for fury, for rage, for yelling and screaming and stamping about? She couldn't. Not here. If she let go, they'd put a needle in her arm and make notes about her having a psychotic episode, no doubt. Here was not the place to give in to anger.

The administrator shifted uncomfortably. "It's not a homosexual disease."

"Not strictly speaking, no. But thus far, only about six or seven percent of persons with the disease in this country got it through heterosexual contact. No doubt that percentage will grow, but just now the incidence is enormously greater among homosexuals. I'm not a homophobe, Ms. Stark. I won't say some of my best friends, and so forth, but I have known and liked people who are homosexual and I feel they are entitled to the same rights and responsibilities the rest of us have.

"However, I'm also pragmatic. I'd feel the same way if I had a red-haired Eskimo for a physician and found out it was mostly red headed Eskimos who had the disease. Any person who reads a newspaper or watches TV knows there's been talk of limiting the practice of health workers with the HIV virus. I think I'm entitled to know if Dr. Humphrey has the virus.''

"Two years ago all our personnel voted to be voluntarily checked every ninety days.''

"That doesn't answer my question.''

"Dr. Humphrey did not test positive at the last check.''

"And his friend, Bryan?''

"There would be no possible way you could become infected through physical therapy.''

"That's not the point! The point is, if one partner had tested positive, the other partner might have become infected in the interim.''

"Bryan's test was also negative. Our understanding is that the relationship is monogamous and has been for some time.'' She offered this tidbit in a slightly superior tone, as though monogamy were a state peculiar to personnel of this hospital.

"Then I'm left wondering what their argument was about,'' Shirley said. "Breakups between longtime lovers, homo or hetero, are sometimes caused by infidelity—actual or suspected. In case it's actual, the matter of past monogamy could well be moot.''

The administrator gestured, palms up.

Shirley read her mind. "That's an area of privacy, I suppose? One can't ask what the argument was about?''

"I wasn't aware there'd been an argument until earlier this week. The FBI uncovered that fact. One of the cleaning people overheard most of it, and now, unfortunately, it's common knowledge. I happen to admire Dr. Humphrey very much. He's a fine physician, and I think this whole matter is a tragic invasion of his privacy!''

Shirley shook her head and plowed on. "How long ago was your ninety-day check?''

"We're almost due to repeat—''

"I suggest you do so. Now. For my benefit. For my peace of mind.''

The woman went away, leaving Shirley in the grip of a bleak depression. She'd been fighting it ever since last fall. She'd been fighting it all through this trip. Anger was a way of fighting it, keeping it at bay. It wasn't, she told herself now, that she was any more afraid of death or change than anyone else, but she was horrified by the prospect of losing control over her own life. She was willing to confront what came, so long as what came was not a lingering and debilitating disease. What frightened her most was the knowledge that when one's body was weakened, one's resolve was weakened as well. She could not allow herself to weaken past that point.

"What's the matter?" said J.Q., who had come in silently and was now standing beside her bed. "You look . . ."

She told him, amazed that she could sound objective with all this bubbling animosity going on inside.

He sat down, wearily, as though his bones ached. "My God."

"I'm probably overreacting," she said. "It was just . . . a shock. Statistically there are probably more homosexuals who are free of the disease than homosexuals who have it."

"I don't know," he replied. "I have no idea. Do you want me to talk to him? The doctor?"

She shook her head. "The administrator's going to do it. The more I think about it . . . Maybe the fact he's a doctor is what caused the argument between him and his friend. Orthopedic surgery is as invasive a procedure as can be done. If HIV-positive doctors were prohibited from doing invasive procedures, and if he, the doctor, got the idea his friend was not totally monogamous . . . Maybe he told his friend he had to stop their relationship, to protect himself and his livelihood."

"Is he going to be tested?"

"I asked them to move up the test date. For my peace of mind."

"You say this big argument took place Saturday

night?'' he asked. ''Do you suppose April could have overheard . . . ?''

She nodded. ''The same thought occurred to me, J.Q., but even if she overheard something, it would have been no reason to kill her. It's obvious that everyone in the hospital knew about the relationship. It wasn't something hidden that they were afraid would get out!''

''The breakup was supposedly a secret.''

''No. I wouldn't say so. Just private. There's a difference. Bryan is angry because he was questioned, probably insensitively and possibly by people who despise him on principle. You've said it yourself: It's a macho society down here. They—I mean *they*, the police—might give the doctor a little room, because of his profession, but not someone who looks like a football player.''

''Why would they have questioned him at all?''

''Because he was *here*. So was Dr. Huphrey. They might have seen something, that's all. And come to that, you and I and Xanthy and Allison will probably be questioned as well. We were also here, which Bryan is now aware of. No doubt he'll tell somebody about us, just to get them off his neck.''

That afternoon, Judy was alone during Shirley's afternoon stroll, making a mere formality of the webbing belt that was supposed to keep Shirley from falling. They passed a comfortably furnished visitors' area on their way down the hall, and when they came to it again on the way back, Shirley asked, ''Would you mind if I sat down here for half an hour? It's a change of view, at least.''

Judy checked her watch and bustled off, saying she'd return in twenty or thirty minutes. Shirley lowered herself cautiously onto the only straight-backed chair. The day's newspaper lay scattered on the table, a file picture of Mrs. Franklin prominently displayed on the front page. Shirley read the kidnap coverage—finding nothing she had not already been told—and leafed through the paper for anything else of interest. Yet another drunk-driving scandal: A man previously arrested ten times had killed three people on his most recent foray. A brief account of the trial of a notorious pot hunter. Guilty, said the jury. A wildlife protection group was petitioning to release wolves into a national forest. Several pictures of wolves, playing with one another, playing with their keeper. Shirley had always liked wolves. Coyotes for clever, but wolves for nobility, in her view.

She laid the paper down and concentrated on what she could see out the window. It was a different view than the one from her room window, and she knew she needed a different view. A different something. No matter how much good sense she talked to herself, her innards remained in a state of seemingly permanent seethe, angry at the world and everyone in it. She was angry with her doctor, with Bryan, with the administrator. Angry at whoever had shot April. Angry at poor April herself, for getting shot. She needed to be by herself, to take herself firmly in hand, but as a patient, she was being constantly bullyragged by this one and that one. Every time she got herself together, some small irritation came along to ruffle her feathers. If she could just hold it together another day, two at most, she could go home . . . well, what amounted to home. Until then, she needed to sit quietly, alone, and generate enough equanimity or good sense to last her another twenty-four hours.

It wasn't fated, seemingly. A heavyset man in robe and slippers dropped himself on the couch across from her, nodded in her direction without looking at her, and picked up the paper she had abandoned. She looked resolutely out the window and ignored him, even when he began to snarl and mutter and turn slightly red around the jowls.

Shirley checked her watch, then craned her neck to look down the hall for Judy. No Judy. It had been almost half an hour, but Judy had been held up somewhere. She fidgeted. The muttering beside her grew louder. Both Judy and Bryan had cautioned her not to walk alone, though she felt fully capable of it. Perhaps it would be better to go than to stay. . . .

"Do you know what those goddamned environmentalists want to do!" the man demanded, turning on her.

"I beg your pardon?"

"Those goddamned environmentalists, do you know what they want to do?"

Shirley considered silence. Perhaps a shrug. Maybe she could claim deafness. The words came out before she could stop them. "They want to protect the environment, I suppose."

"They want to put wolves in the mountains. Wolves. Want to take these damned wolves and turn them loose in the national forest!" His face was very red, lower lip thrust out, eyes glaring.

"That sounds interesting," said Shirley in her most noncommittal voice.

"Interesting! Woman, are some kind of fool? I run my sheep up in those mountains. I've got grazing on ten thousand acres up there! What do you think wolves eat? Dog food? Out of cans? They eat lambs, that's what they eat."

"Deer, also," Shirley murmured. "And rabbits and mice."

"When they can get lamb, they eat lamb," he screamed at her. "Damned fool environmentalists don't seem to realize it's time for wolves to be extinct. Time for 'em. There was time for dinosaurs to go extinct, and now it's time for wolves to go extinct. We don't need them!"

Something snapped, almost audibly. "Personally," Shirley said, "I think it's time for national forest rip-off sheep ranchers to be extinct. We don't need them. We don't need to eat meat at all. We can all eat corn and beans." She snapped her fingers under his nose, towering over him, surprised to find herself standing up, not knowing how she had gotten standing up, but there nonetheless. "Time for you, sir, to quit fattening your sheep on public lands at public

84

expense and go the way of the dinosaurs. We don't *need* you, sir. In my opinion we *need* you less than we need redwood trees and wolves and polar bears and coyotes and wetlands. Tell you something, friend. God made wolves, but pork barrel politics made so-called ranchers who run their sheep in overgrazed national forests!''

Judy caught up with her halfway down the hallway.

"You're not supposed to be walking alone,'' she cried sotto voce. ''What did you say to Mr. Schaeffer? He's having an attack!''

"Oh, I do hope so,'' murmured Shirley. ''That would be very, very nice. Him and Tyrannosaurus rex.''

"He's going on and on about national forests!''

"Lambs can be raised successfully in fenced pastures, or even in barns,'' Shirley muttered. ''As a matter of fact, raised in barns, they have fewer parasites and no predator losses, and they can make a decent return on investment. That's capitalism, which Mr. Schaeffer pretends to believe in. What Mr. Schaeffer *actually* believes in is overgrazing the national forests without paying for the damage he does. Mr. Schaeffer benefits from crony-socialism, but when it comes to something like health care or homes for the homeless, Mr. Schaeffer chants the motto of the conservative greed ticket: *Gimme; let the other guy go to hell.*''

Shirley concluded on a sustained high tone that sounded suspiciously like ranting and raving, even to her. Judy, wisely, made no attempt at argument. She put Shirley in her chair, patted her like a mother patting a child after a tantrum, and departed without a backward glance. Presumably to go to Mr. Schaeffer's aid.

As for Shirley, she lay back in the chair, every muscle letting go, and admitted to herself she felt more relaxed than she had felt in some days. Her volcano had erupted. Her geyser had spouted. Poor Mr. Schaeffer had received all the animosity she'd been saving for the world at large. Now she could go back to simmering for a while. Pathetic, J.Q. would say. Simply pathetic. A woman her age ought to be able to control her temper.

She had no time to feel guilty or ashamed of herself. Her words of the morning were prophetic. There was a subdued knock at her open door, and a gentleman who could only be FBI asked politely if he could talk with her for a few moments. She nodded, grateful for being in her chair rather than in the bed. Having all her life towered over people, she found it strangely upsetting to be constantly looked down upon.

"I was expecting you," she said, staring at the pictured face on the identification he offered. George A. Chalmers. FBI. The same face stared down at her from a considerable height. If she were standing, they would be eye to eye. George A. Chalmers might have been stamped out of a mold. Agent. FBI, for the use of. Neat. Anonymous. A bland and expressionless face, holding itself very still, as in an old sepia photograph. Maybe the Bureau gave them frozen-face lessons. He had no outstanding characteristics. Even his voice was anonymous, an announcer's voice, from anywhere, U.S.A.

"Why were you expecting me, Mrs. McClintock?"

"Ms. McClintock," she corrected him. "Neither of my husbands were named McClintock. That's my maiden name."

He waited. When she said nothing more, he said, "Ms. McClintock, we understand you were here at the hospital Saturday night."

"Saturday evening," she corrected him. "We got here about six. We left somewhere around seven-thirty. By we, I mean myself, John Quentin, Xanthippe Minging, my foster daugher Allison, and her friend April Shaour." She was careful to pronounce it correctly. Shah-oor. "April had a broken arm. It was set by a doctor in the emergency room."

"Where were you while this was going on?"

"J.Q. and I were in the reception area near the front door. J.Q. never left there, that I know of. I made one trip to the women's toilet, just down the hall, across from the emergency room. I made one excursion to the emergency room itself, to see how things were coming along.''

''Who, what, did you see?''

''I saw a man working on the hall floor with a buffer. I saw a woman through the window in the admissions office. I saw the doctor who set April's arm. . . .''

''The doctor's name?'' he interrupted.

''I don't know. I never met her. She was young, in her late twenties. I doubt there's more than one female physician of that age associated with this hospital. It isn't large.''

''The man polishing the floor?''

''My guess would be Hispanic. Short. Solidly built. He had a mustache.'' She shrugged. ''I didn't meet him either.''

Chalmers, George, rubbed the back of his neck wearily, becoming with the gesture a human being rather than a digit. ''You were here about the time it must have happened. Damn. I keep hoping we're going to come up with something.''

''Kidnappings are awful,'' she agreed in heartfelt tones, remembering a time when Allison had been taken by force, held against her will, threatened. ''You feel so impotent.''

''You have some experience?'' He looked up, surprised.

She told him, making a long story very short.

He nodded in understanding. ''At least you had a demand. There was something you could do to get her back. In this case, there's been no ransom demand, nothing. We're up a creek.''

She peered at him, surprised at his revelation. The man was tired, desperately tired. That's probably why he was talking. And because she had had a similar experience.

She said, ''When there's no ransom demand . . . isn't it usually that some woman has stolen the child for herself? Some mother who's lost a child, or a woman who can't have any?''

''That's a valid premise, yes. But nothing clicks. At least so far.''

"No hospital employees who've recently lost a child? No visitors who might fit that category?"

He shook his head, yawning uncontrollably. "The place is so small. In a large hospital, there might be dozens of possibilities. Here?" He gestured. "Everyone knows everyone. Or seems to. There are no new employees and none who have left suddenly. No odd visitors. No one hanging out around the nursery."

"Wasn't there a nurse or somebody in the nursery?"

"She left for about five minutes to take another baby to its mother because, so she said, the mother hadn't been paying the baby enough attention." He laughed shortly. "The mommy already has seven children at home, the oldest six and a half. She probably figured she had a few days coming to her of not paying attention."

"You have children?" she asked sympathetically.

He sighed. "Three. Two boys and a girl. Four, two, and two weeks. The last one was a . . . well, let's say he was unforeseen. He also refuses to sleep at night. The minute you put him down, he starts screaming. I don't remember the last time I got a night's sleep." He yawned, frowned, brought himself back to his subject. "Anyhow, half an hour after the nurse's little excursion, Mrs. Franklin called the nursery and asked for her baby because Grandma and Grandpa Franklin wanted to see him. The nurse went to get baby, and baby was gone."

"That must have been after we left," Shirley said thoughtfully. "There were no visitors' cars in the parking lot when we went out, but there were some turning in to the drive." She tapped her fingers, thinking. "There was one thing. Probably meaningless. Just as we were leaving, a brown pickup came screaming around the corner of the hospital. It almost hit a car that was coming in. I think there were gestures exchanged. J.Q. may have noticed more about it than I did."

"J.Q.?"

"Mr. Quentin. He's out at Rancho del Valle, where we were . . . are all staying. It's about fifteen miles from here, east."

"Will I find the others there as well? You say you were with two girls?"

Shirley swallowed deeply. "One girl. April was shot last Sunday."

Abruptly his expression changed, becoming harder, more demanding. "Shot!"

"I think the sheriff's department has it down as an accidental shooting," she said.

"You were hurt at the same time?"

"My mount was grazed. I got dumped."

He glanced at her knee. "A break?"

"A new knee. Evidently my borrowed mule made bone-meal of the old one."

He looked around, located the straight chair, and pulled it over before her, straddling it to lean on the back. "The pickup is good. We hadn't heard about the pickup. Think about it. Could any of you have seen anything else? Anything at all?"

She shook her head slowly. "We never left the first floor. Maternity's up here, on second. It was just a long, dull wait so far as I was concerned. J.Q. read his paper most of the time. Xanthy Minging was with April. Allison went out to the car and took a nap in the backseat—I suppose she might have seen something if she was awake, and you're welcome to ask her. I prowled back and forth, but the place was empty. I can't swear the others didn't see anything, but I didn't. I sure as hell didn't see anybody carrying a baby."

He put the chair back where he'd found it. "If you think of anything," he said, handing her a card. "I'll be talking to the others as well."

"Good luck," she said. "I hope the little guy turns up."

He shrugged, yawning again, a dutiful man who desperately needed sleep. "We all hope that."

J.Q. and Allison arrived after supper.

"When are you getting out?" Allison asked, pink-cheeked and eager. "There's a really nice room for you, Shirley. You'll like it!"

"Doctor said tomorrow," she answered. "You don't mind missing Carlsbad?"

Allison shrugged. "It's just a big cave. I've seen big caves on TV. Besides, Sarah lets me ride her horse. He's a *paso fino*. It's kind of fun. He takes these little tiny steps. Like a ballet dancer in toe shoes."

Shirley relaxed and turned to smile at J.Q. "What have you been up to?"

"Mr. Shaour and I rode out to the mesa this morning," he said with a sidelong glance at Allison. "Mr. Shaour is not a rider. I imagine he was a little stiff and sore by the time we got back."

"He didn't find anything?"

"Nothing at all pertaining to April, though I showed him precisely where she was climbing and where she fell. He was more interested in looking around where she'd fallen from. He found an interesting crevice with some pots, which he commented on, wondering with the utmost innocence whether anyone would mind if he took one. I pointed out that we were being watched. . . ."

"Watched!"

"By a couple of men, from the pueblo, I presume, in a pickup truck. Which was a little odd, come to think of it, after they told me not to run a vehicle out there. The truck wasn't very picturesque. They should have been on pinto ponies. At any rate, I suggested he would be well advised to leave the site strictly alone, which he did."

"What do you think about the pots?"

"I don't know. That rain yesterday brought a lot of rock down. The pots had been adequately hidden before, I should think. It might be an old burial or ceremonial site. In either case, it was none of our business."

"Um. What else has happened?"

"Last night I turned over the little horse we found, to the Santa Fe sheriff's office. I got a receipt for it. Mr. Shaour and I were almost back at the ranch when I told him about it. He was most interested. Not that he let on."

"What are you two up to?" asked Allison.

Shirley gave her an innocent look. "Up to? Nothing, Allison. You saw the little horse that J.Q. found in the couch of the guest house. We showed it to a man from Santa Fe who knows about such things. He said it might be valuable, so we turned it over to the sheriff's office."

Allison's eyes narrowed. "If it was April's, why didn't you turn it over to her dad?"

"But we don't know that, do we? We have no idea if it was April's or not. She might have stolen it from someone."

"She could have," Allison agreed. "I hope . . . I hope her folks go home and it was just an accident and everybody can forget about it."

"We hope so, too. Did the FBI question you two about the kidnapping?"

George A. Chalmers had indeed visited them shortly after leaving Shirley. He had not, so far as they knew, elicited any additional information.

"He asked me about that pickup that almost hit the car," J.Q. said. "All I could do was agree with you. It was brown, and the drivers of both vehicles made gestures at each other. That's a cultural requirement down here."

"I didn't even see that," Allison said soberly. "I was so tired. Ape . . . April kept me up all night the night before, arguing with me. That's what I told Mr. Chalmers, that I just curled up in the backseat and went to sleep. I guess I was still half-asleep when you guys came out."

"Then maybe we're finished with that matter as well." Shirley found the idea quite attractive. Intellectually she didn't want to be involved with April's death, or with missing babies, or, at the moment, with any other trial or tribulation. She did not want to have to think about a surgeon who might

91

have AIDS. What she wanted to do more than anything else was to sit quietly in the sun and watch something grow. Perhaps with water splashing softly in the background.

"Tell me about this room you're putting me in," she asked.

"It's nice," Allison replied. "It's the owner's daughter's room. It's got a queen bed, one that's long enough for you. It's got its own bathroom, with a big shower stall, one that'll be easy to get into with crutches. And it's got its own patio out back, with a view."

J.Q. said, "Knowing how you feel about uncluttered surfaces, Xanthy and Allison have stored several hundred bits of memorabilia. Restaurant menus. Theater programs. Postcards and photographs."

"Girly stuff," said Allison, with a sniff. She, herself, would never descend to girly stuff.

J.Q. said, "They've put everything away, neatly, in boxes, with a diagram showing where everything was so we can put it back. Seemingly the owners, the Kingsolvers, haven't really spent any time at the place for the last decade. The Kingsolver kids are in their mid-twenties now, married, with families."

"What time tomorrow are they letting you out?" Allison asked.

Shirley shrugged. "I'm not sure. Let's say midafternoon. I'll push for that."

"Do you hurt?" Allison asked, looking worried.

Shirley considered the matter. "No, Allison, I don't really hurt. Mostly I'm just . . . depressed and uncomfortable. You know. The way you feel sometimes when you want to get on Beauregard and ride about twenty miles without thinking about anything. I'm not used to sleeping on my back, but with this thing on my leg, no other position is possible. They give me pain pills, but I'm mostly just taking them to help me sleep. I think I'll be able to keep myself more cheerful when I can look at something besides these four walls!"

After they left, she kept her attention resolutely away from the four walls. She leafed through a magazine J.Q. had brought, thought of calling home to check on her livestock, and decided not to. J.Q. would have done that. He was at least as concerned about the livestock as she was.

More, perhaps. Lately she'd been thinking of relinquishing the livestock. If she sold the ranch, or perhaps traded it, it would be silly to trade for that much land again. Being practical, she had to admit that she and J.Q. were finding it harder every year to get the work done. Spraying for weeds. Mending fence. Fighting off the constant procession of dirt bikers and holiday riders who wanted to use the place for recreational destruction. In former years it had been worth it. She'd regarded herself as the keeper of the flame. But now, with those naked hills all around her, where wildlife habitat had been but was no longer, she felt differently.

She'd miss the cows. What was it about cows? Something about them was intensely peaceful. The sound of them. The smell of their hay-sweet breaths. The feel and look of new calves, all bumptious and eager, a reaffirmation of life. Goats had something of the same feeling, though they were anything but peaceful. Goats were clever. One couldn't relax around goats.

And the poultry. Did she really need chickens? Mostly she'd loved them for the sound of them, the chanticleer greeting of dawn and recognition of sunset. The rustle and cluck of feeding hens. To say nothing of the taste of new-laid eggs.

All that and the sight of an elk herd on a foggy morning, of browsing deer at the edge of a pond, of herons and ducks populating a waterway . . .

Angrily she brushed tears from her eyes. It wasn't there. Not anymore. The McClintock place was a peninsula now, sticking out into a sea of development. Forty-acre horse properties. Five-acre country club sites. And in another ten years . . . Tyrannosaurus rex. Extinct. People like her, extinct. Along with the animals and forests they loved, killed to make room for more men.

She'd have to let it go sooner or later. She wiped at her eyes, ashamed. Crying over it, after all these months. She turned on the TV and found herself watching an inane science fiction movie full of crotch jokes.

She let the head of the bed down and put out the light. The TV show wasn't holding her; she turned it off as well. Only the light from the hallway falling through the drawn privacy curtain lighted the room a little. People went up and down the hall. Silence fell. Nighttime. Time for all good people to be asleep.

She couldn't, quite. Her leg felt as if it were made of obdurate and aching stone. It would never bend again. She knew it would. Every day when the therapists took the immobilizer off, the knee bent, however unwillingly. Right now, however, it felt stiff as a chunk of wood. Part of the current ache was bruised muscle. The mule hadn't been selective.

Someone slipped through the door and stood just on the other side of the half-drawn curtain. She could see the silhouette. She didn't want to talk to anyone. She breathed deeply, pretending to be asleep, watching from barely opened eyes as the shadow came around the end of the curtain.

An instant before the pillow came down over her face, she realized what was happening. Her arms came up, flailing. She thrust the person behind the pillow away, fought the pillow itself, turned her head away, heaved a huge breath, and screamed at the top of her lungs.

A voice from down the hall. Feet running. One set or two? She couldn't tell. She took a breath and screamed again, then fumbled for her call button and pushed it for good measure.

The big night nurse came in at a trot to find her sitting up, gagging.

"What?" she cried. "What?"

"Somebody damn well tried to kill me!" Shirley gargled. "Somebody pushed a pillow down over my face!"

"Now, now. Bad dream. Surely—"

"Look at it, damn you! There it is, on the floor. Here's mine, under my head. I didn't put that there."

The woman picked up the pillow, staring at it. "Maybe you had an extra one."

"Look, lady. I am not drugged and I am not deluded. I am fully capable of telling the difference between dream and reality. I did not have an extra pillow anywhere. Either you call the police, or I do. Which is it?"

She lay simmering. People came to the door and peered in and went away again. See the crazy, paranoid lady. After what seemed hours, the police came, new police, ones she hadn't talked to before, Los Arboles city police. Their questions were perfunctory. Their responses were foreseeable. Supercilious glances. Raised eyebrows. The hell with them.

When they left, she found herself shaking.

"Would you like something to help you sleep?"

She laughed, on the edge of hysteria. "Sleep! If I'd been asleep, I'd be dead!"

They didn't believe it. They wouldn't let themselves believe it. She wouldn't argue with them. What was the point?

She raised the head of the bed upright and turned the television back on, unable and unwilling to close her eyes. Despite weariness and worry, damned if she was going to give whoever it was another chance.

4

"I'D LIKE TO keep you another day," said Claude Humphrey, M.D. It was the third time he'd said it.

"I'd like to go home this afternoon," Shirley replied, as she had to each previous statement.

"We had to do some repair work inside that knee, and you may have wrenched it. . . ."

"I may have barely escaped a murderer. I would rather be wrenched than dead."

"I'm sure you're mistaken about all this."

"So your nurse said. All I know is, since last Sunday, I seem to have been getting further and further entwined in either a murder or a kidnapping or both. Yesterday I was questioned by the FBI. Last night somebody tried to do me in. I have no idea why, but I have no intention of giving him, her, or it another chance."

He stared out the window with practiced impassivity. "I felt we needed time to discuss your concerns. About . . . the HIV virus."

Shirley frowned. She had completely forgotten the HIV virus, which, considering her outrage yesterday, would be rather embarrassing to confess. "At the moment, that's taken a back seat," she equivocated. "If you want to reassure me, just have a test and see that Bryan has a test."

"Your fears are illusory. . . ."

"Right. No physician ever gets AIDS. No physician ever infects a patient. There is a miracle clause in the Hippocratic oath that prevents such occurrences."

"Sarcasm isn't necessary." He drew himself up in offended dignity, wide mouth compressed, bald head gleaming, looking exactly like the sobriquet Judy had awarded him. He was egglike! Poor Humpty, his love life all broken to pieces, and not all the king's horses . . .

She sighed. "Look, Doctor, I'm sorry if I sound . . . sarcastic. I really don't want to be hard on you. As far as I know, my new leg is wonderful and I'm thankful to you for your skill. I know I've got no lease on life. I don't expect to live forever. But if I've been exposed to this disease, I want to know it. I think that's reasonable."

"A test won't tell—"

"I know a test won't be final proof. I know it will have to be repeated over time to establish you haven't recently been infected. But a negative test will be reassuring. And I'm sure you want to reassure me, as you would any patient."

He cleared his throat, looked out the window, then down at his notes. "I want you to have a prothrombin test in a week to be sure you're taking the right dose of Coumadin, which should be continued for another three weeks. The prescription is here, together with a prescription for pain pills. Either I or some other orthopedic surgeon should see you in a month, do new X rays, see how the knee is healing."

"If I'm still here in New Mexico, I'll come to you."

His haughty look accused her of hypocrisy. "Bear no more than a third of your weight on that knee. Don't go for long walks or get yourself stranded so you have to walk. I had an idiot patient who drove up in the mountains in a heavy snow and got stuck four days after he left the hospital. His new knee did not stand up well to a five-mile hike." He fumed silently, as though it had happened yesterday. "Do your exercises. Keep the immobilizer on as much as you can for another week or so, particularly if you're in any danger of being bumped or put off balance. You're looking at five more weeks' healing time, during which the knee needs protection. I'd stay away from crowds."

"I always do," she replied honestly. "Whenever humanly possible."

"You ran a fever that was atypical. Of course, the injury was atypical, as well. The usual pattern is a quick rise and a steady fall, but yours went up and down like a roller coaster for a few days. It's down now, but we want to be sure it stays that way. Take your temperature twice a day, and call my office if you have any fever at all. The therapists' notes say the knee bends sixty degrees now. During the next few weeks, work at getting it to ninety degrees, but take it easy. It's not necessary to force it. Simply sit in a chair sufficiently high that the leg will drop by gravity. Since you're quite tall, you may need to put a high cushion on a chair or a platform under it." His voice ran out and he stared out the window once more.

"Is that all?"

"Except for removing the staples from your—"

"Staples!" Shirley used staples mostly for barbwire fencing, and the picture in her mind was decidedly uncomforting.

"We use stainless steel staples to close incisions. They hold better than stitches. They're easier to sterilize. The nurse will take out the staples before you go. And Mrs. Stark will call you with the test results from . . . hospital personnel."

"Thank you."

"Your prescriptions will be with your discharge order. Be sure to pick them up before you leave."

Humpty departed, dignity unscathed, marching to silent and different drums.

Judy arrived with such suspicious promptness, Shirley suspected her of having been listening outside the door.

"Just me today. Bryan's still at home, sulking."

"That's a bit snide."

"Well, he is! He was responsible for this whole mess, and he knows it. We're all being tested early, just because of him and Humpty."

"All of you?"

"Starky says it has to be everybody, to avoid discrimination."

"Why is Bryan responsible?"

Judy looked briefly self-conscious, the look of a born gossip who has just enough conscience to feel guilty but not enough to keep her mouth shut. "The way I heard the story, Humpty wanted Bryan to go to the opera with him. If you live in Santa Fe and are anybody at all, you have to go to the Santa Fe Opera. Anglos, that is. Otherwise you're a vulgar nobody. But Bryan said opera bored him and he'd rather go to the gym, and Humpty ought to come with him or Humpty's not going to stay strong enough to pull bones into their sockets and stuff. It does take strength, and lately Humpty's been having his partner do a lot of the pulling and pushing. So then Humpty got mad at Bryan because Bryan spends all his spare time working out, and Humpty thinks he ought to improve his mind. So then Bryan told Humpty maybe he'd be happier with some fat old egghead." She smirked, "No pun intended. So now Humpty's walking around with this martyred expression, and Bryan isn't coming to work at all."

"How do you know all this?"

"They had their big fight in Humpty's office with the door wide open, and one of the cleaning people heard them. She told somebody, and that somebody told somebody, and—"

Shirley, feeling herself dissolving into an endless chain of somebodies, had to put an end to it.

"I'm leaving this afternoon," she interrupted, shutting off the continuing saga.

"I don't blame you. You had some nut in here last night?"

"I had someone in here last night. I think I'll be safer where I can lock the doors."

"Well, that's the funny part, you know, because the doors are locked! Visitors all have to leave by eight, and at eight-fifteen, they lock the doors. What time was the person here?"

Shirley tried to remember. "I was watching this silly space movie." She described it.

"I remember that one. My little brother was watching it, and it came on at nine. So the doors had been locked by then."

"The person might have come in earlier." Shirley did not say what she really felt: that her assailant might be on the staff, or have a key.

Judy wrinkled her brow and switched to her professional persona with an almost audible grinding of gears. "Well, if you're going home, do you remember your exercises? Do I need to write them down for you?"

"I remember them. Despite all the side issues, you and Bryan have been very good to me. Very effective. I'm sure it's mainly due to you two that I don't feel at all disabled."

"You will." Judy sat down, leaning forward to emphasize her words. "You will feel disabled. You'll feel depressed."

Shirley, remembering her mood the previous night, blinked and swallowed.

"You'll start to do something you used to do all the time and it will hurt. You'll reach for something and realize you can't get it. You'll be sort of up and down. It happens to everybody. It's easier if you know it's coming."

Shirley, chastened, nodded.

"In your case, you're still anemic, so it may take you a while before you really feel good. Take vitamins. Drink a lot of orange juice. Eat iron-rich foods. Spinach and broccoli and frijoles. Eat a lot of fiber, too, because you'll be getting less exercise than you're used to.'' She sighed. ''I'm sorry about everything, mostly about last night. We can't figure that out, really. You don't think it could have been him, do you?''

''Him who?''

''Mr. Shaeffer? He was really mad.''

It took Shirley a moment to remember who Mr. Shaeffer was. ''How would he know what room I'm in? Besides, he doesn't strike me as the suffocating type. He's more of a shoot-first-and-ask-questions-later type.''

''Could there maybe be a nut loose?''

Shirley shook her head. ''I don't think so, Judy. I don't think it was random. I think the person was after me, personally. I honestly believe someone is frightened that I may tell the FBI something. Someone thinks I know something about the kidnapping.'' Which is why April got shot, too. Something told her so, despite all the red herrings.

''But you don't know anything?''

Shirley gestured a vast ignorance, arms wide. ''I've already told everything I know. Everything. I have no facts I have not revealed! Spread that word around, will you? It may get whoever it is off my back.''

''I will. It'll be easy, because nobody wants to talk about anything else. Even Mrs. Grant, that woman whose little boy didn't get stolen, it's all she wanted to talk about. How the nurse was mad at her and brought her baby to her room, and that's all that kept him from being stolen.''

''That's the mother of eight?''

''That's right. She's a case. Couldn't quit talking. Didn't even pay any attention to the little boy, but couldn't quit talking about his almost being kidnapped.''

''Why is she still here? I thought maternity patients went home the day after.''

''She went home yesterday. They kept her awhile because she had an infection and they wanted to give her IV antibiotics. There's something strange about her. Like she's mad all the time, but holding it in. Not talking to anybody. I was there when her husband came, and she wouldn't even look at him. Well, maybe having that many kids that fast would make you mad at the world!''

Shirley thought this not only possible but probable. "You do therapy for maternity patients, too?"

"Sure. Tummy exercises. Bends and twists. How to get rid of postpartum flab. You know."

"Did the other mother go home? What was the name? Franklin?"

"She went home yesterday, too. Oh, hey, I've got news for you! There was a ransom note!"

Shirley's mouth dropped open. "Now, how in hell would you know that?"

"It came here!" Seeing Shirley's expression, she nodded vigorously. "Honestly. It was on her door this morning. Not in an envelope or anything. It said get a half million together and wait for a call at home."

"What do you mean, it was on her door!"

"On the door of the room she was in until yesterday."

Shirley still didn't understand.

Judy explained. "Look. Mrs. Franklin had a cesarean, right? She was due to go home Monday. But this whole business made her hysterical, and she's got a tendency toward high blood pressure anyhow, so her doctor decided to keep her here awhile. It's not like money was a problem with that family! So he discharged her yesterday and she went home around suppertime, but then this morning the cleaner found the note sticking up out of the chart rack on the door! She showed it to everybody!"

"Chart rack?"

Judy gestured toward Shirley's door, standing as it always did, open. The wooden chart rack was there, a clipboard sticking out of it, so obvious, she'd never noticed it.

"Anybody could have left a note there," Shirley said.

"Right. Especially during visiting hours last night. People wander in and out of maternity all the time."

Shirley mused, 'If the door was shut, or only slightly open, or if the curtain inside was pulled across to hide the bed, the person who left the note might not have known she was gone."

"Right."

"But wait a minute. Once she'd gone home, there wouldn't have been any patient record in the rack. Wouldn't that tell the person there was no one in the room?"

"Not necessarily. Sometimes the nurses take the records for a while, to bring them up-to-date. They aren't always in the rack."

"I'll be damned."

"You sound surprised."

Shirley nodded. "I am very surprised. Aren't you? Did you ever hear of a kidnapping where the ransom note didn't arrive for a week? Usually kidnappers leave the note when they nab the kid. Either that or they phone right away." She scratched her head, wondering. Was that really the way it was? Or was that only in movies? What sense did it make to delay?

Judy said, "It is kind of odd, isn't it? You wouldn't think a kidnapper would want to keep the baby any longer than they had to."

"Almost as though . . ."

"As though what?"

Shirley shook her head. It was a vagrant thought that wouldn't form up. "Nothing. Maybe it'll come to me."

"Do you need some help getting yourself together?"

Shirley laughed. "I could use some help getting myself together, yes, but I'm afraid it's hopeless. If you mean getting my possessions together, J.Q.'s coming for me. He'll do it as well as anyone can."

J.Q. managed her removal quite well, with the assistance of two white-clad wheelchair pushers, up to the point of getting her into the car. Then it was discovered that neither the clothes she wore nor the Velcro monstrosity on her leg would slide on the velour car seats. It took all three of her handlers to stuff her inch by inch into the backseat, like a sausage into a casing, where she lay like a beached pilot whale, staring at the car ceiling.

"Are you all right?" J.Q. asked anxiously.

"My left ear is resting on the window handle," she growled. "I wish you'd brought a pillow. Since you didn't, I suggest we limit conversation and get home as quickly as possible."

He put the car in gear and they went while Shirley attempted to think up any other positions that might be more ridiculous or undignified. It was only fifteen miles. Perhaps twenty minutes, or twenty-five. Surely one could stand anything for twenty minutes, or twenty-five.

After ten minutes, cursing wildly, she demanded that he stop.

"Help me unstrap this damned devilish contraption!"

"You're supposed to leave that on. . . ." he said uncertainly. "Aren't you?"

"I'm suppose to get home in one piece. Take it off!"

He took it off. She bent her knee gingerly, achieving the sixty degrees the therapist had considered appropriate. She eased herself higher, watching the knee bend itself, surprised that there was so little pain. A mere twinge. She leaned against the seat back and sighed.

"You're pale," he complained. "Is your knee supposed to bend like that?"

"I'm . . . anemic," she replied quietly. "And yes, it's supposed to bend like that."

"If it's supposed to bend like that, why do they have it immobilized?"

"I think it's so it won't get twisted by accident. Or bumped. I'll put the thing back on when we get home. Maybe. Promise me something, J.Q."

"What?"

"Promise me, if I get some disease that wastes me away. If I get so I can't walk and people have to heave me around. If I get so I can't go to the bathroom by myself. Do me in. Please."

He patted her, shut the door, and got back into the driver's seat. "I promise," he said. "You didn't even need to ask."

She gloomed the rest of the way down the valley, wondering why hospital personnel had given her so much information of doubtful usefulness while no one had addressed the problem of getting into and out of a car. Surely most joint replacement patients went home in cars. Perhaps whatever happened in the hospital driveway was someone else's responsibility. Her gloom persisted when they arrived, only worsening as she maneuvered herself out of the car and found that J.Q. had produced a wheelchair out of thin air.

"It's just for a few days," he soothed. "While you get to know the house. So you don't get tired."

"Have you been talking to the doctor?" she asked suspiciously.

"I merely inquired if there was anything I should know to provide a supportive environment," he said in his officious, I'm-taking-charge voice. "I was told I should try to prevent your overdoing."

"I don't overdo!"

"You very seldom do anything else."

He wheeled her slowly down a walk that led behind the main house, into a tiny, low-walled patio, and through one of a pair of French doors. She was in a spacious, high-ceilinged room with bedroom furniture at one end and a sitting room arrangement in a windowed alcove at the other. Her own belongings were set out on the dresser and bedside table: her comb and hairbrush, her notebook, a book she'd been reading before the . . . the accident. When J.Q. turned her about, she could look across the little patio toward a dramatic view of the canyons to the west. The foreground just beyond the wall was occupied by peacocks dancing, tails fully fanned, bowing and bending, rattling quills in a frenzy, hopping first on one foot, then on the other, all the while staring impressively down their beaks, like Back Bay matrons at a benefit tea. The room smelled fragrantly of cedar with an overlay of chicken soup.

"We tried to think of everything." Allison said from beside the bed, where she was energetically and unnecessarily plumping pillows that were already plump enough. "Mingy and I ironed your sheets and got you three extra pillows. Mingy made chicken and dumplings for supper."

"Mingy?" gasped Shirley. She herself would never dare call Xanthippe Minging *Mingy*.

"She says I can call her Mingy now. Since I'm graduated from Creps. Her nieces call her that. Anyhow, I bought the cedar incense. Sarah threw corn outside your window so the peacocks would stay there and dance for you. And we've got surprises."

"Surprises?" Shirley croaked. She was having strongly contradictory feelings, wanting to laugh and cry at the same time. How could she sulk in the face of such energetic effort on her behalf! All this caring minutiae! "You have surprises?"

Allison nodded, eyes bright. "We do, don't we, J.Q.?"

He nodded solemnly. "Oh, yes. Of various kinds."

Harry Fielding's head protruded past the doorframe, then Sarah's.

"Can we come in?"

"By all means." Shirley beckoned.

"Were the peacocks showing off?" Sarah asked.

Shirley swallowed the lump in her throat. "They're still at it."

Harry grinned affably. "Sarah's been feeding them there for three days so they'd assemble for you." He waved the unlit cigarette he habitually carried, or sucked on. "We were just saying how good it is to have somebody staying here.

When was the last time the Kingsolvers were here, Sar? It was eighty-nine, wasn't it?''

"I think so. And they were only here for a weekend then.''

"It's an extremely attractive place,'' Shirley said, looking around herself. "Why do they keep it if they're not going to live here? Or at least visit.''

Sarah seated herself on one of two couches that faced each other in the large, windowed alcove. "Winston and Gwen Kingsolver bought it as a retirement home. They were from Chicago, and they used to spend summers here with their children. Summers, and winter holidays, and spring vacations. That was before Harry and I even knew about the place. Then Gwen Kingsolver got cancer. We only met her once, twelve years ago, not long before she died.

"Winston Kingsolver and the kids came here a few times after that, then a couple of years later, he remarried. Her name is Trina. We've met her two or three times. Winston keeps saying maybe they'll want to live here someday, but Trina never will. It was Gwen's place, and Trina wouldn't want to live in Gwen's place. And the kids aren't that fond of Trina. . . .''

Harry agreed. "Also, she's a city person. She doesn't much like animals, she hates insects and snakes. She's afraid of 'em. She gets hysterical.''

Sarah nodded. "Right. The last time they were here was one May when we had a lot of miller moths. You'd think they were black widow spiders! I admit they're disgusting, but they're not harmful! She got up in the middle of the night and made Winston move with her to the Hilton in Santa Fe, where there wouldn't be any bugs. And then, too, she's from California. If she goes anywhere, it'll be there. She likes things slick. This place is real old New Mexico. It'll never be slick.''

Shirley assessed her surroundings once more. The ceiling had carved vigas and cedar *latillas* laid in herringbone pattern. The two-foot-thick walls were plastered and painted white. The floor was brick, a soft terra-cotta glossed with wax or laquer into a mellow glow. No. It wasn't slick. "How old is it?"

Harry seated himself next to Sarah. "The house you stayed in with the girls and another little house we use for storage, those were built sometime around 1750. The kitchen in this house was built maybe 1800, along with a couple of the bedrooms in this wing. The rest of it is anywhere from sixty to a hundred years old."

"It wasn't built as a guest ranch then?"

"Oh no." Sarah settled herself comfortably. "There was an overseer's little house, and a cook house, and a bunkhouse or two. Over the years, the land got sold off and the buildings sort of got added to and added to. Now there's only fifty acres left. When winston and Gwen bought it, he remodeled all the outbuildings to make individual little houses of them, with new kitchens and bathrooms. They thought it would be nice, you know, when they retired. They would invite their friends and their children's families and rent them out in between times. Winston Kingsolver is in the construction business, so he knows all about building. The place was kind of a hobby with him."

"That was before you came."

"Mostly before. Afterward he was preoccupied with Gwen's illness. There were lots of little odds and ends to finish up when he hired Harry and me."

"Hired!" Harry snorted.

"Well. Not hired. Made us a deal. We live here, Harry's got his military pension, and I've got a little income from some family property. Winston said if we'd run the place and use its income to pay our expenses and maintain the place, we could essentially live here free, and that's the way it's worked out. We've enjoyed it. Even though we've decided it's time to move on."

"Move on?" Shirley asked.

"Our kids are out in Oregon. Harry says it's time to move a little closer. Get to know our grandchildren better."

Harry, watching Shirley from the corners of his eyes, looked uncomfortable at this attribution of sentimentality.

Xanthippe Minging appeared in the doorway. "Well. I wondered where everyone was!"

"We've been visiting," Sarah said, getting up and smoothing her shirt over her ample hips. "Are we still invited to supper?"

"You are. The only question is, do we bring it in here, or does Shirley come to the dining room?"

"About as far as from your hospital room to the nursery," said J.Q. with a doubtful look in her direction. "You have been walking at least that far, haven't you?"

Shirley nodded, suddenly inexpressibly weary. "I have been, but . . ."

"No matter," he said. "The wheelchair is available for occasions when you'd rather not walk." He turned her around to face the hall door.

"My Lord, J.Q., I'm not disabled!"

"You're tired," he said softly. "You are allowed to be tired, and Harry is here to help, so it's no trouble."

"Take two of us to get you over the threshold," said Harry, grinning at her as he flexed his arm to show off his Marine Corps tattoo. "But from there, it's a straight push."

For the first time Shirley noticed the raised threshold of the door, an eight-inch barrier. "The house we were staying in before had the same high thresholds. Funny. I hardly noticed them until now."

Sarah said, "That's the authentic pueblo style. Small doors, no bigger than could be covered with one deerskin, and raised thresholds to keep the rain from running in—and maybe to keep the snakes and scorpions from crawling in, too. Thick walls to stay warm in winter, cool in summer. Natural tree trunks, vigas, instead of a ceiling. Between them, natural brush or twigs or splits, *latillas*, to support the dirt roof. The whole bit." She waved and went off down the corridor.

"Really?" Shirley asked Harry. "This house has a dirt roof?"

He made a face. "Well, the owners before the Kingsolvers covered it with urethane, but yes, the dirt is still up there."

"Don't dirt roofs leak?"

Harry made the face again. "Of course they leak. In the traditional pueblos, they put *latillas* over the vigas, then brush or straw over the *latillas*, then a good layer of clay that's raked smooth. The idea is, the clay sheds the water, and if the roof slopes right, the water runs off before it has a chance to soak in. So long as there's very little rain, I suppose it would work all right. Of course, if you have a downpour like Thursday, it doesn't work at all! Rain in New Mexico is a mixed blessing, depending on whether you . . . have a flat roof or not." It came out sounding unnecessarily bitter, and he gestured apologetically. "Sorry. I get damned sick of patching somebody else's roofs."

"It's like sod houses," murmured J.Q. "My great-grandmother lived in a sod house in Kansas. Must have been very similar."

Shirley held out her hand for her crutches. "All right. We'll trek to the dining room, but I'll make it easy for you. I'll get myself over that threshold, and you can push me from there."

She adjusted her crutches, recalling the litany Judy had taught her during their last therapy session. "Climbing stairs with a bad leg is just like they taught you in Sunday School," Judy had said. "The good go up to heaven, the bad go down to hell. So, good leg first up. Bad leg first down."

The dining room was in what Shirley thought of as the front of the house, nearest the parking area, down a short hallway from the kitchen she had seen when she used the phone to arrange the ill-fated horseback ride. They sat down to a family-style dinner of chicken and dumplings, corn casserole, and salad.

Though the food smelled mouth-watering, Shirley didn't feel hungry. She took enough to seem appreciative, and picked at it while the others talked about one thing and another. J.Q. mentioned the observers who had watched him and April's father at Blue Mesa. Harry merely frowned at his plate, but Sarah seemed to be confirmed in some previous opinion.

"The pueblos do not like people trespassing," she said. "That much I do know. Lots of the guests who stay here want to see a pueblo, and they're surprised when we tell them they've already come right by Pojoaque Pueblo or San Ildefonso Pueblo or San Pedro Pueblo without noticing it. Most tourists have seen pictures of the Taos Pueblo or the Acoma Pueblo, and they think all Indian pueblos look like that."

"Which, at one time, they probably did," Xanthy said.

"Pueblo just means town, doesn't it?" asked Allison.

Xanthy nodded. "That's all. But a lot of the towns along the Rio Grande were destroyed by the Spanish, or by disease, and the people were scattered. When San Pedro Pueblo was renewed, they only found a few people who were descended from the original inhabitants."

"Renewed?" Shirley asked, intrigued.

Sarah said, "My ex-housekeeper, Emelia, told me all about it! Back in the forties, the land was still owned by the San Pedro Pueblo, but there were only two or three old people left living there among a bunch of Anglo and Hispanic . . . oh, interlopers, I guess you'd say. Squatters. Anyhow, those two or three got a lawyer and ran the Hispanics and Anglos off, and they located enough descendants to return and renew the pueblo. The people who came back didn't speak Tewa, or know the religion, so the people from the other Tewa-speaking pueblos taught them. Of course, there's still a lot of Hispanic influence."

"Which seems to be resented," J.Q. remarked. "There

was something in the news, some local Indians who painted graffiti all over the statue of a conquistador?"

Sarah snorted. "San Pedro Pueblo has a group of young militants. Mostly they sneak into the plaza in Española late at night and paint dirty words on the statue of Don Juan de Oñate. They want the pueblo referred to only by its old Indian name. They want to return to their roots."

Harry shook his head, saying almost angrily, "They say it, but they don't. They don't want to live the way their ancestors did. They don't want to get rid of Chevvy trucks and television and refrigerators."

"That's true," Sarah agreed, as though reluctantly. "And Emelia says there aren't very many purebred Tewa people anymore. They've mixed with the Spanish and the Mexicans and even other Indian tribes. The Spanish made them take Spanish names, and Emelia says a lot of them speak more Spanish or English than they do Tewa or Tiwa."

"Do you go to the dances?" Allison asked.

Sarah wrinkled her nose. "Harry goes. It makes me uncomfortable."

Shirley raised an eyebrow.

"It's the way I was raised, I guess," Sarah said. "The old so-called Protestant ethic. You know."

"Work and responsibility," said Shirley. "Pay your bills on time. Don't get married and have children until you can afford it. Don't have more children than you can afford."

"All that, plus go to church on Sundays. So I keep thinking of my church back in Iowa with a bunch of tourists sitting in the back of the sanctuary during baptism or Holy Communion, laughing and talking, the women wearing halter tops, all of them throwing cigarettes and candy wrappers around and setting off flash bulbs. Even if they were respectful, I'd think I'd resent their being there, because worship isn't for spectators."

"I go to the dances," Harry said in a slightly contentious tone. "Hell, if they're going to put on a show, why not?"

112

"I think a lot of the disrespect is because people don't understand the music," offered Xanthippe, helping herself to more dumplings.

"What's to understand?" Harry asked.

"That's what I mean. We Anglos, or Europeans, tend to judge the solemnity of religious observances in terms of our own musical heritage. The Indian music we hear seems monotonous and nasal. . . ."

"Indian singing isn't very pretty," Allison offered. "J.Q. and I were listening to it on the car radio. It's all one or two notes, and it all sounds the same, over and over."

Xanthippe said dryly, "I've made the the same remark about rock music. I'm sure if I understood it, I would notice the subtleties."

Sarah sat back, shaking her head. "I never thought of that. . . ."

Shirley, noting that Harry was beginning to look annoyed, said quickly, "Xanthy, this is delicious chicken."

"Thank you, ma'am. My mother's recipe."

"I've never tasted dumplings like this before."

"There have never been dumplings like this before. They've been adapted to the Southwest, in deference to Sarah. She says one mustn't cook anything in New Mexico without cheese, onions, and green chiles. I think we also threw in a little yellow cornmeal."

"Everything has chiles? Even ice cream?" Allison asked, aghast. "I thought we were having chocolate!"

Sarah laughed. "We can do without chiles on the ice cream. Especially since I made Harry's favorite pecan-caramel sauce."

After the ice cream, J.Q. wheeled Shirley back to her room.

"That was pleasant," he said. "I hope it made you feel better."

"They're nice people," she said wearily. "Though it's

113

obvious Sarah likes the milieu better than Harry does. And frankly, I'm so tired, I don't know if I feel better or not.''

He watched her closely as she got herself from chair to bed, where she stretched out, concentrating on letting go her tight muscles, relaxing her arms and legs.

''What's worn you out?'' he asked. ''On the way down the hill, I thought it was just aggravation, but you look exhausted.''

Staring at the ceiling, she said, ''I didn't get any sleep last night, J.Q.''

''Why?'' He looked up alertly, disturbed at her tone.

''Somebody . . . somebody got into my room at the hospital last night and tried to smother me with a pillow over my face.''

He merely stared, dumbfounded, unable to speak for a time. His lips formed words, but no sound came out.

''You called the police?'' he asked at last.

She nodded. ''Over the objections of the nursing staff, who thought I was dreaming it.''

''You weren't dreaming it.''

''No.''

''Why are you just now telling—''

''What good would it have done to tell you last night? Or earlier today? I wasn't going to get you or Xanthy up in the middle of the night, and I sure didn't want Allison scared to death. We haven't had a moment alone until now, except on the trip down the canyon, which wasn't a good time. I decided last night I was going to tell you and only you, first chance I had. I figured we'd handle it.''

''I appreciate your confidence,'' he said with a bitter twist to his lips. ''What did the police do?''

''The two officers took my statement, glanced at one another in a significant and superior fashion, and went back to whatever they'd been doing before. Possibly playing poker down at the station. Or cutting out the Playmate of the month to tape to their locker doors.''

"You don't think they believed you."

"It was the Los Arboles police, and no, I don't think they believed me. If I'd been upright instead of recumbent, it might have helped. It might have helped if it'd been any of the law we'd already talked to. Santa Fe. San Pedro Pueblo. FBI. But it wasn't. One thing I wanted to know from you: When did the Shaours leave?"

"Yesterday. Shortly after he got back from the ride to Blue Mesa."

"I forget what you told me. Did he say anything when you mentioned the golden horse?"

"Well, it was interesting. You met him, so you know this kind of pale complexion he has. It's that thick, cream-colored skin that looks like it never tans or changes color. He'd gotten himself pretty hot and dirty, climbing around out there, without getting at all flushed, but the minute I mentioned the golden horse, these red patches popped out under his eyes, like heat rash. Kind of like those round red spots they paint on wooden soldiers. He was either excited or angry, probably angry. I pretended not to notice even though he had to feel what was happening to his face. He obviously wanted to ask all kinds of questions, but he wouldn't let himself. He kept opening his mouth and then shutting it again, thinking twice."

"What did you tell him?"

"Just what we'd decided. That I'd found the thing in the couch, that I'd had it looked at by an expert, that I'd turned it over to the sheriff's people. He asked which sheriff's people, and I told him. When we got back, he went into his house like a snake down a hole, and when I got back from Duran's, they had all their stuff in a rental car and were departing."

"You don't know whether they actually left the area, though."

"The only thing I'm sure of is they left this ranch. Why?

Do you think it could have been one of them who attacked you last night?''

"It could have been, though I have no idea why either of them would have done it. You're the one who told them about the horse. I don't know anything you don't know. And neither of us have the thing. Judy, the therapist, thought it might be a patient I insulted during my afternoon walk.''

"You didn't.''

"Well, J.Q. It sort of popped out. He was a sheeprancher, going on and on about predator control. He's one of those who'd have the taxpayers pay to kill off all the wildlife in the world rather than buy guard dogs.''

"Can't keep your mouth shut, can you!'' He stood up and stared around the room. "I'm going to sleep in here tonight.''

"How will you explain that?''

"I don't think any explanation is necessary. I don't intend to make any fuss about it. If anyone notices, I'll say I offered to be within call for a few nights. Until you felt more secure.''

"God, you make me sound like a hysterical grandma.''

"Do you care? You know Allison and Xanthy aren't going to think anything of it.''

"Not really.'' She heaved a sigh. "Tell you the truth, J.Q. Your being nearby would make me feel better. That business last night got me badly off balance. If I had really been asleep, as he thought I was . . .''

"You're sure it was a he?''

"No. It could have been a woman. Medium height. But either not strong enough or not resolved enough to fight me once I yelled.''

He have her a long, level look. "Do you need some help getting ready for bed? Xanthy told me to be sure and offer her help if you'd like it.''

She shook her head. "I'll manage. I can undress myself. I can get into my pajamas. I can brush my teeth and my hair.

116

I can't wash my left leg below the knee, but it isn't terminally filthy yet. Tomorrow I'll have Allison bring a bucket of hot water and scrub it for me.''

''I'll make up one of these couches for myself, then. When everyone's all settled, I'll come in.''

He nodded and took himself off, leaving Shirley to explore the attached bath and the small dressing room, where the few clothes she'd brought on the trip were neatly hung or stowed in top drawers, within easy reach. To remove the immobilizer she had to sit on the bed with her leg stretched out before her, but when it was off, maneuvering was so much simplified that she was unwilling to put it back on. She propped the device against the wall, crawled into bed, and protected her leg with one of the extra pillows.

She was almost asleep when she heard the door open.

''It's me,'' murmured J.Q.

She mumbled an answer, then listened to rustles and heavings as J.Q. got himself placed. Shortly he began to snore, breathy eruptions as regular as the ticking of a clock.

Reassured by the sound, she let all the sleepless anxious hours well up and drag her away.

J.Q. was gone when she woke in the morning. She became aware of that about the same moment she realized her left leg was paralyzed. Momentary panic gave way to amusement when she found the paralyzing factor was the same orange cat who had stared at her from the patio gate a week ago today. When she twitched her imprisoned leg, he lifted his head, half opened huge amber eyes, and pulsed a baritone purr-burst in her direction.

''Good morning,'' she offered. ''I don't think we've been introduced. . . .''

''Baron Valter!'' said Sarah from the doorway. ''How did he get in here?''

''I imagine someone left a door ajar or a window open,''

Shirley murmured. "Don't move him. He's fine where he is."

"Well, he's not been in here for years! Not since the King-solver girl was here last!"

She put a small tray on the table by Shirley's bed. Hot coffee and two tiny muffins with a molded pat of butter. Shirley exclaimed in honest pleasure. Sarah went pink in the cheeks and turned her attention back to the cat.

"I'm surprised he even remembers being in here. He belongs to Jeanette Kingsolver. His name is Baron Valter von Shenanigan the Third. His daddy was just a kitten when Harry and I came here."

"Baron Shenanigan the Second, I trust."

"Right. His grandpa, the first Shenanigan, was a barn cat, but little Jeanette adopted his son and made a house cat out of him. This one is a grandson."

"Papa and Grandpa both departed?"

"Right. Grandpa was an old, old cat. I think he died of old age. We're not sure what happened to this one's daddy, though Harry suspects wild dogs. Harry has a running battle with wild dogs. He says they're worse than coyotes. Some lambing seasons he's out there most of the time, popping off at dog packs. Anyhow, all three of the Shenanigans had extra toes on their feet. Valter there has seven toes on each front foot."

"You've kept the cats all this time?"

"Part of our deal with Winston was that we care for the animals. The sheep were Gwen's—they're Shetlands; she was a handspinner—and the rest of the animals were the children's pets. Including the koi fish in the patio pond. And peacocks and guinea hens."

"I wondered why peacocks. Why not chickens?"

"I wondered the same thing when we came here. We always had chickens in Iowa, so I bought a couple dozen pullets and let them run with the other birds once they were big enough. Peacocks and guinea hens roost up high. Come evening, they're thirty or forty feet up in the cottonwoods yelling at each other, no matter what the weather's like. My chickens, though, either they didn't roost, or they roosted down low, on a fence rail or something, and coyotes and raccoons and skunks and weasels picked them off two or three a night, and before we knew it, they were all gone. Harry tried popping off the raccoons, too, but there's more of them than you can shake a stick at. No, the neighbors tell me the only way to have chickens here is to have a fenced poultry yard and a good tight chicken house for nighttime.''

"Which you don't have?''

"Oh, sure, there's one down there by the hay shed, but Harry and I don't care that much. I mean, with Harry's cholesterol, he's not supposed to eat eggs at all, and I'm not that big on eggs either, and when you keep the poultry in a chicken house, you have to clean the chicken house.'' She made a face. "Not my favorite job, not since I was twelve and had to do it for spending money, and not Harry's cup of tea at all! Besides, the guests really enjoy seeing the birds wandering around loose, and the peacocks and guineas are real good at that.''

"They reproduce?''

"Oh, my, do they! There's a peahen nest out behind the gate in the patio right now, and there's at least one guinea hen nesting in tall grass somewhere. We had nine peafowl chicks last year and eleven guinea chicks. Keets, they're called. Peahens are good mothers. I've seen cats and dogs come in with their heads all bloody from getting too close to the chicks. I'm surprised how many of the chicks live to grow up.''

"I'm surprised you're not up to your behind in peacock!''

Sarah laughed. "Oh, they get thinned out. I don't doubt some of them have wandered far afield and been shot and eaten. What's good enough for Henry the Eighth is good enough for San Pedro Pueblo, right? I haven't tried peacock yet, but the guineas are good eating when we get too many of them. Like pheasant. And we can always sell the extras. If we can catch 'em.''

She started to leave, then caught herself. "I'd forget my head if it weren't nailed on! There was a reason I brought your coffee. I wanted to explain that Harry and I won't be here today. There are guests in three of the houses, but we've checked with all of them, and nobody needs anything. They're all going off hiking or riding today, anyhow, so nobody will be coming over, bothering you. Also, Vincente and Alberta are spending the day with friends in Albuquerque, so you'll have the place to yourself.''

"Where are you off to?''

Sarah plunked herself down, loosened her moccasin, and scratched at her instep. "Well, first we're going to see our ex-housekeeper, Emelia Grant. She just had a new baby boy last week. . . .''

Bells clanged in Shirley's head. "Is she by any chance a mother of eight children?''

"She is! How did you know?''

"Oh, scuttlebutt at the hospital. You say she's your ex-housekeeper?''

"We hired Emelia as housekeeper when Harry and I first came here. She worked for us for five years. Not fast, but fairly reliable. Then we had a money misunderstanding. . . .''

Shirley cocked her head.

Sarah sighed. "What happened was, her brother wrecked his truck, and he needed five hundred dollars to fix it, and Emelia wanted me to cosign a note at the bank for her. Emelia's mother was in bad health. The family depended on him and on the truck. It was the only transportation they had. Of course, by that time I knew her brother, I knew her mother and the older sisters.''

"So you cosigned?''

"Against the advice of the banker, yes. I told him Emelia was good for it, or she'd work it out. She made one payment and stopped. So I told her she'd have to work it out, and she looked at me with those big brown eyes and said she couldn't afford to work for nothing. I explained she wasn't working for nothing, she was working to pay her debt, but she said she couldn't do that. I told her in that case, she'd have to work for someone else, because I couldn't afford to pay her twice, which was perfectly true. Harry and I were in hock; we had to use the money from here to maintain the place, so until we got our heads above water, we were pinching pennies! So I cleaned the casitas myself for a while until we got a little ahead and hired Vincente and Alberta. It was a slack season, so it wasn't too hard on me. I don't know whether I was angry at me or angry at Emelia or just hurt.''

"But you're still friends?"

"Well, sort of. It was what one might call a cultural misunderstanding. Once she'd arranged for the car to be fixed, she figured that was it. Once she got me and the banker on the hook, she figured she wasn't involved anymore. I asked around, and people said yes, that's fairly typical. Among her people, the ones who have give to those who have not, and though everyone knows who gave and who got, there's no direct debt. Being able to give confers . . . what? Esteem? I suppose that's it.''

Shirley remarked. "What a very Judeo-Christian point of view.''

Sarah shook her head with a wry laugh at herself. "Isn't it? At any rate, the banker knew what she'd do, and he warned me. I don't know why I thought Emelia should behave any different. Anyhow, I feel responsible.''

"For what? Her eight children?''

Sarah laughed at herself. "Maybe even that. Harry hired Antonio Grant as our maintenance person the year before Emelia left. Emelia's mother died soon after that, Emelia inherited the family trailer at the pueblo, and next thing we knew, Tonio had moved in with her.''

Shirley furrowed her brow. "You've been here twelve

years, she worked for you five, then she started having children and has eight?''

''One every eleven months or so since. Right.''

''Can they afford a family like that?''

''According to me, of course not. According to her, she makes out. At least, I suppose she does. She's given three of the children to her relatives to raise. They wouldn't have taken them unless it was all right, would they?''

''Her husband . . . Grant? He accepts it?''

''Even though it's an Anglo-sounding name, Tonio Grant is from Mexico. He and Harry have stayed in touch, and I hear about what he's doing from Harry.''

''Macho?''

''Oh, yeah. Very into his manhood and his honor, which are pretty much the same thing around here. He has to show he's virile. That's really important, and so is keeping his womenfolk pure.''

''How does he do that?''

''Well, he keeps his wife pregnant all the time, and if he had teenaged daughters, he'd keep them locked up. Though I think he's given away all the girls but one.''

''How do they support all the family?''

''Emelia hasn't had a job since she left me. Tonio's quite a good worker in a slapdash sort of way. He quit working for us to take a job in construction. It pays a lot better, but unfortunately, it isn't steady. So when he works, they do well, and when he doesn't, they don't, I suppose. They seem to get by; heaven knows how.'' Sarah sighed, shaking her head. ''Anyhow, I have a few things for the new baby, so that's where we're going first. After that, since it's our thirty-seventh anniversary—''

''Congratulations!''

''Thank you. . . . Harry and I are going out for lunch in Santa Fe. Then we're going to a movie. That'll take up the rest of the day. Vincente and Alberta are gone, as I said, so you're really on your own.''

Shirley said, "I think we can manage. And thanks for being so hospitable."

"Well, if we are, it's just . . . we felt . . . we felt awful about what happened. I mean, Harry was all over that child about sneaking and spying, I've never seen him so angry, and then there she was, dead. And when those parents of hers showed up! My God in heaven, what a pair. I've seen one of those birdbrained peahens more concerned over a lost chick!"

"I feel pretty bad myself," Shirley confessed. "The very minute she was shot, I was telling her she had to learn to behave herself."

"She did need to do that! I still can't figure out what she thought she was doing spying on that couple. They were just an ordinary couple, at least by New Mexico standards."

"New Mexico standards?"

"Well, you know. In Iowa, where I'm from originally, any interethnic couple is suspect. But New Mexico's been mixing the Anglos and Indians and the Hispanics for generations. . . ."

"Good morning," called Xanthy from the door. "Are you ready for a second cup?"

She came in waving a coffeepot and an empty cup. "J.Q. and Allison are making brunch. They're determined to produce a bacon-and-onion quiche. What with all the rolling out, it's becoming a major production. I thought I'd duck out and leave them to it."

Sarah rose, waved, and departed as Xanthy sat in the vacated chair. She filled Shirley's cup, then her own.

"How do you feel?" Xanthy asked.

"Actually, not bad."

"J.Q. told me what happened at the hospital."

"He didn't say anything in front of Allison?"

"Of course not. No. Have you any idea what all this is about?"

"Not one. The only thing I can figure is that since we

were at the hospital Saturday night when the baby was taken, we're supposed to have seen something.''

''What did you see that I didn't?''

Shirley pondered. ''If it isn't the kidnapping, then it has to be that business with April.''

''I wouldn't put anything past that father of hers. . . .''

''Where was he when she was shot?''

Xanthy shook her head. ''I spoke to him within a few hours of when it happened, and he was in Turkey, stopping there, so he said, for a few days before returning to the U.S.''

''You know he was really there?''

''I got the number of the hotel from Mrs. Shaour's mother, and I placed the call myself. I said his name, Suleiman Shaoor, the phone rang, and he answered. Of course, it could have been someone pretending to be him. I don't know his voice that well. . . .''

''He could have an accomplice. . . .''

''To what?''

''Smuggling.'' Shirley gave her a brief rundown on the subject, including a physical and character sketch of Dennison McFee.

''I wonder . . .''

''What, Xanthy?''

''You know, it just occurred to me. What if April isn't his daughter?''

''Why would you think that?''

''Appearance. The man and wife look so much alike. The Shaours, I mean. Men often pick women who look like their mothers, which means women who look like themselves. It's not coincidence.''

''You're right that April didn't really resemble them.''

''She didn't. She had freckles. Her hair had reddish lights in it. Her eyes were greenish. Both theirs are brown.''

''This is pure speculation, Xanthy.''

''Not entirely pure. Something must explain the man's attitude toward her. If she was someone else's child and if he had always resented that fact, his resentment might explain his behavior.''

''It could explain her mother's behavior, too. Repressed grief. She did want to cry, but he wouldn't let her.''

''You think he beats her?''

''No idea. I'm quite sure he dominates her.''

They subsided from this spate of invention, each into her own cup of coffee.

''Are you going to figure it out?'' Xanthippe asked after a considerable silence. ''You do figure such things out, usually.''

''I really . . . don't want to,'' Shirley mumbled.

''I think you have to.''

''Really!'' Shirley drew herself up, slightly offended.

''For Allison's sake.''

''Allison?''

''Shirley, she's having nightmares. Three times, now. Each time, she's dreamed someone is after her.''

Shirley doubled her fist and pounded on the bedclothes. ''Damn. I hadn't even considered that she might . . . Damn!''

''I think it's because no one knows why. She's left with these vague feelings that maybe someone just hates little girls. . . .''

''I feel impotent,'' Shirley mumbled. ''When I do solve things, J.Q. says I do it by thrashing about, stirring up mud, until something goes splash. I can't thrash about from a wheelchair. It takes at least two legs to thrash.''

''Send us out to thrash for you,'' Xanthy suggested.

''You're staying awhile, then?''

''So long as Allison doesn't mind sharing a room. Also, I feel responsible. Leaving just now would be . . . inappropriate.''

''You think Allison will be less fearful if we know who did it?''

''Oh, I do indeed. Wouldn't you? You and J.Q. had

125

planned to stay in New Mexico for a few weeks longer anyhow."

"I don't look forward to going home, that's sure."

Xanthy sighed, turning her empty cup on the table with a restless hand. "I can understand that. In the last five or ten years, the whole character of our area has changed. Another five or ten years, it will be a foothills suburb of Denver, no different from Mt. Vernon or Evergreen. When I built my little house near the school, it was lost in the woods. I woke up in the morning to birdsong. Now there are houses on either side and I wake up to Mack Clennons yelling at his wife, or the two Pfeiffer boys on their dirt bikes. The crazy part of it is, both the Clennons and the Pfeiffers say they moved to the country for the peace and quiet of nature."

Shirley gave her a rueful smile. "I can't go on living at the ranch feeling the way I feel now, that's certain. The problem is, I can't figure out what else to do with myself, Xanthy. I never saw myself anywhere but there. I planned to die there. All those years in Washington, I looked forward to coming home. All the time I was elsewhere, it was the ranch I longed for. And now . . . now it's like somebody died. Like a person who's not there anymore. Only the husk remains. . . ."

"And?"

"And what?"

"You were thinking something else. Your eyes went on talking when your mouth stopped."

Shirley laughed. "I was thinking I should be honest with myself. When I'm being honest, I have to admit things were getting . . . laborious for me and J.Q."

"It's a big place for two people."

"It was beginning to feel that way. Even before all that business happened last year, we'd begun to talk about cutting down on the livestock and letting some of the pastures just go."

Xanthippe nodded to herself, staring into the distance. "I'm a strong believer in serendipity."

"Meaning?"

"Meaning keep your eyes and ears open. I tell the young people that all the time. Watch. Listen. Good things often happen if you're just in the mood to notice them."

Shirley was chewing on this when Allison's voice preceded her down the hall:

"You guys coming to breakfast?"

"I'm not even up!" Shirley grumped as Allison appeared at the door.

"Fifteen minutes, it'll be done!" Allison announced importantly.

"What can I do to help you?" Xanthippe asked.

Shirley heaved herself more or less upright, threw the covers off her pajama-clad legs, and stared at them as though they might speak for themselves. "You can give me a few minutes in which I'll try to make myself respectable."

They complied and departed, leaving Shirley to totter into the bathroom and examine herself closely in the three-way mirror the Kingsolver daughter had either inherited or considered necessary. If Shirley had inherited it, she would have removed at least two of the three mirrors. One view was quite depressing enough. Her facial bruises had faded to a light avocado shading along the cheekbone and around the eye, making her look merely jaundiced instead of abused. Her hair was flattened and oily from all the days spent in bed.

Growling, she turned the shower on hot, shed her pajamas, and set one crutch aside to stand propped against the shower wall while she sudsed her hair and face and let the hot, soapy water run down her body. Perhaps she would spend the day here. Hot water had never felt so good.

Getting out of the tiled cubicle posed a problem. The other crutch had fallen out of reach and had to be fished back with the one she held, a lengthy and frustrating process. Someone had put a chair near the tiled vanity, however, and she could sit down to towel her hair and use the dryer, which she found already plugged in and neatly positioned where it was reachable. Bless Xanthippe or Allison or J.Q. or whoever had arranged things. The clothes she'd brought with her included an ankle-length cotton caftan, which was far easier to get into than trousers. The last chore was to fish her slippers out of the closet with a crutch tip and wriggle her feet into them.

Total elapsed time, fifteen minutes. She emerged clean, combed, still damp around the hairline, face slightly pink from the hot water, to find J.Q. waiting for her.

"You want a ride?" He gestured toward the wheelchair.

She shook her head firmly. "Today I walk."

"You don't have your leg protector on." He patted the monstrosity leaning against the bed.

"Bring it. I'll put it on when I get where we're going. It's easier walking without it."

"Then I'll come along to be sure you don't fall and break your leg all over again."

Carefully watching the placement of her crutches, she followed J.Q. along the corridor she had traveled last night, past the library, through the cavernous, almost windowless living room, and into the dining room once more, where Allison and Xanthippe were dishing up the quiche.

"We'll all get fat, eating this way," she commented, seating herself with a sigh of relief and sticking out the leg for J.Q. to strap the monstrosity around.

"Allison and I thought your appetite needed tempting," Xanthippe offered. "Multivitamins are by your plate."

"Yes, Mother," Shirley murmured.

Allison giggled. "I'm so glad you're home," she said.

Shirley started to say, "This isn't home." She managed to keep the words from coming out. She knew what Allison meant. Wherever they all were, that was home to Allison, and God bless her.

Instead, she asked, "Do you like it here?"

"It's fun." Allison nodded, carefully cutting off the tip of her wedge of quiche and setting it aside for last.

Shirley, watching, reflected that Allison did the same thing

128

with wedges of pie, though not with wedges of cake. A private little ritual, come from heaven knows where. Like the afikomen, after Passover. Shirley herself always started with the tip of the pie and ate back toward the crust. One might make a heresy out of that. Like the Lilliputians with their eggs, opening them at the little end. Was it the little end? And what was the name of the other people, the ones who opened their eggs the opposite way?

"Shirley?" said Xanthippe for the third time. "What are you thinking?"

"About Lilliput," she replied. "About opening eggs at the right end. About rituals and what they mean to people."

J.Q. laughed. "All the eggs in the quiche were opened in the middle. Xanthy asked how large a piece you want."

"Modest-sized, please, Xanthy. It looks and smells just as wonderful as last night's dinner did, but I've done nothing to work up much of an appetite."

They ate quiche, and cantaloupe garnished with fresh mint and lime crescents. They drank coffee. They read the Sunday paper, to much commentary, finally leaving Shirley scrunched over the crossword while the others cleaned up the kitchen. Looking up from the table, she could see a paseo of poultry outside the window, crowned heads high, long tails dragging, back and forth, back and forth. The young people in Española also had a paseo, though they drove up and down main street in their low-rider cars, exchanging looks and shouts, insults and invitations.

The poultry had no sooner departed than the large orange cat came stalking across the room and jumped on top of the table, from there to Shirley's lap, where he lay down to knead her knees with careful paws. Shirley looked over its head at the shaded canyons where vast blue cloud shadows fled like enormous bats.

"What?" whispered J.Q. from the buffet beside her.

She looked up helplessly, surprised at the flood of emotion

129

that had come from everywhere and nowhere. "It's nice," she whispered. "You're all . . . you're all lovely."

"We have our moments." He put away the dishes he was carrying and went back into the kitchen.

She leaned back and reciprocated the Baron's knee massage by kneading his back and shoulders.

"You've got a friend," said Allison.

"Baron Valter von Shenanigan the Third," murmured Shirley, half-hypnotized by food, warmth, and cat.

"This afternoon we thought you might like to go to the flea market," Allison said. "We'll wheel you. Xanthy really wants to go, but she doesn't want to go alone."

Shirley raised her eyebrows. Somehow, she had never thought of Xanthippe Minging as a flea market type.

"It's not a typical flea market, from what I understand," said J.Q. "Harry and Sarah tell me it's more like an open-air multiethnic market. Stuff from Mexico. Indian crafts. New and near new clothing. Furniture."

Shirley gently dumped the Baron and sat up straight. "Sounds interesting. However, if we're going among people, I'll have to dress in something besides a robe . . ."

"One of our surprises," Xanthy announced. "Allison and I stopped at Sears the other day and picked up a pair of jeans that are cut very full in the leg. They're made for someone about twice or three times your girth, but the leg fullness will go over your leg gadget."

"I can leave it off. . . ."

"No. You might get bumped, and we'd all be more comfortable if you're properly protected. Since you're going to be sitting down, nobody'll notice the baggy seat."

Shirley swallowed the objections that came automatically: too much trouble, too much concern. She led the way back to the bedroom, where Xanthy produced the trousers and she and Allison got Shirley into them. From the waist up, she looked reasonably normal.

"I won't be able to get into the car," she remarked, suddenly remembering her traumatic trip down the hillside. "The leg sticks out too far."

"Fiddle," muttered Xanthippe. "Let me think."

She went off down the hallway, grumbling to herself. In moments she was back, bearing a sewing kit from which she took scissors, a tube of something, and a roll of something else. She ripped open the inside seam on the left leg halfway up the thigh, turned it back, smeared stuff from the tube down both sides, and then cut off a proper length from the roll and pressed it between the two sides.

"Velcro," she announced. "Now you can open the seam to get the thing on and off. We'll leave it off until we get there, then we put it on you and fasten the seam up. Nobody will know."

"Xanthy . . ."

"Yes. What?"

"Do you always go around with fabric cement and Velcro and—"

"When I'm in charge of a group, yes. Also adhesive tape and bandages and sanitary products for the girls and antiseptic and fungicide and replacement buttons and snaps and elastic for waistbands. And press-on patches for rips in jeans or shirts and sunblock lotion and stuff for poison ivy and allergies, not to mention ordinary needles and thread. I keep adding to my emergency kit, and still every trip I find there's something I should have had with me that I hadn't thought of."

Their departure was delayed while J.Q. and Allison went through the house, shutting and locking, and while J.Q. searched for the key Harry had given him, finding it at last hung on its hook by the kitchen door.

"Where it belonged," said J.Q. in a disgusted voice.

"Where are you putting it?" Shirley asked.

"In my wallet," he said, showing her as he did so.

They drove south toward Santa Fe. Just short of the opera house turnoff they came to a large, level tract of land west of the highway, one-third of it fenced off as market, the other two-thirds as parking lot.

They parked, got Shirley first into her leg protector and then into her chair, and went through the gate into the market enclosure, past persons selling tires, persons selling chainsaw carvings, persons selling pottery. Past persons selling Indian-style jewelry made in Taiwan. Past persons selling Indian-style rugs made in Korea. In both cases the word *Indian* was in large type and the word *style* was vanishingly small.

Xanthippe murmured something and disappeared into the crowd toward a truck laden with quilts.

At another truck, this one covered with Mexican serapes and blankets, J.Q. bargained for a brilliant red, green, and blue one for Allison. At a booth selling *biscochitos*, Allison bought a sack and shared the anise-flavored cookies with Shirley and J.Q.

"Is the crowd too much for you?" J.Q. asked.

Shirley reflected. Actually, it wasn't. People seemed to see the wheelchair as something to be avoided. They broke around it like water around a rock, and she was being jostled far less than if she'd been on foot. "I'm fine," she said, believing that she was. The sun was warm but not hot. The people were a crowd but not a mob. She was all right.

They went all the way down one long lane, stopping here and there to look at this and that, then rounded a corner and ran into Harry and Sarah.

"My God," Harry muttered. "The whole world's here today. Old housekeepers. Recent guests. And you guys."

"I thought you were going to a movie," Shirley said.

"We were," Sarah murmured, her eyes ranging past Shirley to the crowd around them. "But when we stopped at Emelia's place, her daughter said she was here, so we thought we'd come here first. . . ."

"It'll be hard to find her in all this," Shirley remarked. "There must be close to a thousand people here."

"I agree," growled Harry. "I tried to talk her out of it, but Sarah's got a gnat in her throat."

Shirley looked up at him, for the first time conscious of his tone. The man was angry.

"What's the trouble?" she asked.

It was Sarah who answered. "When we got to Emelia's place, three children were there alone, two of them babies in diapers. The oldest one, little Clara, is six and a half, and she said her mommy was here, buying some clothes for the boys."

"You didn't like her leaving them alone?" asked Shirley.

"I did not. But that's not all!" snarled Sarah. "There was a new color TV in the living room. There was a new truck in the driveway. But when I asked how the baby was, Clara told me her mommy doesn't have the baby anymore."

"What did she mean?" asked Allison.

"That's what I want to find out! Oh, I see her. There she is, Harry." She bustled off, crying over her shoulder. "Excuse me. 'Bye."

Harry went purposefully after her.

"Why wouldn't she have the baby anymore?" Allison asked again.

Shirley said, "According to Sarah, Emelia has given several of her children to her relatives to raise. Sarah doesn't think it's right."

"What does Emelia's husband think?" J.Q. asked.

"I got the impression he's less interested in his offspring than he is in keeping his wife pregnant. Of course, that's Sarah's interpretation." She craned, trying to see through the crowd, without success. "What's happening, J.Q.?"

"Sarah is trying to talk to a woman, presumably Emelia. Emelia's having none of it. She's turning her back and walking away. Sarah's after her, Harry tugging at her, trying to pull her away. Emelia's saying something. Wow. Whatever that was, it set Sarah back on her heels. She's red in the face.

Harry is definitely pulling her away. She's crying, but she's leaving. The end of that engagement."

He looked down at her with a wry smile. "Satisfied?" Then, seeing the expression on her face, he asked, "Hey, what's wrong?"

Shirley shook her head. She didn't know what was wrong, though something was. A few minutes before, she'd been fine. Now she felt . . . closed in. Panicky. Maybe it was only the crowds. She was accustomed to looking over people's heads, but all she could see was people's bodies, endless packs of torsos and swinging arms. Maybe it was only her weariness, now come back all at once, like a tide.

"Sorry," she murmured into his ear as he bent above her. "Sorry, J.Q. I hate to spoil all your fun, but I need to get out of here. Maybe you can take me back to the car. I'll wait while you guys finish your shopping. . . ."

She put her head in her hands, trying to figure out what it was. Not the noise. People weren't all that loud. Not the pain, though there was pain. Something.

Movement brought her out of her abstraction. He was taking her back to the parking lot.

"Allison's with Xanthy," said J.Q. "I told them I'm taking you home. I'll come back for them in about an hour. We shouldn't have rushed you like this. We should have given you a few days of peace and quiet instead of bringing you into this mob."

"It's not that," she said.

It wasn't that. It wasn't the people. It was a tide of apprehension, a flood of worry and fear, come out of nowhere, sparked by something she couldn't even identify. Something happening. Something going on. Something she should know about, but didn't.

134

5

WHEN THEY DROVE up in front of the house, Shirley rejected use of the wheelchair. "I can get into my room, J.Q. You go on back."

"You can't get in anywhere until I unlock some doors," he replied, fishing through his wallet for the key. "I did put the key in here, didn't I?"

"I watched you do it."

He found it as they approached the kitchen door. When he put his hand on the latch, however, the door opened.

"Don't tell me we locked everything else and forgot to lock this one!" he muttered.

"I watched you lock it," she said expressionlessly.

They went through. The kitchen was as they had left it.

"You stay here," he said. "I'll be back." He went off through the dining room, disappearing through the far door.

Shirley sank into one of the chairs at the kitchen table and waited. The house was utterly silent. No sound came through the open door from outside, either. It was siesta time for birds and beasts. Certainly siesta time for all the cats lying along the wall in the sun.

"Nothing," called J.Q. from across the dining room. "The outside door to your room was open, so somebody's definitely been in here."

"They didn't break in," Shirley commented. "Whoever it was had a key."

J.Q. made an angry gesture. "Hell, Harry leaves the keys hanging by the kitchen door. People go in and out of the kitchen all the time, because that's where he keeps the rental records and the credit card machine. Anybody could pick one up."

"It's hard to imagine why they'd want to," she said, rubbing her forehead. "Sarah and Harry have both remarked that the Kingsolvers removed all their valuables when they stopped coming here regularly. There's no stereo, no silver, no jewelry."

Both of them avoided, as though by mutual consent, the subject both were thinking of: the attempt on Shirley's life. If they didn't say it, perhaps it wouldn't be true.

Shirley said, "I think I'll go back to the bedroom, J.Q."

"Let me wheel you back there."

"All right," she murmured, surprised to find herself agreeing. She let him take her as far as the high threshold, then went the rest of the way by herself.

"What was the man's name, the one with the pueblo police?" she asked as she sank onto her bed with a long exhalation, like a leaky balloon.

"Apodaca. Ray Apodaca."

"He wouldn't talk to me, would he?"

"I didn't get the impression he was very forthcoming, no."

"Since I woke up this morning, I've been thinking about last night's conversation at the dinner table. About the pueblos and the tourists and Sarah's saying how she felt or would feel about tourists coming to her church. I got to wondering whether someone—one of the young militants she mentioned, for example—might get so upset about April's stealing that bag, or maybe just her being there, that he might have shot her. A twenty-two is kind of a kid's gun. A varmint gun."

"I'd consider it more of a target gun." He sat down and stroked his mustache. "I suppose it's possible, but it would seem more likely if she hadn't been a little girl. It's hard for me to visualize even a militant taking out his anger on a child. Besides, if someone was angry at her for just being there, why not be angry at me and Shaour for just being there?"

"Symbolically, maybe she wasn't a little girl. She was a white person. Besides, there were two shots. Maybe the intent was to shoot any or all of us."

He frowned. "You get into the area of ethnic hatreds and anything's possible, I suppose."

"I had another thought: Suppose the little bag wasn't all she found. Suppose she saw the same pots you did. Suppose she took something else from out there, but we didn't find it?"

"What? It would have to have been something small enough to fit in her pocket. Something she could have hidden after she got home. The fact I found the bag still in her pocket argues against that. Besides, both the houses we were staying in at the time have been cleaned since. Surely anything she might have hidden would have been found. What's led you in this direction?"

"I suppose it's all the talk we've been having about cultural differences. People do not see things the same way. Emelia's children, for example. Sarah thinks Emelia is awful, first for having so many and then for giving them away. Emelia herself pleases her husband by staying constantly pregnant. Sarah thinks it's irresponsible to leave two little ones in the care of a six-year-old girl. Emelia thinks otherwise. She was probably left in charge of babies when she was no older than that. It would be neglect in the Anglo world, but is it neglect in the Indian one? If we judge them, then we must allow ourselves to be judged by them. They see us as money-grubbing environment wreckers.''

"You are anything but—''

"I'm not, no. But a lot of white people are. A lot of Hispanics and Indians are, too, but that's not their stereotype. We tend to lump Indian people together. They tend to lump us together. What one does, everyone is guilty of. I want to talk to someone who's familiar with that culture, but you're right. The pueblo policeman probably isn't the right person.''

"Maybe some young person?''

"Maybe.'' She sighed, staring at the ceiling. "I wish I could talk to Emelia herself.''

"If you don't get any more from her than Sarah did, I don't think it would help you.''

"Emelia might have a key to this house.''

He stared at her, mouth open.

"Shut your mouth, J.Q. You look like a flytrap.''

"We just saw her at the flea market!'' he objected. "She can't be the one who came in here. . . .''

She snapped, "Keys are quite portable. She could have given it to someone.'' She put her arm across her forehead.

"Why!'' he exploded. "Damn it, Shirley. Why!''

"I wish I knew,'' she said from beneath her arm. "Do you suppose I'll be safe here until you get back with Xanthy and Allison?''

He stalked out wordlessly, returning in a few moments with one of his handguns.

"I didn't know you had that with you,'' she commented.

"It was in a locked compartment in my suitcase,'' he replied. "Habit, more than anything. I never let the kids see it.''

"A good thing.'' She sighed. "If April had known it was there, she'd no doubt have stolen it and robbed a bank.''

"Put it under your pillow. I'm going back to pick up Allison and Xanthy. Half an hour at the outside."

She disposed of the gun as he'd suggested and lay back on the bed, reminding herself of the therapist's words at the hospital. She would be depressed. She would feel disabled. She would be up and down. This morning had been briefly up. This afternoon was down, a snarly, pressured, squeezed feeling. If she were a zoo animal, she'd be crouching in the corner of her cage, all teeth showing. If she were a wild animal, she'd be hiding, peering out, waiting for the hideous something to arrive. Perhaps this was how dogs and other animals felt before an earthquake. Perhaps this is what made them howl.

When she felt like this at home, she went riding. She went out and looked at cows. She went up into the woods and smelled the air. Here, she could do nothing but fume impotently. Even thrashing around until something went plop was beyond her. She felt imprisoned.

Why was it that people felt death was worse than imprisonment? Death was normal; it came to everyone sooner or later. For some it was welcome as an end to physical pain or mental confusion. To Shirley it now seemed that imprisonment was cruel and unusual. Being unable to do, unable to move . . .

Outside her door, the gate shrieked open on rusty hinges.

She opened her eyes a slit. Someone was coming into the little patio. As the person was silhouetted against the light, she could see only the outline, male and tall, moving slowly, deliberately. She slipped the gun from beneath the pillow into her hand, letting the hand lie along her side. The dark shape came to the door, opened the screen, twisted the knob.

He had a key. He inserted the key and came into the room, stopping short when he saw her.

"Stop right there," said Shirley, the gun in her hand now very visible.

An indrawn breath.

Then laughter, a bit forced, but laughter nonetheless.

"You must be Ms. McClintock," he said. "I'm your host. I'm Winston Kingsolver."

Shirley gulped, started to put the gun down, then changed her mind. "If you're my host, I owe you an apology. If you're just saying so, however . . ."

"Identification?" he asked, reaching slowly for his inside breast pocket. "Driver's license?" He took out his wallet, removed the license, and passed it to her between two fingers, the other hand still held high.

Winston Kingsolver. Address in Chicago. Nice picture. Handsome man. About her own age.

Shirley found herself blushing as she put the gun down.

"I'm sorry. We're getting a little paranoid. When we came in, we found the doors open, but we knew we'd locked up."

"My fault," he admitted. "I unlocked the kitchen door, and then came back through here. When we lived here, summers, this was our main route out to the back. My daughter Jeanette always complained about our tracking through her room, but it's the only one with an outside door on this side of the house."

"I had no idea you were coming. I'm afraid we've occupied your quarters."

"No, no." He waved away her protestations. "I didn't intend to stay. I hadn't even made prior plans to visit, but I ended up in the neighborhood, so to speak. Actually, I was in California, and I decided to stop off in Albuquerque on my way back home, rent a car, and come up to take a look at the place. I haven't seen it in . . . oh, three or four years, I guess."

"It's a delightful place," Shirley said, sitting up and pulling pillows behind her. "Except for our various tragedies, we've enjoyed it enormously."

"Sarah told me," he said, looking vaguely around himself. "Do you mind if I sit down?"

"Not at all," she said, shaking her head at herself. "I'm

140

sorry. I'm afraid both my wits and my manners have left me!"

"It's not every day I get a gun pointed at me," he admitted as he dropped onto one of the twin couches. "Sarah told me about the little girl. That seems quite enough of a tragedy by itself; has there been something more than that?"

Shirley leaned back comfortably. "More, yes. Odds and ends of happenings starting with April's death. No one knows why she was killed. My companions and I don't believe it was accident, though I think the sheriff's office would like to believe so. If it wasn't accident, it might have been because the girl saw something she shouldn't have, or overheard something. She was incurably nosy. She sneaked and pried, and, I'm afraid, she stole things."

"So Sarah said." He shook his head. "A regular little delinquent."

"Understandably," Shirley said. "If one has met her father, one knows why."

His lips thinned into a hard line. "That's often what it comes down to, isn't it? You were hurt at the same time, Sarah says. A new knee, is that it?"

"I hope eventually it will work like one. Right now it feels anything but new."

"My son-in-law ran himself into a tree, skiing. He had to have knee surgery, and Jeanette said it took several months before he could simply ignore it." He gestured at the room. "I must say this room is neater than I ever saw it when my daughter lived here."

"We'll put everything back when we leave. In the meantime, it's a delightful environment to recuperate in."

"We always liked it, the kids and I. But they're grown-up now, grown-up and married and very busy. And since the Fieldings are leaving, well . . . I think it's time to sell it."

"They're definitely leaving?"

He thinned his lips once more, this time in irritation. "I've no right to be disappointed. They've been good, faithful caretakers, above and beyond the call. They accepted my offer to let them live here because they'd had some financial reverses and needed to stretch their income. Now, evidently, they've recouped and want to move closer to their children. Who am I to argue with that!" He laughed ruefully at himself. "Nonetheless, it feels like . . . like an interruption. Now I have to do something about the place." There was pain in his voice.

"It's hard to sell a place with memories," said Shirley softly. "It's like breaking faith, somehow. Believe me, I understand. I'm in the same fix myself."

When J.Q., Xanthy, and Allison returned in some haste and anxiety, they found Shirley and Kingsolver chatting companionably about a pueblo artist friend of Kingsolver's, the pistol lying forgotten on the bed.

"You can have the room I've been using," J.Q. offered their unexpected visitor, after introductions and exclamations. "If you'd like to stay the night in your own house."

"Actually," Winston Kingsolver replied, "I checked the calendar in the kitchen, and it seems the little house by the drive is unoccupied and has been for several weeks. It'll be just right for me for a day or two while I look the place over and see what shape it's in so we can set a fair price on it."

"You're welcome to join us for dinner," Xanthy offered. "We're having roast lamb."

"An offer I can't refuse," he said with a bow in Xanthy's direction and a significant glance at Shirley. "Now, I believe I know where the house keys are kept, so I'll pick up some sheets and towels from the laundry room and go get myself settled." He nodded at them and went out the way he had come.

"We thought there was a burglar," Allison blurted, when he had gone. "Or somebody come to get at you . . ."

"He never thought a thing about it," Shirley commented. "It's his own house. He simply unlocked it and walked through it, as I might have done. He couldn't have known how on edge we all are."

"You two seemed to be getting on very well," said J.Q. stiffly. "What was all that about the Indian artist?"

Shirley nodded slowly. "Potter," she corrected. "I'd mentioned to him that I wanted to talk to someone from the pueblo. Someone who knows the local culture and wouldn't mind talking about it to an Anglo. He knows an Indian artist, a potter, born and reared in San Pedro. She's worked with Anglos a lot and isn't paranoid about them. He, Kingsolver, says he'll call the woman. Assuming she's still alive and kicking, that is. He hasn't talked to her in a number of years."

"Ah," he murmured, his face clearing.

"Well, if we're going to have company, we need to do some preparation," Xanthy said. "We need to be festive! We need to look through the pantry and see what we can find!" She drew Allison out with her, the echoes of their voices trailing behind them like smoke from a locomotive, slowly wisping away to nothing. The long hallways with their hard brick floors were virtual whispering galleries, transmitting sound from one end to the other undiminished.

"I held the gun on him," Shirley confessed to J.Q.

"I suppose you're sure he is who he says he is."

"He showed me his driver's license."

"That open kitchen door put a chill up my backbone, I can tell you that." He sat down with a thump. "I was afraid your assailant from the hospital had come back to finish the job."

She nodded soberly. The idea had more than merely crossed her own mind. "I'm sorry Xanthy and Allison's afternoon got wrecked."

"Shirley, they were trying to amuse you! The whole trip was for your benefit, to get you out of your glooms. You know Allison's tendency to fret, and when you went to the hospital, she was worrying herself into a real crisis, unable to do anything else, not eating or sleeping well. Xanthy distracted her by getting her involved in inventing 'surprises' for you. The flea market was one of them.''

''I thought Xanthy wanted to go.''

''Oh, Xanthy thought it would be fun, but mostly fun for you. As it happened, she told me on the way back that she lucked out. She found a local quilt cooperative that's agreed to make a certain pattern of quilt for her, one she's been wanting for years. Pure serendipity, she says.''

''Serendipity.''

''Right.''

''Have to watch out for that,'' she murmured.

''Are you sleepy?''

''Tell you the truth, J.Q, for some reason, I'm wiped out. I think I'd like a nap.''

He left her. She dozed, half-in, half-out, aware of movement and sounds, incapable of responding. Serendipity. She thought of serendipity. Of Winston Kingsolver and serendipity. She drifted.

''Shirley?''

She opened one eye. It was Sarah. A very unhappy Sarah.

''Whassa matter, Sar?'' she said, struggling to get both eyes open.

''Can I talk to you?''

''Sure.'' She cleared her throat, blinked several times. ''Tell you what, bring me a hot washcloth. My face feels like it's set in cement.''

Sarah complied. Shirley sat up and applied the steaming cloth, then blinked and wiggled her jaw experimentally until her face felt like flesh again. Where her face had been bruised, the skin felt fragile and flaking.

''What's the trouble?'' she asked.

''Emelia.''

''Told you to get lost, did she?''

''It's probably my own fault. Harry didn't want me to even talk to her there, in public, but I was just so . . . so angry. And something's wrong! I know there is!''

144

"Like what?"

"It's how she acted! I asked her, if she had the money for a new TV set and a new pickup truck, surely she had the money for a baby-sitter so she didn't leave her children alone! Damn it, Shirley, that trailer house has a kerosene heater in it. One of those children could set the place afire, and they'd all be dead by the time the fire department arrived!"

Hardly in midsummer, Shirley thought. Though things that bad did happen to children left alone. "So?"

"So she looked past me and said she wasn't going to be gone long. So then I asked her where the baby was. She knows I don't like the thought of her giving her children away. She said it wasn't her baby anymore."

"Meaning she's given it to some relative or friend."

"I don't know what it means! Even though she gave her other daughters to her relatives, she never said *they* weren't her children anymore. When they have family gatherings, all the children are there, and they know they have brothers and sisters who live with other people. It's all extended family, and I have to admit there's no neglect involved! It's just another way of doing things!"

"Sarah, if you can admit that, why are you so upset?"

Sarah took a deep, shuddering breath. "It's ridiculous, isn't it?" She rubbed her eyes, compressed her lips. "It's the children, I guess. I'm a nut over babies. Harry says that. When people come here with babies, I always offer to baby-sit; I don't even charge for it! I used to volunteer at the hospital, in the nursery, but they stopped their volunteer program. Some insurance problem. I'm sort of like . . . oh, Harry and his cigarettes. He quit smoking, but he can't quit carrying them around. I can't quit carrying babies around. There haven't been any babies here for months, and I miss it so." She wiped her eyes. "So when I saw those two babies, left alone with little Clara, I got . . . Harry says I got hysterical."

"I can understand how you felt."

"And then it's how she acted. She looked at me and Harry and said she didn't want white people bothering her ever again because all they did was cause her trouble. That she could tell me things about some white people I wouldn't even believe."

"But you didn't give up?"

"Harry was trying to drag me off. I asked her where they got the new TV set and the truck."

"And?"

"She just stared at me and didn't say anything. Not anything. Didn't even answer me."

"It's not how friend treats friend, true."

"No."

"But it is how one behaves when one is very uncomfortable."

"I suppose."

"What do you think she did with the baby?"

"Gave it to someone. Someone who needs a baby."

"Someone in the pueblo needs a baby?"

"Well, the infant mortality rate is high in the pueblos. Their health care isn't the greatest. Their diet isn't the greatest, either. Their prenatal health care is a scandal. That's partly why I get so . . . so upset. There's a lot of diabetes and alcoholism. . . . Someone may have lost a child and want a replacement."

"Well, that could be good for the baby."

"I suppose it might. If they're good people. Not alcoholics. But how would anyone know?"

"Why did the truck and the TV upset you? Do you think they were dishonestly come by?"

Sarah ran a hand across her forehead. "Not really. She plays bingo all the time, and I suppose she finally won one of the ten-thousand-dollars pots they have every month or so."

"I thought gambling was illegal in New Mexico."

"Not on pueblo land. The pueblos decide what's legal on

their own land, and they run big bingo. A perfectly legal way to get some of their own back from the white people. Well, some of the white people and a lot of Hispanics.''

''Surely you're not angry that she won?''

''No, of course not! I'm angry that the money got spent the way it did. Why a new TV and truck? Why not something for the children! A savings account for emergencies. Or dental care. Or even a new trailer, one that isn't a firetrap! For what they paid for that truck, they could have bought a used trailer that's bigger and in better shape. . . .''

Shirley sighed. ''You can't change people, Sarah. You really cannot. When you calm down, you'll realize that.''

''Harry says the same thing,'' she cried bitterly.

''No point beating your head against a wall.''

''That's also what Harry says. But people do change! I've changed. Harry himself changed. He used to be so money-hungry, I can't tell you. All the time trying this or that. Stocks. The futures market. Real estate speculation. All those books and videos they advertise on late night TV that tell you how to get rich quick. About the third time the bottom fell out of our lives, I talked him into our living within our means instead of trying to be a millionaire. That's when we accepted Winston's offer and moved in here. I think Harry's a lot happier, not that he'd ever admit it.''

''Well, this is a place to be happy in,'' Shirley commented.

''I don't know how he'll feel when we move, even though he suggested it. And I do want to spend more time with my grandbabies. Oh, Shirley, I do miss babies so. At our ages, we don't have that much time left.''

''How old are you, Sarah?''

''I'm sixty-three. Harry's a year older.''

''You've probably got a good twenty or thirty years,'' Shirley laughed. ''Enough time for great-grandchildren.''

''Not likely.'' She shook her head. ''Our kids were slow

starters. They didn't either of them have babies until they were over thirty-five."

"I think you'll be better off worrying over your own family than worrying over Emelia's."

"I shouldn't have let her upset me so, but when I saw that little girl there all alone with those two babies . . ."

"I know." Shirley nodded soberly. "I'm sure it would have affected me that way, too. Lots of bad things can happen to children left alone. But Emelia's right, too. It's her life, her culture, her children. You've got to butt out, Sarah."

Sarah nodded miserably, breathing fast, mouth already forming the next sentence, obviously not yet talked out.

Shirley, however, had had enough of Emelia. "Did you hear about Winston Kingsolver showing up?" she asked quickly, before Sarah caught her breath.

Sarah smiled, changing tracks. "I hear he scared you to death."

"He came very close to doing just that," Shirley admitted. "We've invited him to supper. I hope you and Harry'll be there."

She shook her head. "Harry was taking me to lunch, for our anniversary, but since we got all involved, he's taking me to dinner instead. I'll see Winston tomorrow."

She got up, smoothed her dress, and left, pausing in the doorway to whisper, "Thanks. For your shoulder."

"Anytime," Shirley told her insincerely.

Sarah went out still snuffling, leaving quiet behind. The screen door onto the patio eased open. The Baron had his paw around it, pulling it far enough open for him to slip through.

"Smart-ass," remarked Shirley.

He jumped up onto the bed and lay down beside her, purring a soft rumble that made the bed vibrate. Her eyes sagged shut. She dozed, fully aware of the Baron and the bed and the soft breeze coming through the open door, at the same time seeing a parade of golden horses and Indian pots. The procession emerged from a dark cavern, marched across a desert, and disappeared into a misty canyon, horses cantering, pots cantering. She wondered vaguely how they managed that, but it didn't seem important enough to wake herself up over.

It was a smell of roasting lamb that did wake her, finally, though all she did for a time was lie perfectly still, enjoying the aroma and the fact she didn't have to do anything about it. Her mother used to say that whenever anything smelled that good, it was probably about to burn. Which might be what made barbecue so popular. Everything always smelled as though it was about to burn, or had already burned.

"We thought we'd eat at six," said J.Q. from the door.

"Fine with me," she said, forcing her eyes fully open. "I had a nap. Two naps. Two halves of one nap."

"I see you did. It's twenty to six now."

"Is it really, J.Q.? Lord, I must have been tired! But I slept last night."

"You thought you did, but I'll bet you were lying there listening for trespassers."

"It's possible." She sat up, yawned, stretched. "I'll have another shower and be with you in twenty minutes. Winston's joining us, right?"

"Right," he said grumpily.

"He said he'd try to get in touch with his potter friend today. I told him to see if she'd come talk with me anytime, tonight, tomorrow, whenever."

She was talking to his back. J.Q. was not interested in Winston Kingsolver's arrangements. J.Q. was not interested in Winston Kingsolver. Winston Kingsolver made the hair on J.Q.'s neck stand up. Interesting.

Once showered, shampooed, and combed, she found it was possible to suspend a pair of jeans by the waistband at the end of a crutch and fish them carefully over her left foot. The right foot could be inserted, and then it was only a matter of getting hold of the jeans to pull them up. Dressed in cus-

149

tomary garb and feeling almost her normal self, Shirley made her way slowly out into the corridor, past a bedroom, door open: a queen bed, curtains and coverlet that looked hand-woven, sand-painting designs on the walls. This had to be the room J.Q. was using; his hat was on the desk. Bath across the hall. Next bedroom, door open, two queen beds, a big room, larger than the one Shirley was in, with an attached bath. This one was frilly, unlike the rest of the house. Shirley tossed a mental coin, and it came up Trina. She had redecorated this room after Winston's first wife died.

If Shirley were doing it, she'd put it back the way it had no doubt been before. Frilly didn't fit with exposed vigas and split-cedar *latillas* and the softly belled shape of the adobe fireplace. On down the hall, furnace room, laundry room. Then a door that had a closed, private look to it.

She'd come the wrong way! The closed door led into Sarah and Harry's living quarters.

She turned back, past the bedrooms and her own door once more. Then the library. Nice. Lots of bookshelves. Big old desk. Dark green leather chairs and couch. An Indian rug over the ubiquitous fireplace. At least she assumed it was Indian, though she'd never seen one in those colors. Apricot, several shades of green, violet. In Shirley's mind, Indian rugs were gray, brown, black, white, and red. Period.

She stepped through the open door at the end of the hall and down into the living room. Too dark for her taste, too few windows. Whoever built it had been enamored of the adobe churches of the Southwest. If someone put an altar against the clerestory-lit wall, it wouldn't look out of place. What could one do with a room this size to make it livable? It was furnished, but it had a temporary, unplanned air to it. The double door opened out onto the patio, and Shirley paused there to stare across at the far wing, where the Fieldings lived. Sarah had said they had a bedroom, bath, living room, and tiny kitchen of their own, but she, Sarah, preferred to use the big kitchen except when the Kingsolvers were in residence. Shirley could empathize. She hated small kitchens.

She made her way slowly across the living room to the far door. A glassed-in porch—portal—and then the dining room, festive with candles. Everyone was in the kitchen but J.Q. He'd pulled a dining room chair over near the window and was buried in his newspaper.

"Smells good," she murmured.

"Ayeh." He folded the paper and put it on the windowsill. "I encountered several guests out in the parking area who made similar comments."

"How many living units are there? In addition to this house?"

"Five rental houses," he said. "Actually six units, if you count the suite the Fieldings are using. Seven if the little house they're using for storage was fixed up. It's got plumbing in it already, so it wouldn't take much doing. Eight if you count the house occupied by Vincente and Alberta."

"I wonder how much business they do."

"Why?"

"Just curious." She shrugged. "What would you guess, J.Q.?"

"Oh, I don't know. Not much in the winter. The place is only about half an hour from the ski slopes, but I've noticed skiers aren't happy unless they can jump out of their hot tub directly onto the lifts. Besides, the place isn't right for skiers. It's too . . . contemplative. Peaceful. They probably do quite a bit of business in the spring and summer and early fall. Figuring what we paid as an average, they probably gross somewhere between sixty and eighty thousand a year."

She nodded slowly. "That would support the place. And buy groceries."

"Depending on what they pay the help. Maintenance is high in a place like this. All these damned flat roofs. Swimming pools eat up money, too. Why do you care?"

She shrugged again. "Just curious. You know me, J.Q. Always nosy."

"Right." He pulled out a chair for her as Winston Kingsolver came in from the kitchen bearing a bottle of wine.

"Look what I found in the cellar!" he crowed, holding up the bottle like a trophy.

"I didn't know this place had a cellar," said J.Q.

Kingsolver beamed. "It's hidden. There's a trapdoor in the floor of the so-called butler's pantry. Got a rug over it. I don't know why or when, but somebody put a wine cellar under there, and I must have left a few bottles . . . when? Must have been twelve, fifteen years ago. Nothing down there but the cobwebs now, because I brought up what was left: six bottles of this."

"What is it?" Shirley asked. "Not that it will mean anything to me when you tell me. J.Q.'s the connoisseur."

"He gets to taste it then." He flourished a glass, poured an inch into it, handed it to J.Q., and waited expectantly.

J.Q. frowned, sipped. Frowned harder. Sipped again. His face cleared. He smiled. "Lord," he said reverently. "That's nice. Pauillac, is it?"

"It is! I was afraid it might have gone, but isn't it great? I figure we can get to all six bottles while I'm here."

"You're staying awhile?" J. Q. asked.

"A few days. I want to get an appraisal on the place, but I won't be able to talk to anyone until tomorrow. I'll try to get someone out here before I leave."

He put the napkin-wrapped bottle at the end of the table and went back into the kitchen, where they could hear him laughing at something Xanthippe or Allison had said.

"If he's getting it appraised, he must mean to sell," J.Q. said softly. "I guess it's definite that Harry and Sarah are leaving. Seems to me it would be hard to leave the place."

Shirley replied as quietly. "If you owned it, yes. If you only worked here, perhaps not. Harry isn't that crazy about it, and Sarah very much wants to live closer to her children and grandchildren. She doesn't think she'll have many years in which to be grandma, and she doesn't want to miss any of them."

"Never had that urge myself, but I can understand it."

"So can I." Shirley wondered if she would have felt the urge, if her own children had lived. If Allison married and had children, both she and J.Q. would spoil them rotten! But that wasn't what he'd meant. He'd meant he'd never had the urge to move in on his children's or grandchildren's lives.

"So when are they going?" he asked.

"Rather soon, I think. Winston was slightly irritated, the way people get when something unexpected happens that has to be handled right away. I think if he'd known about it longer, he'd have been more matter-of-fact and less annoyed."

"Harry didn't say a word about it to me."

"Well, he wouldn't necessarily, would he?"

"Oh, I don't know. We got very chummy the day we were fixing the plumbing. He talked about a lot of things he planned to do in the future. Fishing trips. A cruise to Alaska. But he didn't mention leaving."

"You know how things like that go. You talk about them and think about them and then you wake up one morning with your mind made up. Maybe that's what happened."

"Possibly." He stared out the window for a moment without speaking, then turned. "I'll go see if I can help out in the kitchen."

"Good," she said to his back. "I'm starved."

They ate fresh asparagus, roast lamb with herbs, and a mixture of long- and short-grain rices with nuts and raisins.

"Marvelous," said Winston. "And the wine's right with it, too."

"I think it holds its own," laughed Shirley, who had had three glasses and enjoyed each one of them.

They ate a salad of bosque pears, Gorgonzola cheese, and Boston lettuce. J.Q. and Allison had made an apple pie.

"Do you people eat like this all the time?" Winston asked as he leaned back and eased his belt.

"J.Q. and I cook up a storm sometimes," admitted Shirley. "But today is mostly thanks to Xanthy and Allison."

Xanthippe flushed, enjoying the accolade. "Shirley and J.Q. are too busy with their buried treasure to bother with cooking."

Winston raised his eyebrows. "Buried treasure?"

Shirley found herself telling the "found in the couch" version of the golden horse story, to which Xanthippe added a few words about the Shaours.

Winston shook his head. "But you don't think that's the reason for the girl's shooting? No. Nor would I. Much more likely to be something to do with Blue Mesa. When Gwenny and I first bought this place, we used to take long hikes out over the surrounding countryside. Being easterners, we didn't understand about pueblo land. It wasn't fenced or posted, and we had no idea anyone would mind our walking on it. Well, one day we were hiking out there—"

"Around Blue Mesa?" J.Q. asked curiously.

"Not actually that near, no, but on San Pedro Pueblo land, and we had quite a nasty confrontation with one elderly man and two younger ones he'd obviously brought along for muscle."

"They threatened you?" Shirley asked.

"No. It wasn't a threat, it was more of an indictment. A list of charges, starting with the conquistadores! They told us they'd been watching us, and we had no business there, and then they went into a long harangue about their grievances. Gwenny tried to explain we didn't know we'd been trespassing, all they had to do was tell us, but they were in no mood to let us go without the full harangue."

Xanthippe said, "I have the feeling there are a lot of misunderstandings like that, some of them rising from the fact that people aren't speaking the same language in a very real sense. The pueblos around here speak Tewa; the ones farther north, Tiwa. The pueblos south and west of Santa Fe speak Keresan. Zuni speak their own language, and Hopi speak a Uto-Aztecan language. And those are just the pueblo peoples.''

"People who live in towns," said Allison.

"Agricultural people who have lived in towns for a thousand years or more, yes. Then there are the nonpueblo peoples, the nomadic warrior-hunter-gatherer people, the Apache and Ute to the north of here, and the Navajo. The Navajo have become pastoral, of course, but they were originally raiders, very warlike. Add English and Spanish to that mix, you've got good grounds for misinterpretations.''

"Which of the Indians are descendants of the Anasazi?" asked Winston. "Gwenny was always fascinated by the Anasazi.''

Xanthippe nodded. "Anasazi are only one of half a dozen ancient cultures. From what I've read, it seems lately Zuni and Tewa and Keresan peoples have all made it a habit to claim affiliation with any ancient ruin that's discovered. They can't all be descended from the same ancient ones, however, or they wouldn't have such different languages now.''

"Possibly some of them are mistaken?" asked J.Q.

"That's one possibility. Another possibility is that ancient sites were occupied sequentially by different language groups. One group would move away because of drought, and another group would come along later and resettle the same place. That would give two language groups a legitimate interest in a single ancient site.''

"Can't they find out?" asked Allison eagerly. "Can't the archaeologists find out which ones belong to which?''

Xanthy smiled ruefully. "Well, there's some difficulty with that. For example, there's a so-called catacomb site in Arizona that both the Hopi and the Zuni claim affinity to. Each tribe explains the site differently, each tribe ascribes different meanings to the petroglyphs, and both tribes forbid any interference with the graves. In effect, what this does is prevent scientific evaluation of the history while leaving the grave sites open to looting. In addition, one tribal leader has been heard to remark that the archaeologists aren't open enough about their discoveries.''

J.Q. laughed. ''Meantime, the poor archaeologist is being very tight-lipped because he doesn't dare say, 'Look, we think this site may belong to somebody else's ancestors, not yours.' ''

''That's about it,'' agreed Xanthy. ''Reality being compromised by mythology, which is nothing new, as any scientist or politician can tell you.''

''So New Mexico isn't as complaisantly tricultural as presented by the chamber of commerce,'' Shirley commented.

Xanthippe swallowed a last morsel of lamb. ''There's some enmity between Navajo and Hopi over land, some between Indians and Anglos over water, some between Hispanics and Indians over erecting statues of men the Hispanics regard as heroes and the pueblo people regard as genocidal villains. And some dislike, of course, by the Indians of the Anglo tourists for just being insensitive.''

''But the San Pedro Pueblo people dance for tourists,'' argued Allison. ''And the Santa Clara people—''

''The Hopi don't, not anymore,'' said Xanthy. ''They've put up signs telling the white people to stay away.''

Shirley grinned. ''And we don't know what the people at the Tewa pueblos are actually saying, do we? They could be asking a spirit to send a large scorpion to sting that mostly naked white woman wearing the halter top and shorts. Or please to let the man firing off all those flash bulbs be bitten by a rattlesnake.''

Xanthippe put down her napkin and said firmly, ''I'm sure they'd never be so rude. Though I for one wouldn't blame them. Who's doing dishes? I cooked, so I'm exempt.''

''You and me, kid,'' said J.Q. to Allison.

''Not at all,'' claimed Winston. ''Three of us at the very least. I know my way around this kitchen.''

The three of them cleared the table while Xanthy and Shirley poured more wine and sipped at it quietly, watching the sun submerge itself behind a blue sea of mountains.

"Didn't know you were such an authority on local Indian groups," murmured Shirley. "Your erudition never ceases to amaze me, Xanthy."

"I'm certainly not erudite on this subject! I did read up on it a little, before we left Colorado, just to acquire some general information for the young people. I confess, the more I read, the more fascinated I became."

"Why all those different languages?"

"Well, assuming there were several migrations from Asia over the Bering Strait, each migration may have had a different root language. Then considering that various tribes have been here for at least ten thousand years, there's been a lot of time for languages to change and deviate. Heck, we couldn't understand Chaucer if he rose up and spoke to us today, and that's only what? A few hundred years?"

"It doesn't sound long."

"Linguistically, it's long enough. What the linguists do, as I understand it, is make lists of words and see if various people have similar words for the same thing. Do they have words for hunting, or for a kind of tree? Do they have any word at all for war or slaves? Some of the peoples were more peaceful than others. Some of them practiced slavery of captured women and children; many of them had human sacrifice and torture killing of enemies."

"The white man didn't interrupt an idyll in Eden, then."

"Not in that sense, no."

"All the Indian populations had respect for nature, however. They didn't overpopulate."

Xanthippe smiled ruefully. "If they'd had another five hundred years, who knows? The Maya in Yucatán may well have overpopulated."

"I didn't realize that."

"There's a theory they did, just before they fell into disaster. Just as we're about to."

"You believe that?"

"I do indeed. I think the turning point happens when more people live in cities than in the country. At that point, men begin to lose respect for nature. City kids are reared outside nature. They believe they don't need it, that nobody needs it. City kids elect leaders who also don't need it. Stupid men, ignorant men, men who say it's all right to chop down all the trees because if you've seen one, you've seen them all. Put one tree in a park for people to look at and chop down all the rest because we can make money that way. People who see nature only as a money resource, who claim to respect human life but actually cheapen it because the more people there are, the cheaper life gets. . . ."

Shirley, who had herself often feared that within a century, there'd be nothing on earth but man and his food crops, felt a wave of pure despair flood through her. She gasped at it, took a deep breath, and said through gritted teeth, "Xanthy, if I think about what you just said, I'll probably agree with you. If I agree with you, it will be very hard to care whether this damned leg gets any better or the rest of the body goes on living!"

"Oh, Shirley, I am sorry!" she cried. "I'm being despicable! I've no right to inflict my horrors on you."

"It's unlike you," Shirley agreed, white-faced. "That's why it's scary."

Xanthy wrung her hands, literally, ending with them at her forehead, in an attitude almost of prayer. "I started feeling this way when April got shot. I was shocked because I felt myself not caring the way I would have cared even . . . even ten years ago. I can't seem to shake it. I said you should solve this thing for Allison's sake, and you should, but I wish you'd solve the thing for me, too. Then maybe I could forget it in favor of something more hopeful."

Shirley patted Xanthy's arm and took another sip of wine.

She would make her next attempt when Winston found her someone to talk to.

"My public name is Geraldine Olivarez," said Shirley's visitor. They were sitting in Shirley's bedroom on the twin couches, a Monday morning pot of coffee and plate of muffins between them. "My Tewa name, in English, is Dawn Wind, but you can call me Gerri."

Shirley tried not to smile, without success. The woman seated across from her in her bedroom was as wide as she was tall. She was close to Shirley's own age. Together, they were Mutt and Jeff. Jack Sprat and wife.

Gerri kept her straight face. "When they named me Dawn Wind I only weighed about seven pounds. It's like my brother. In English his name means Little Horse; he should be called Big Bear now; he weighs more than I do. Winnie said you wanted to talk to somebody about the pueblos?"

"Winnie?"

"Winston Kingsolver."

"You know him well, then."

"I am pleased to do him a favor. When he and Gwen were living here, they contributed a lot of time and money to the Northern Pueblos Arts Council. I'm one of the founders. We put the group together to lobby for laws preventing non-Indians from capitalizing on Indian art. You know, Anglos making Acoma-style pots; Hispanics making Navajo-type jewelry or blankets."

"I saw some of that at the flea market."

"Last year we made them clean up their act, and it looks like we're going to have to get them again. Anyhow, there were several of us on the Council who got to know Winnie and Gwen pretty well. She really loved this place. We used to have some of our meetings here. Anyhow, I told him I'd be glad to talk with you."

Shirley pulled a muffin slowly apart, thinking. "It was kind of him to ask you and kind of you to consent. I'll start

159

out by apologizing. I've got no right to ask these questions; I'm sure they're intrusive and unwelcome. The last thing I want to do is be offensive, but we've got a very unwelcome mystery on our hands.''

Gerri's face was impassive as she said, ''I'll tell you if I get offended.''

''Did Winston tell you about the little girl who got killed?''

''He mentioned it, but I already knew about that. There was some talk about closing that trail down. It crosses San Pedro Pueblo land. Whenever something happens to a tourist on pueblo land, you always get some who want to close it off.''

''I can understand that. The police hassles alone would be irritating.''

She shrugged. ''You get county sheriffs and FBI and city police and pueblo police mixing it up, it can be a mess. We'd already had FBI this week, asking pueblo people if they'd seen anybody strange, heard babies crying, you know.''

''That was over the kidnapping.''

''Right. For some reason, they thought somebody might be hiding out in the pueblo, or on our lands somewhere. Somebody could hide out there, but they could hide out in the national forest just as well. This time of year, all you'd need would be a tent or a camper.''

''When I asked Winston if I could meet someone from the pueblo, I was thinking of some fairly simple questions concerning what the little girl might have been up to on pueblo land. This last couple of days, the whole matter has become more complicated. Now I also want to ask some questions about a pueblo woman married to a Hispanic man. . . .''

''Mexican?''

''I guess. Is there a difference?''

''Sure. Somebody whose folks were from Mexico but he was born here, he'll call himself a Chicano, maybe, or a Hispanic. Somebody who came here from Mexico, he usually calls himself a Mexican, even if he's a citizen. That's what we call him, too. So you've got an Indian woman from where?''

"San Pedro Pueblo.''

"Married to a Mexican?''

"And they've had eight children. Only she's given four of the children away. That's what I want to know about.''

Gerri looked over Shirley's shoulder. "About her giving them away?''

"Right. What do her people, her pueblo, think about her giving them away?''

Gerri let her eyes rest on the distance, twiddling her thumbs, pursing her lips. "Well,'' she said after some time, "if she got sick or if her husband treated her children badly, people from the pueblo would probably take the kids without her even asking. There wouldn't be any fight, but the kids would get moved out and cared for.''

"The pueblo wouldn't condone abuse.''

"No. It's not our way to beat children.''

"But if the mother isn't abused, or sick, and just goes on having babies, one after the other, like a chicken laying eggs, and gives them away . . .''

"People will not like that.''

"Why is that?''

"The thing a lot of white people don't understand, our people are what you call puritan. We're modest. We don't go around undressed or show off sex feelings in public. People doing that offends us. We don't put sex up front in our lives. People hugging and kissing in public, pictures of people kissing on billboards or in ads, that's offensive to us. We don't traditionally have lots of children, either. Our men are expected to be religious, and when a man's religious, he has to stay away from his wife during certain times when he's preparing for ceremonies and dances. Times likes that can take weeks, even months. There are ceremonies and dances going on all the time, so if a man is really religious, it's a cultural form of birth control. Also, we pueblo women nurse our babies a long time—at least, we used to—and that kept women from getting pregnant.''

''I see,'' Shirley murmured, to show she was paying attention.

''But you take one of our women married to a man who isn't religious and she feeds her babies bottles and she gets pregnant all the time and gives her babies away, people are going to be unhappy with her.''

''Like maybe the third or fourth time she tries it?'' Shirley asked.

''I think maybe more like the second time,'' said Gerri firmly. ''You can think of it like it's a big family. Some family members are good for the family and some aren't. A woman like that isn't really good for the family. Her actions bring us disrespect. That upsets people.''

Gerri's face was no longer impassive. She looked upset.

Shirley sighed. ''You know who I'm asking about, don't you?''

''It'd be hard not to. There's only about two hundred people in the San Pedro Pueblo, including the children. I know all of them.''

''So what happened to her little boy?''

''Nobody knows for sure,'' said Gerri quietly. ''Her husband told some people he gave the baby to his family, down in Mexico, but he hasn't been down to Mexico since it was born, so how did it get there?''

''But nobody's done anything about it?''

''About what? One thing we're sure of, she wouldn't hurt the baby. If we go stirring up a fuss, we may have the white police down on us, the FBI, who knows? We don't need outsiders mixed in something like this. Winston says you won't drag them in. I hope he's right.''

''I don't plan to,'' said Shirley uncomfortably. ''Tell me, are there are a lot of mixed marriages?''

''Quite a few. More than we like. And quite a few intertribal marriages, too.''

"Someone from San Pedro marrying someone from Santa Clara, for instance?"

"We wouldn't call that intertribal. The language is the same, the religion is the same. Santa Clara marrying Taos would be intertribal. Taos is very private, very secret. If one of us married one of them, we couldn't live in the pueblo, they wouldn't let us do that. Or Santa Clara and Hopi would be intertribal. Two languages. Two different religions."

"Are such marriages difficult?"

"It depends. If the people aren't religious, it doesn't make any difference, does it? Or if the men are outsiders but they show respect for their wives' tribal customs, it works out all right. A real outsider won't take part in the ceremonies or dances of his wife's people, but his children will grow up taking part. But when one of us marries a white or a Mexican who doesn't respect our ways . . . that's difficult." Gerri gave Shirley a long, measuring look. "When are you going to tell me what all this is about?"

"I'll tell you now, but I'd rather you didn't speak of it to anyone."

The woman didn't change expression or answer. She was making no promises.

Shirley shrugged. "You know about the little girl, April Shaour, who was shot to death. We can only think of three reasons why it might have happened. One was what happened the day before, Saturday, when she wandered onto San Pedro Pueblo land, out in Blue Mesa, and found a little leather bag, possibly in a cave that also had a lot of Indian pots in it. The bag contained pot shards, inlaid animal bone, a bear carved from stone, a turquoise ring. She took the bag. We found it in her pocket, after she was killed. She may have stolen something else, also, but all we found was the bag. Maybe the theft made someone murderously angry at her, or at all of us."

No response from Gerri.

"Two: she saw something she was not supposed to at the

hospital where she was treated for her broken arm. I was attacked while I was in that hospital. The most notable thing that happened there was the kidnapping of the Franklin baby, but I am struck by the fact that *two* baby boys, born within hours of each other, have gone missing. That may be just coincidence. On the other hand, it may have some meaning.''

Gerri thought this over before rousing herself to ask, ''You said three reasons.''

Shirley paused for a second, deciding the matter of the golden horse needed no wider circulation. ''The third reason would have been something that happened back home, before she came on this trip. In which case, I'll probably never know the reason, but then, I'm not responsible for it, either.''

''You don't mention accident.''

''My friends and I were mentioning accident up until somebody tried to smother me with a pillow in the hospital last Friday night. Then we stopped mentioning accident.''

Still impassive, Gerri regarded her for some time before asking, ''What did you really want to find out from me?''

''When I asked Winston to find me someone to talk to, I wanted to know about that little bag, whether April's stealing it made someone really angry. Now I also want to find out whether the baby is really missing or whether the mother in question gave him to a relative.''

''I can answer part of that. I've heard nothing about anyone being angry over the girl stealing anything. And Emelia did not give her new baby to anyone in our pueblo, no.''

''Then my next question is, is there any connection between the baby being missing and the family buying a new truck and a new TV set?''

''You think she *sold* her son?'' The impassive look was gone; she was outraged.

Shirley shrugged. ''Parents have been known to sell babies.''

"Not Indian parents! That's not the way our women behave!"

Shirley started to remind Gerri that Emelia already had a reputation for not behaving as Indian women behave, but decided against it. "Perhaps she won big at bingo, as someone has suggested."

"We know who wins big, and it wasn't her."

"You see my problem," Shirley said.

"I can't see what the two things have to do with one another."

"I can't either, but I think they do."

"As for the leather bag the little girl found out there at the mesa, I don't know what to think about that. If it was religious, it could make somebody angry, but it doesn't sound like something religious."

"No?"

"No. No pollen, no cornmeal, and Blue Mesa isn't a place you'd find anything religious, anyhow. Besides, even though religious men get angry when people invade their privacy, they're not the kind who'd . . . go shooting some child. Pueblo people are peaceful! They don't fight or abuse women or children. Women have more real equality in our culture than in lots of others."

Shirley didn't contradict her. How could she?

Gerri went on, "You said something that bothers me. You said there were pots out there, at Blue Mesa?"

"According to my friend, yes. The little girl's father wanted to go out there, to see . . . where she'd been lost." The man's actual reasons would only complicate the issue. "My friend J.Q. got permission from the pueblo and took April's father out there on horseback. J.Q. says there's been a recent rockfall that disclosed a place where there were a lot of pots."

"At Blue Mesa?"

"You sound . . . as though you don't believe that."

"I don't. Pots. I mean, we use pots in our homes. Pots

165

are for storing things, for cooking things. They're made to be useful, or were, originally. Also, historically, we buried pots with our people. That's where you find them, in our homes, or in ancient homes, or in graves."

"How about storage areas? Granaries?"

"In houses, sure. Or nearby. But who goes a mile or two out in the desert to store food? Nobody ever lived out there that I know of."

"You're saying you know of no reason for there to be pots out at Blue Mesa."

The woman actually smiled. "I'm saying I know of no reason for there to be pots at Blue Mesa."

"My friend said a pickup truck followed them out there."

"A pickup truck?" Long, thoughtful pause. "What kind of pots were they?"

"I don't understand?"

"Big ones? Little ones? Micaceous?" Seeing Shirley's questioning look, she explained. "Clay with mica in it. It makes shiny little spots. Were the pots red or black or white? Smooth? Rough? Incised? Carved? Painted designs? What kind?"

"I'll ask my friend," Shirley said helplessly. "He didn't say. He just said pots. When I find out, should I tell the pueblo police?"

She shook her head. "No. Ray Apodaca doesn't know about pots. You try to tell him, he'll shut his ears on you. He wants this whole thing to be accidental. I know about pots. You tell me."

"Getting back to our previous subject, would taking money for a child be illegal?"

"Of course it would be illegal!"

She had actually raised her voice! Shirley made a mollifying gesture. "Sorry. I didn't know. I know there are differences between state and tribal law."

"In a matter like this, they'd probably be alike! We would not permit Indian children to be sold, no. Militants and re-

166

ligious both would consider that to be . . . genocidal. And the women in the pueblo would be very angry at any woman who did that!''

"Even if the child is only half-Indian."

"If his mother's a member of the tribe, so is her son." She shook her head gravely, waving an admonitory forefinger. "A century ago our pueblo was destroyed by disease, and the survivors were scattered. In the forties, the land was restored to pueblo ownership and the descendants of the survivors were sought out. I was one of them."

Shirley settled herself. This had the tone of a many-times-told tale, and even though she'd already heard about it, she'd better listen.

Gerri went on: "I was living in Colorado. My father had died, my mother had married a Hispanic man. She didn't want to come back, but my brother and I did. Our people came from all over. Colorado. Arizona. Texas. Some of us were living in other pueblos. By that time, some of us had Mexican blood, and white blood, and blood from other tribes, but we were still descended from San Pedro. Our great-great-grandparents lived here. Now we live here. We are the vines from this root. Our kinfolk from San Ildefonso and Santa Clara and San Juan, they taught us our old Tewa language and our own religion. Any child of a Tewa woman is a Tewa child; any child of a San Pedro woman is a child of San Pedro. The little boy we're talking about, he's a child of San Pedro. Emelia cannot 'sell' him away from the people. He belongs to the people."

"I see."

And she did see. If Emelia had sold her child, it was definitely not something she would want the people of San Pedro to know.

She said as much to J.Q., after Gerri Olivarez had gone, leaving behind a card that gave the name, address, and phone number of the Dawn Wind Gallery in San Pedro, where Geraldine Olivarez and three other artists, each doubly named in Spanish and Tewa, were listed as working in clay, fiber, wood, and stone.

"You think Emelia didn't tell her people?" J.Q. asked.

"I think Emelia would not have told people about this for anything. Whatever she did, she doesn't want the pueblo to know."

"You have other thoughts on the matter?"

"Yes indeedy. I think her husband knew about it. I think it is even possible that her husband arranged for it. Listen, J.Q. Find out from Sarah where Emelia lives, will you? Do it casually if you can, and don't let Harry hear you. He doesn't want Sarah involved, not that I blame him."

"What are you going to do?"

"You and I are going over to see her. If we're lucky, we'll catch her at home alone."

"It's lunchtime," he objected.

"We'll pick up something on the way. Or, if you can wait, after we talk to her, we'll go into Santa Fe and have luncheon out. I could use a break from this solitary clumping around."

"I thought we'd been quite solicitous," he said stiffly.

"You've all been wonderful! Which is part of what I need to have less of. I feel like some unwieldy china ornament, some great porcelain white elephant, carefully being washed and dried and laid away in cotton batting! I feel stifled! Come on, J.Q. Find out where she lives."

He stomped away, disapproval in every step. She sighed and picked up a book. When he was in that kind of mood, she couldn't expect him back promptly, even if he found out promptly. He would delay. He would do something else, to prove how busy he was and illustrate his displeasure. As though he hadn't done it quite enough already.

She was deeply involved in the book by the time he returned, almost an hour later.

"I had to look at pictures of her family," he said, without apology. "Including the babies."

"Did you coo?" she asked wickedly.

"I fell back on my usual remark."

"Let me see. Your usual remark is 'Now, that's what I call a baby'?"

"Correct." He had the grace to look slightly abashed.

"Did you find out where Emelia lives?"

"I did. Do you want to walk to the car?"

"Yes. I'm tired of being carted."

Actually, she reflected, however slow the crutches were, they were no slower than the wheelchair, which had to be maneuvered around corners and folded up in the back of the car. She made the trip to the driveway in five minutes, pausing as necessary.

"How far?" she asked.

"Ten minutes. Or less." He turned the car and started out the driveway.

"Damn," said Shirley. "We should have asked Allison if she wanted to come along for the ride."

"She and Xanthy have gone into town for groceries. I left them a note saying we'd be home later."

"That's good. Poor kid. Her vacation has been disrupted, hasn't it? She was very nice about missing out on Carlsbad."

J.Q.'s expression of studied disapproval softened. "Allison is one of the world's great kids. No; the world's great young ladies."

They drove on the highway, west for a mile before turning off across a cattle guard, past a signboard telling outsiders to stop at the tourist center, past the one-story building designated as the San Pedro Pueblo Tourist Center, past a number of small houses on both sides of the gravel road, left onto a rutted road that led past half a dozen mobile homes, obviously immobile for decades, and over a low east-west ridge that hid the final dwelling from its neighbors. When they parked, they saw the wide bulk of Blue Mesa filling the sky to the north, nothing between but sagebrush and chamisa.

Shirley took the proffered crutches and stood staring at the mobile home before her, its corroded metal sides, its cinder-block foundation and steps, the two-sided shed at one end, obviously intended as a carport but filled instead with a dozen large Super-Soft toilet tissue cartons, a broken bicycle, two bald tires, a half-inflated child's wading pool, and other assorted junk. She clumped her way to the piled cinder-block step and paused, hearing children inside. There was a good deal of loud, wordless crying, but at least one voice was pleading for something or someone.

"Hello," she cried, thumping on the screen door, which rattled loosely beneath her hand. "Hello."

A diminution in the sounds. At least two babies were still crying: one bellowing, one whimpering.

"Hello," she called again, turning to beckon to J.Q., who was ostentatiously remaining aloof from her visit. *I'm only the chauffeur*, his stance proclaimed. *I have nothing to do with this*. Well, at least he wasn't pointedly writing in his notebook with his back to her, the way he did sometimes when he didn't want to be part of whatever she was doing.

She beckoned more strongly.

Something in her face moved him, for he joined her at the door.

"Hello," she cried again. "Is anybody home?"

A barefooted girl child appeared inside the screen door, wearing pajama bottoms and a dirty T-shirt, dark hair messily tousled, face dirty and tear-streaked.

"*I'm* home," she said in an almost inaudible voice.

"Is your mommy here?" Shirley asked softly.

"She won't wake up," the child said. "My brothers are crying and she won't wake up. She's all . . . she's all over blood. . . ."

Shirley's skin crawled as she tried the latch. Open. "Would you like me to come in and see if I can wake her?"

The child neither agreed or disagreed, but she led the way as Shirley climbed laboriously up the cinder-block steps and came inside. A small room with too much in it. Pillows and blankets at each end of the couch marked children's sleeping places, at least one in addition to the baby who lay there whimpering and hungrily sucking a fist. Not quite a year old, Shirley thought, as she turned to follow the little girl, passing the large, very new TV, which was already imprinted with circles from wet glasses and beer cans, through the tiny kitchen, neat enough, though swarming with flies that were gathered over a stickiness on the counter. Two bedrooms at the back. The little girl stood in the door of one of them, tears running down her face.

Shirley went only partway to the disheveled bed, near enough to see the open window, the pillow over the face, the gaping bloody slash below it. She turned and pushed the little girl out before her, hanging her head, breathing through her mouth, trying not to be sick, not to be dizzy.

When she had caught her breath, she called, "J.Q. We need to take the children outside."

He appeared with the baby on his shoulder, glanced into the bedroom, then went into the other tiny room and came back with a toddler, not yet two, his nose wrinkled in distaste. Both the children smelled strongly of dirty diapers.

"Where does your mommy keep the diapers?" Shirley asked the girl, trying to keep her voice level.

"We ran out," said the soft little voice. "Papa didn't come home with any."

Shirley was looking for another child. "Isn't there another baby?" she asked. "Don't you have another baby brother or sister?"

"Raoul. He's almost six. He went with Papa."

Shirley collected a roll of paper towels from the kitchen counter, moistened several of them, and went outside.

"Strip them down, J.Q. It's warm enough they can run around bare-ass. I'll hold the fort while you go find a phone." She took a deep breath, surprised to find she could not control her trembling. She asked the girl, "Do the babies still have bottles, sweetie?"

The child nodded. "I'll get them. There's some milk."

171

"That's fine, honey. You do that."

J.Q. was wiping bottoms with an expression half of pity, half of disgust while the two little boys howled with outrage.

"Pueblo police?" he muttered at Shirley.

"I suppose. Tell them to bring someone to take charge of the children. And bring diapers!"

He left her sitting on the cinder-block step, turned the car, and was gone. The little girl came out with a container of milk and two nursing bottles glazed with dried milk and furred with detritus. Shirley tried to summon the willpower to go into the house and wash them, but failed. Whatever bugs the bottles were carrying, the babies had already been exposed to, she assured herself. The little girl set the bottles on the step and filled them with cold milk, then handed one to each baby. The noise stopped abruptly. The smaller child sat on the sand, concentrating on the bottle. The older one staggered around, waving it between sucks.

"Mommy didn't wake up," said the little girl. "I think she got hurt."

"What's your name, honey?"

"Clara. That's Roberto." She pointed at the staggerer. "And that's Joey." Joey made a contented sound and peed strongly onto the dirt in front of him, bending forward to play in the resultant puddle.

Shirley decided to ignore it. "What's your other brother's name again? The one who went with your papa?"

"Raoul. And I've got sisters, too, but they don't live with us. Rosa, she's almost three, and Maria, she's three and a half, and Lupe, she's four and a half. Almost."

"Where do they live?"

"With the aunts."

"When did your papa leave?"

"Last night. Before supper. He took the new truck. Mommy was mad."

"What was Mommy mad about?"

"Boxes. And the truck. And the money."

"He hasn't been back since?"

The child shook her head wearily.

"Have you had anything to eat today?"

"I ate a apple."

Shirley put her arms around the child and held her. She could hear the flies in the kitchen, like a hive of bees. The stickiness on the counter probably wasn't jam. There had been a cloud of flies in the bedroom, on the blood. No screen on the bedroom window, she reminded herself. Someone had come in that way, probably. Someone had washed his hands in the kitchen.

"Was anybody else at your house this morning, or last night? Besides your mommy?"

"Just Papa's friend last night. Outside in the car."

"What's the friend's name?"

"I don't know."

"Ah. Do you know what he looks like?"

"He's just a man," the child said, tears welling in her eyes. "Can't you wake her up? Is she hurt? Is she dead?"

"I'm afraid so, sweetheart."

"I want Papa."

"I know, honey. I know. I want him, too. Right now."

6

"WE MAY NOT make it home in time for supper," Shirley remarked to J.Q. sometime toward the middle of the afternoon.

They were sitting in the car outside the office of the pueblo police. Clara had wept herself to sleep in the backseat while they waited for someone to come pick her up. The little boys had already been taken away by other persons, relationships uncertain.

"What do you think happened?" J.Q. asked softly, with a glance over his shoulder at the exhausted child.

"I think Emelia and her husband got into an argument, or maybe just a discussion, over what Sarah said at the flea market. Emelia said something that made him angry, probably something about returning the truck and using the money for something else. Maybe all she did was repeat what Sarah had said, and he took it as a threat from Sarah. He likes trucks. In his culture, trucks are the status symbol. So he

174

decided to go somewhere, maybe back to Mexico, taking the truck out of danger. The truck and his eldest son.''

"But not the little boys?" J.Q. frowned at the windshield, then burrowed in the glove compartment and brought out a box of tissues. "Not Clara?"

"The boys are still in diapers. That'd be my guess as to why not. I don't picture this truck-loving fertility symbol as being great at changing diapers."

"Do you think he . . . you know?" He glanced over his shoulder again.

"No. I don't think he's abusive. If he had been, I think it would have come out when I was talking with Gerri. Why should he be abusive? Ninety-nine percent of the time, Emelia was probably doing her best to please him. Besides, the way she was killed isn't the way these macho males kill people. They don't sneak around; they kill in a fury, in a frenzy. They go berserk, they take hostages, they run amok. . . .''

"But this was cold-blooded."

"Very. Cold-blooded and calculated. There were children sleeping in the living room. Clara was asleep in one bedroom, her mother in the other. Anyone looking through the screen door or the windows could have seen that."

"Why didn't he come through the door?"

"It was locked. Breaking the lock might have wakened the children. He didn't want any noise, so he came through Emelia's window, put a pillow over her face, slit her throat, went into the kitchen, leaned on the counter with his bloody hands, washed his hands, and left quietly, leaving the screen door unlocked, as we found it. The pillow was still there; the screen was off the bedroom window. I went around back while I was waiting for you. The screen was lying on the ground, one of those flimsy stamped metal frames, like tinfoil. Easy to pull out."

J.Q. was carefully wiping dust from the inside of the windshield, refolding the tissues to get it all. He nodded toward a car that was pulling up. "Isn't that your friend? What's her name?"

"Winston's friend. Geraldine Olivarez. Gerri. Right."

Shirley got out of the car, propped herself on her crutches, and moved a few laborious and painful steps toward the approaching woman. Sitting in the car all this time had stiffened her legs. They felt as rigid as broomsticks.

"Gerri. You heard?"

"The whole pueblo has heard. Have you talked to Ray Apodaca?"

"We can't help him . . . them much. They're really not listening to us. They think her husband did it."

"And you don't?"

"No. My best guess is that she and her husband had an argument about the new truck, and he took off with the oldest boy."

"That'd be Raoul," said Gerri in a thoughtful voice. "Raoul is his favorite. Or maybe his mother's favorite. He always takes Raoul with him when he goes to visit his family in Mexico."

"Well, that's where he probably is now. I doubt he even knows his wife is dead."

"Why would anybody kill Emelia?"

"Because despite your pueblo culture, she either sold her baby or allowed it to be sold. Whoever bought it from her or from her husband doesn't want her talking because the whole deal has become very complicated and nasty."

Gerri shook her head slowly. "When we were talking this morning . . . I thought you were making most of it up. I couldn't . . . I couldn't accept that she might be involved in something like that. It's a mess."

"Is someone going to take little Clara? The poor little thing is worn-out and grieving. She needs some hot food and a comfortable lap."

"That I can do."

"They said her aunt was coming. You're her aunt?"

"I'm not her mother's sister, but in the pueblo we're all one family, so yes, I'm her aunt." She shook her head slowly. "After we talked this morning, I called Ray Apodaca. I told him what your friend saw out at Blue Mesa. Ray is as puzzled as I am about that. There's no reason for there to be any pots out there. Blue Mesa's sacred to us in the same way all our historic lands are sacred, but not in any ceremonial way. It's not one of the ancient holy places. In fact, Ray made a point I should have thought of earlier: Blue Mesa itself is a place our people generally avoid. There's a lot of scary stories about Blue Mesa."

"Taboo?"

"No. Not at all. That's what I'm saying! A *holy* place would be taboo. This is more like . . . well, you Anglos have stories about haunted houses? Or places that are bad luck? We have places we avoid, certain canyons or mountains. I'm not talking Navajo stuff, not witches or skin walkers or anything like that. Just someplace that's kind of scary. Blue Mesa's like that. Storytellers scare children with the giants that live there. And another thing Ray said, he doesn't know who could have followed your friend out there in a pickup truck, but he's pretty sure it wasn't anybody from the pueblo. A few years back we had an ecologist come talk to the pueblo people about maintaining our lands. Ever since then, we try not to tear up the land when it's wet."

Shirley leaned on one crutch, raising the other hand to rub at the ache in her forehead. "Now, isn't that interesting."

"He still thinks the little white girl got killed by accident, but at least I got him to say he'd keep an open mind about it."

Shirley leaned one way, then the other, easing the pain in her legs, before she led the way back to the car and opened the back door.

Gerri reached inside and shook Clara gently. "Hey, Clara. Come on. Let's go home and get you cleaned up." She pulled the child half-upright, then into her arms.

177

"We'll talk, hey?" she said over her shoulder.

Shirley nodded, climbed back into her seat, and sat silently while J.Q. drove them slowly away from the pueblo.

"You hungry?" he asked.

"Not really," she said. "All that mess back there kind of destroys one's appetite."

He made a face. "It must take a particular kind of person to slit a throat."

Shirley nodded. "I was thinking about that. Somebody who routinely kills animals might find throat slitting easy, do you think?"

"I've killed animals. Game animals. Chickens. I don't consider it routine."

"You don't do it often, J.Q. Not even chickens. I mean, someone who kills animals all the time. Someone who lives in a society where if you eat meat, you kill it and cut it up yourself."

"Like where? Farmers don't even butcher their own meat much anymore."

"Not in this country, no."

"Mexico? I thought you said her husband didn't do it."

"I don't think he did. But there are lots of people around who grew up in that culture, J.Q."

He grunted, a sound that might equally well have been agreement or disagreement. "If you don't want to stop for something to eat, what do you want to do?"

"I want to lie down. My legs feel like they're carved out of wood."

"Good enough." He drove silently, several times opening his mouth as though to speak, then shutting it again.

"What?" she asked.

"I'm wondering if you have any idea what's going on."

"Oh, I've got theories coming out my ears."

"Would you mind sharing your insights?"

She grimaced. "If you'll accept it all as conjectural. From everything I'm told, Emelia is one of those people who slip out from under responsibility. With Sarah, it was responsibility for a debt. With the pueblo, it was responsibility for some of her offspring. She didn't even care for the children she kept; Clara did.''

"The house was neat enough.''

"Oh, yes. I don't mean she's lazy. She probably works quite steadily, doing what has to be done. But she limits what has to be done to what she can manage with the least effort. There's something almost admirable about that. Anyhow, I conjecture she sold the baby, or agreed to its being sold, before it was even born. But she wants to be thought well of—most of us do—and according to Gerri, the pueblo would not have approved of her giving her baby to any outsider, and they'd have been angered at its being sold. So she fell in with a plan where she wouldn't be held responsible for the baby's disappearance.''

"Because the baby would disappear from the hospital?''

"Right. She was already saying the little boy wasn't hers while she was in the hospital. It was her saying that that actually makes me think her husband made the deal. I can hear him saying, 'I've sold it, it's not your baby anymore.' And then there's the business about a baby who did disappear from the hospital a whole week before a ransom note appeared.''

"You think they got the wrong baby.''

"It's the only scenario that fits the facts. The person who has made the deal, or his henchperson, hangs around until the nursery is unsupervised, then goes in and gets a boy baby, that is, a baby in a blue blanket. Because of an officious nurse, there is only one blue-blanketed baby present, and because there's only one—and perhaps because the henchperson is inexperienced or rattled—the kidnapper doesn't look at the identity bracelet.''

"Henchperson?'' J.Q. asked, with a wry twist to his lips.

"It could have been male or female. Anyhow, in this case, nobody looked at the bracelet until later. That's when they realized they had the wrong baby, not the Grant baby, the Franklin baby! As the nurse said to me, a very important baby!''

''Mucho dinero!''

''Exactly. Worth one hell of a lot more as a kidnap victim than as an adoption candidate. What can you get for an adoptable baby? Fifty thousand, maybe? And of that, I suppose five or ten thousand goes to the mama.''

''I thought the big demand was for Anglo babies.''

''Lord, J.Q., did you look at those two little boys back at the trailer? Handsome! Clean them up and anybody in his right mind would pay fifty thousand, assuming they wanted a baby at all!''

''But the ransom request was for half a million. . . . ''

''Because by that time the kidnappers had seen the TV or read the papers, and they knew the Franklins were VIPs and wealthy to boot.''

''Are you going to talk to what's his name? The FBI guy?''

She nodded. ''George Chalmers. I suppose I should. I told Gerri I wouldn't drag them in, but that was before Emelia was killed.''

''You think Emelia knew who *they* were?'' he asked as he turned in to the driveway. ''They, the kidnappers?''

Shirley shrugged tiredly. ''She had to know something. She got the money. Or her husband did. One of them did. Somebody must have made the pitch, even if it was only a voice on the telephone.''

''You don't think she won at bingo?''

''Gerri says she didn't.''

''Or a lottery or something.''

''If she did, there'll be a record of it somewhere. Chalmers can figure it out.''

They drew up in front of the main house. Shirley made no move to get out of the car.

''There's this other thing,'' she said. ''Gerri Olivarez says there's no reason for there to be any pots out at Blue Mesa.

It's not a burial site, it's not a place anyone ever lived. And, contrary to what Harry told us, Gerri says Blue Mesa is not sacred, it's merely a place the locals generally avoid, kind of like we do a haunted house. Finally, no one knows who was in the pickup truck that followed you and Shaour out there. It wasn't anyone from the pueblo.''

He stared blindly through the windshield. "The pots were black designs on white,'' he said. "They were large.''

They stared at each other in bleak surmise.

"The rockfall was fresh,'' he said. "I'm sure it wasn't there when we found April. Some of the rock was actually on the ledge where we found her, and I'm positive it wasn't there before.''

They were silent again. "Pot-hunter pots?'' she asked at last.

"If they were old, you'd be talking real money,'' he muttered. "Real money.''

Shirley examined her fingernails, thinking furiously, finally giving it up. "J.Q., do me a favor, will you? I can't wait to get my shoes off. I think my feet are swollen into them. Will you call Chalmers and McFee? Please? I'd like us to talk to both of them.''

She got out and started down the sidewalk that led around back to her bedroom, wincing with each step. Her feet were indeed swollen. Once inside her room, she collapsed on the side of her bed with an involuntary exclamation, partly relief, partly pain. Now, if someone would just help her get her shoes off!

She was still sitting there, staring at her feet, when J.Q. came in, took her phone off the hook, and handed it to her. "Chalmers,'' he whispered.

"Hello,'' she said, holding the phone slightly away from her ear as an angry voice ranted at her ear. She put her hand over the mouthpiece. "What did you say to him?'' she mouthed at J.Q.

He shrugged. "Just told him about Emelia being dead.''

She nodded. "Mr. Chalmers. George! J.Q. isn't telling you there's a connection, he's saying that I think there's reason to believe so. . . . If you're not interested, George, that's fine with us. . . . No, I think there's a great deal of evidence to indicate there's a connection. . . . Not all of it circumstantial, no. Not by a long shot . . ."

Shirley took the phone away from her ear, put it down on the bed beside her, put a pillow on top of it, lifted her weary legs onto the bed, and lay back. "He's having hysterics," she said. "Poor man. I think we'll let him cool down. J.Q., will you pull my shoes off? I can't reach."

"Why not hang up the phone?" he asked, unlacing.

"Because he might just call back. He sounds like he hasn't had any sleep for days and his boss just gave him a going over. Possibly for letting down his hair with me. Which he did. To my considerable surprise at the time. So now he's mad at me. That's understandable, but I don't have to listen to it."

"You're showing great forbearance."

"He has a new baby who keeps the family up every night. He's on a kidnapping case of a very wealthy family that's probably bringing all kinds of political pressure to bear, all of which is being passed down the chute onto his neck. People with that kind of clout don't seem to understand that using the clout is sometimes the worst way to expedite anything. When a man is already doing all he can, pressure just makes him nasty-tempered and unreliable."

"Will you hang up the phone?"

"When I'm ready. Never mind about McFee. When the phone is usable, I'll call him. There's a phone book here."

He nodded and departed. Shirley shut her eyes and tried diligently to think of nothing at all. When she picked up the pillow sometime later, she heard only silence. Not even a dial tone. Both Chalmers and the phone company had given up on her.

* * *

"Chalmers has shown up, hat in hand," J.Q. came to tell her about five o'clock. "You want to see him?"

She asked drowsily, "What kind of mood is he in?"

"Apologetic. And you're right. He looks tired."

"Bring him on back. I don't feel like going up front to talk with him. And ask Xanthy or Allison to watch for Dennison McFee. He told me he'd drop in around suppertime."

J.Q. brought Chalmers back to the bedroom, together with beer, glasses, cheese, and crackers.

"I told Xanthy you missed lunch," he said. "She and Allison bought deli cheese and crackers this morning." He dropped onto one of the couches and gestured to Chalmers to seat himself.

Shirley poured herself half a beer and leaned forward, cheese knife in hand, to give Chalmers a looking over.

"You look awful," she said sympathetically.

"I feel awful," he said, hangdog. "I want to apologize. I shouldn't have blown up, but I've been putting in twenty-four days on this thing. And Mr. Walter Franklin, the baby's grandpa, has invoked the governor. The governor has, if you can believe it, called the president of the United States, who has called the director of the FBI, who has spoken to the head of our field office, who has—"

"Come down on you?"

"Oh, only with hobnailed boots and a sledgehammer. I suggested he might want to reassign the case, but all he did was yell at me." Chalmers yawned uncontrollably.

"And your baby's still staying up all night."

"I told my wife from now until the case is solved, I'm staying at a motel. I've had it."

"We really might be able to help."

"That's what I realized about the same time it came to me I was talking to an open phone line. Sorry. I was just set to go off the next time anybody said anything."

Shirley poured him a beer, waved away his expostulations, then told him the story as she had told it to J.Q., beginning

183

with April's probable involvement on Saturday and concluding with Emelia's death.

"An accidental kidnapping?" he asked, dumbfounded.

"In my opinion, yes. The way to get at whoever killed April is to find the kidnapper. The way to find the kidnapper is to find out who killed Emelia Grant. Whoever killed Emelia Grant either knows where the Franklin baby is or knows somebody who knows."

"I'm supposed to do this on your word alone?"

"Chalmers, if you weren't so tired, I'd be offended. In some circles, my word might be good enough, but I don't expect you to take my word for anything! I do expect you to interview the nursery nurse about Emelia's attitude. Interview the neighbors and the pueblo people to find out where and when Emelia or her husband got the money for the TV and the new truck. Find out where she got the truck and how much she paid and whether it was in cash. Establish the fact that her baby is gone and that no one knows where it is. You can elicit the same stories I heard, but you can get them firsthand. Surely you're not on this thing alone."

"Not by a long shot. Though whether I can convince anyone else the two things are connected . . ."

"Three things. Don't forget April! April, the kidnapping, and Emelia." Shirley rubbed her forehead, reminding herself that she, too, was involved only because of April. "Has the kidnapper asked for the money to be dropped?"

He yawned again, then peered around as though looking for hidden microphones. "My director thinks I was entirely too open with you before, even though it seems to be paying off now. So whatever I say doesn't leave this room, right?"

"Right," grunted J.Q.

"The money is to be turned over day after tomorrow."

"Wednesday?"

"Right. Don't ask me details. I can't tell you."

"If the baby comes back then, the whole question of who did it will be moot?"

"Not for a minute. But Grandpa Franklin will probably quit calling the governor at that point. Which will help, God knows."

"What are the odds you'll get the baby back?"

"Up until you told me about this woman being killed, I'd have said they were pretty good. You really think this connects up to the little girl getting shot?"

"I think it has to. Nothing else fits the facts. She could have seen something at the hospital. After her arm was set, she was out of sight for five minutes or so, in the ladies' room. She could have seen something there, or heard something."

"Like somebody making off with the baby?"

"Um." Shirley rubbed her forehead. "There was that man I mentioned to you, the one who was polishing the floor? He was right there; did you ask him?"

"He's the owner of the pickup, and yes, we did ask him."

Shirley frowned, puzzled. "He was in a real hurry. He left the floor polisher sitting in the hall. Didn't even put it away."

"We asked him why he was in such a hurry, and he said his watch was slow, he was late meeting a friend."

Shirley looked doubtful. "I don't suppose he's left town or anything?"

"No. His name is Max Benez. He's got family around here—a brother, I think. He's worked for the hospital for four months, and he still works there. He lives alone. We talked to him. We went to his house. No baby there, no sign of a baby ever having been there."

"You might ask him if he saw April, though I think he was already gone by the time she came out of the emergency room." Shirley shook her head. Something about the story was wrong.

"What's the matter?" asked J.Q.

"I keep thinking there's something I should remember," she said. "One of those sneaky images that just slips in at

185

the edge of your mind and then disappears before you can get a good look at it.''

J.Q. shook his head. "We were together, Shirley. Except when you went to the ladies'.''

"And nobody was in there but me.'' She threw up her hands.

Chalmers got up slowly. "I'm on my way to rent a motel room,'' he said. "If I don't, I'll be fired. Of course, if I do, my wife will divorce me. She gets just as tired as I do of the baby yelling all night.''

"Will you take advice about that?'' Shirley asked.

"We've tried everything. The only thing that calms him down is being walked. The minute we put him in his crib, he howls!''

"Have you tried sleeping with the baby?''

"Sleeping with?''

"Put the baby in the bed with you and your wife, or either one of you. Her, if she's nursing.''

"The books all say—''

"The books are wrong. Recent research has established that the books are wrong. Both babies and mothers sleep better if they sleep together. Every society in the world knows that except ours. If you're desperate, try it.''

"But . . .''

She shrugged. "I'm not going to argue it with you. If you want a night's sleep, try it.''

"Won't we roll on the baby?''

"According to what I've read, there's no case, anywhere in the world, where a baby has died from being rolled on by his or her normal, healthy, sober parent. Pigs roll on their babies, not people. Or any primate, for that matter.''

"Where'd you get that?'' J.Q. asked, as Chalmers left, bemused.

"I've always known it,'' she said. "My mother knew it. It isn't natural for a baby primate to sleep alone. Their lungs

186

and heart and brain aren't synchronized yet. In nature, they're carried and held and touched and moved all the time.''

J.Q. lifted an eyebrow. ''You told Chalmers there was research.''

''There was. At the University of California, a year or so ago. I think I saw it in *Discover*. I read it and laughed. I always laugh when some male scientist proves something my mother or grandmother knew. It's especially funny when it's something any ape knows.''

J.Q. shook his head at her, disbelievingly.

''Well, J.Q., we get the magazine. You could have seen it, too, if you ever read anything but the *Wall Street Journal*!''

''I do,'' he said stiffly. ''Sometimes.''

She snorted at him. ''What are we having for supper?''

''I don't know what it's called, but it's a recipe Sarah gave Xanthy. It has chicken in it, and chiles, and sour cream. It's beginning to smell very good.''

''Winston's joining us?''

''Xanthy says he called from town; he's having dinner with some old friends.''

''I'm glad,'' she said with a sign. ''I don't have the energy to be passably social. I've slept for hours, but I still feel worn-out!''

He gave her a worried look. ''You're anemic. We're supposed to be feeding you liver and spinach and beans.''

''Tomorrow,'' she said, shaking her head at him. ''Don't fret, J.Q. Tomorrow I'll eat all the right things.''

Suppertime came and went, the food up to Xanthy's usual high standard. Xanthippe and Allison offered to do the dishes, and Shirley was about to leave the table to J.Q., a bottle of brandy, and his western edition of the *Wall Street Journal* when Dennison McFee arrived.

''What a wonderful place!'' he exclaimed, when he had accepted coffee and brandy and joined Shirley and J.Q. at the table.

"Before you leave, have a look at the living room," Shirley said. "It's interesting, but I've been wondering what one might do to it."

"Do to it?"

"Look at it. You'll see what I mean."

He drew his mouth into its triangular grin, fished the little leather bag out of his pocket, and passed it across the table to her.

"What do you think?" J.Q. asked, his eyes on the bag.

"I asked some friends. Not religious stuff, according to them. Carbon dating will give you the age of the bone, but only plus or minus two hundred, three hundred years. The bone was probably used as a scraper. The animal figure is the right size and type to be a hunting fetish. The collection as a whole is representative of authentically Anasazi artifacts. If it's old."

"How does one tell?" Shirley asked, puzzled.

"Well, carbon dating, as I mentioned. And the pigment used to make the designs on the pots changed over time, too. It can be chemically tested. Art changes, like anything else. Crafts change. Things like pots and baskets and carvings can sometimes be dated by changes in style and technique or even material. Dates arrived at by that method may be more subjective and less accurate than . . . oh, say, tree ring dating, or dates arrived at by careful excavation, but they can be useful, just so long as one doesn't put too much weight on them. If one suspects forgery, one might look for microscopic signs of whatever tools were used to carve the animal figure and the ring. Was stone used to carve stone, or was metal used, or—"

"Or even power tools?" asked J.Q.

"Or power tools, right. My friend didn't find any sign of metal tools. He says they look old. . . ."

"How old?" Shirley asked.

"He said Pueblo II, Pueblo III, which would be around seven hundred to a thousand years. They could be older."

"How about the pottery shards?" Shirley asked.

"The same. They could be hundreds of years old, or they could have been done last week. Without provenance, no one is willing to guess. We've had some interesting cases in Santa Fe in recent years. Responsible, respectable dealers have purchased pots they were sure were old, paying tens of thousands for them, only to find they were created by skillful forgers within the last five or ten years."

"How did they find out?"

"Something not quite right about the designs, leading to suspicion as to provenance, leading to a falling out among thieves. One laying it on another to avoid prosecution. It's made all the dealers and collectors extremely wary. These days, a seller with artifacts dishonestly come by might have to go farther afield."

"But if authentic, they could be sold."

"If authentic, they could be sold, whether they were honestly come by or not."

"Interesting," Shirley said, putting the contents back into the bag and hefting it thoughtfully in one hand. "I don't know how to thank you, Dennison."

He cocked his head. "We'll think of something. May I see this living room you're talking about?"

She nodded toward the door at the far end of the portal. J.Q. went to open the door, followed by Dennison, who peered inside, exclaimed something in a muffled voice, and disappeared into the room, with J.Q. behind him.

Shirley poured herself a small tot of brandy and sipped at it, listening to the sounds of their voices as she turned the little bag over and over in her hands. What was it? What did it represent? Was it what she and McFee had thought it might be originally? A sample? *"Look, here's some of the stuff I found. Pots like this. Carvings like this. Some bones and stuff like this."* And if the person could offer provenance, could say where and when and by whom the things had been found, perhaps show pictures, offer witnesses, even if they had been stolen, unscrupulous dealers would buy them.

The two men were returning from the living room, Dennison chortling, J.Q. looking pleased with himself.

"It's a wonderful house," the art dealer said. "J.Q. showed me the library, too. From the outside you'd have no idea how spacious it is! I see what you mean about the living room. Almost a pity the place doesn't belong to an order of monks or nuns. It would make a perfect chapel."

"It echoes," Shirley remarked dryly. "All it needs is a boy's choir."

"It does have that feel to it. Speaking of feelings—" he lowered his voice to a conspiratorial level. "—your feelings about the golden horse seem to have been correct. I passed the word along to a man I know rather well. My ex-brother-in-law, who has continued to be my friend despite various familial displacements. He's with customs, and though he didn't exactly come all over loquacious, he did say enough to let me know they already had Mr. Shaour in their sights and have been planning for some time to drop a net over him and over the much larger smuggler fish for whom, allegedly, he works. It isn't only Scythian gold, evidently. It's a much larger matter than that. The thieves are using the present political situations in the former Russian provinces to cover thefts from major museums. You did not hear it from me." He tapped his nose, huge lenses gleaming, looking more than ever like a predatory bug.

Shirley nodded. "Ah. You told your brother-in-law about April?"

"He already knew about it, because they were keeping track of where the Shaours went, and why. He tells me in the opinion of their particular powers that be, the Shaours could have had nothing to do with their daughter's death."

"One theory down," Shirley said to J.Q., after Dennison had finished his brandy and departed. "Which we'd more or less assumed. That leaves only two more theories to go."

* * *

Tuesday dawned through cloud, a heavy, muggy day, so calm that the moisture hung in the air and gathered on the skin. An Oregon day. An East Coast day. A day as unlike ordinary New Mexico days as it was possible to be.

After breakfast, Shirley took a slow, thoughtful walk around the Rancho del Valle property, stopping at the sheep pens and the poultry house, examining the hay shed, looking over the fences along the river bottom pastures.

"What are you up to?" J.Q. called to her from up the hill where he was sitting in the patio outside her bedroom. "You're supposed to be taking it easy."

"I am, J.Q. Just wanted to see the sheep."

He wandered down the hill, mug in hand, and joined her.

"Shetlands," she remarked of the sheep. "Sarah says they're descendants of the registered stock that belonged to Gwen Kingsolver. She was a hand-spinner."

The multicolored flock had nosed Shirley's hands and sniffed her legs, as tame as house cats. Black ones, brown ones, tan ones, only as high as her knees, certainly neither meat nor dairy animals, but their wool was soft and fluffy as down.

The sheep continued to follow her as she wandered along the fence. J.Q. dallied behind, scratching a ram behind his horns.

"What kind of pigs are these?" she called.

"I didn't know there were pigs," he said, surprised.

"Come look!"

He joined her at the corner of the pasture where a stout fence fronted an old log barn. Inside the enclosure two huge red pigs, boar and sow, lay on their sides in the sun, smiling.

"I didn't know pigs smiled," Shirley said, regarding the quarter-ton sow with interest.

"Just like Miss Piggy," J.Q. offered.

The sow opened its upper eye and snorted gently.

191

"She looks like she's about to . . . What's the word for pigs?"

"Farrow," answered J.Q. "She'll probably have a dozen."

"The boar looks friendly. I thought male pigs were fierce and had tusks."

"They're removed at birth. Snipped off with toenail clippers, as I remember. It doesn't hurt the piglets, and it makes the boars safer to handle."

"How did you know that?"

"We had pigs at my uncle's farm, when I was a boy. I used to stay with him and my Aunt Elda, summers."

"He's a big fellow, isn't he?" She leaned over the fence and scratched the pigs with her crutch, turnabout, boar, then sow, then boar again. Both snorted pleasurably, squirming onto their backs so their stomachs could be reached.

The group remained as it was for some time, two humans, two swine, lost in mutual contemplation.

"What are you up to?" J.Q. asked at last. "You're definitely conspiring about something."

"Winston wants to sell this place," she said. "And as it happens, I may want to sell mine."

"Ah," he said softly. "Well, well." He stared blindly at the horizon. "I should have thought . . . you would want something more . . . similar."

She leaned on the fence, trying to find words. Anything similar would only remind her. Anything alike could only be lesser, somehow. A second choice. A continuing reproach. But if one changed everything . . . changed place, changed culture, changed the basis of one's life, changed . . .

Perhaps if one changed almost everything, one would not be reminded quite so much. Perhaps then one could go on, find new things to delight in rather than grieving for the old.

She turned to him. "Fifty acres would be big enough for Allison's horse, for horses for us, too, if we want them. Not

192

the cows, of course. We'd miss the cows, but they were getting to be . . . well, a lot of work."

"Not too much work," he argued. J.Q. liked cows.

"A lot of work," she repeated. "Every year, a little more work. We've even talked about full-time help, J.Q. You know that."

His jaw clenched stubbornly. "How about the goats?"

"We could bring some of them. Go through the flock and pick the nicest ones. This place is big enough for a few goats, a few sheep, pigs . . . maybe. I've never had pigs, but they look interesting. There's not enough grass pasture and there's no hay pasture, but we could buy hay to supplement what's here. Maybe even find some hay pasture for sale not too far away. We can bring the chickens. I like the fancy birds that are already here. They're interesting. I like the cats. The Baron has been very attentive to me during my convalescence. We'd bring Dog, of course."

"You'd run it as a guest ranch?"

She noticed the pronoun he'd used. "I'm only talking, J.Q. I haven't made anybody an offer. If you don't want to . . . if you think it would be unbearable . . . I wouldn't do it. But anyplace like the ranch . . . anyplace like that would just remind me, us, all the time."

He dug his heel into the soil, leaned on the fence once more, his jaw set stubbornly.

She said, "We could run it as something, J.Q. It's not what I think of as a guest ranch. More a hobby farm with guest houses. It could pretty well support itself. We could either keep Vincente and Alberta or, if they didn't want to stay, we could hire another couple. It would be nice to have a resident couple on the place. God knows I'm not that great a shakes at housework, and if someone was here all the time, we could take vacations. We could explore the West. All my life I've said I'd do that someday."

He looked around himself, considering. "Sarah said they'd

considered running it as a bed and breakfast. You weren't thinking of that?''

''Not if I have to do breakfasts! Neither of us are what one might call morning people.''

''I'm an early riser,'' he said defensively, as though replying to insult.

''You *rise* early. You rise at cockcrow! You're polite to animals by eight, but you don't *people* until about ten, after three or four cups of coffee, and you're not really sociable until at least noon. No, I wouldn't consider a bed and breakfast. Besides, the houses are fully equipped with kitchens.''

''One might offer a complimentary cocktail hour instead.''

''That's a thought. Beer, wine, and nibbles. Hire someone to make juicy nibbles by the thousand and freeze them until needed.''

''Tapas,'' he murmured. ''That's what they call them in Spain.''

''Call what?''

''Hot, savory little things for cocktail time. There's a problem with cocktail hours, though. Guests have children, and children are no fun at cocktail hour. We'd need an activity director for the young ones. A nanny. A sitter.''

Shirley laughed. ''Sarah says she's been providing baby-sitting service to anyone who needs it. She was complaining about not having had any guests with babies for a long time.''

''They had one last week,'' J.Q. remarked. ''At least, that's what stopped up the plumbing.''

''What did?''

''A baby diaper. I told you. Somebody put a disposable diaper down the drain.''

''When was that?'' she asked curiously.

''Early last week. Weekend before last.''

She shook her head. ''I suppose it could have been in there for a long time.''

''I doubt that very much. We put the snake down the toilet and ran into the obstruction within five or ten feet. If it had been there very long, the place would have overflowed long since."

"Which house, J.Q.?"

He furrowed his brow. "The one farthest from the drive. On the other side of the little bridge."

"Which one was April spying on, early Sunday morning?"

"I don't know. You told me about it."

"Sarah told me about it. She didn't mention which house."

"Well, you can eliminate the two we were in. And the one next to us, the family with the teenaged boy. That leaves the one across the acequia and the one nearest the drive."

Shirley said, "It wasn't the one nearest the drive. That's the one where Winston is, and he said it hadn't been occupied for several weeks, according to the calendar."

"So April was spying on the one across the acequia."

"The remotest, least visible of the five. Which had a baby diaper down the drain."

"From which the people departed, precipitously, following April's nosiness." J.Q. scratched his head and stared at the sow pig as though she might have the answer. "Which was the morning after the kidnapping. You think . . . you think they had the baby?"

"*The* baby? What baby? Their own baby? Someone else's baby? We don't know when Emelia's baby went missing. Did she ever bring it home from the hospital?"

"We could ask Sarah. . . ."

"Don't ask anyone," said Shirley, firmly. "We are not going to lift up our tails and go trotting around making loud farting noises, J.Q. I'm convinced April was killed because somebody thought she knew something. We give the impression we know something, we may find ourselves dead on the ground with a bullet through our heads. I think we don't say nuttin to nobody."

"Not to Xanthy?"

"Not to her or anyone else. To Chalmers, maybe, but only

195

to him! Not Sarah, not Harry, certainly not Allison.'' She scratched the sow pig's belly again. The pig rumbled delightedly.

''The ransom is being paid tomorrow.''

''I wish we could figure this damned thing out by tomorrow. I have this awful feeling April's killer is going to get away.''

''If April was killed because of something she knew, why were you attacked?''

''We've been over it and over it! Because of something someone thought I knew. And that had to be something I'd seen or overheard or been told. Right?''

''Those are the only possibilities I can think of.''

''Seen or overheard myself. Or been told by April. It's much more likely April would have spoken to Allison or Xanthy than to me. The only time I was alone with her was during the ride down from the reservoir. She said nothing to me then, and in any case, we could not have been overheard at that time. So the likely reason is *not* something April told me but something I, myself, overheard or saw.''

''Your logic is impeccable,'' he said dryly.

''When we took April to the hospital, the only time I was apart from you, I went to the bathroom. There was no one in the bathroom. There was no sound in the bathroom. No people, person, thing.''

''You went down to the emergency room.''

''Then I was in the same room with April and Xanthy. I saw or heard nothing they didn't see or hear.''

''Who saw you there?''

''Just the man working the floor polisher. And the doctor. And the laundry woman.''

''What laundry woman!''

Her jaw dropped. ''I forgot the laundry woman.''

''I say again . . .''

''A blond woman came in a corner door of the emergency room, pushing a laundry cart. She went through the door where I was standing, almost running me over. She had braids around her head, I remember that."

"And when you went out?" he demanded.

"She was gone. And the man with the polisher was gone."

"And when we went out, ten minutes later, the pickup came around the corner like a bat out of hell. And the pickup belonged to the floor polisher man."

"Wait, J.Q. Wait. Something, something. What is it? All that business about the man's watch being slow. There's a clock over the emergency room doors. Great big bastard of a clock, lighted; he couldn't have missed it. Now, where in hell could they have gone, either of them, that April might have seen them?"

"Obviously into the toilet. Why would the woman have gone in there?"

"Maybe for the usual reason one goes to a toilet. But suppose she had the baby! It would have been dressed in hospital clothes, so she might have gone in there to change its clothes. Or she could have been waiting there for somebody to bring her the baby, or to give someone else the baby."

"Any of which April might have seen."

"And knowing April, she'd have said something nasty, drawing attention to herself. Let's suppose she did see one or both of them acting suspicious, and then she saw one or both of them again, in the little house across the acequia. She sneaked around, they knew they'd seen her before, they left in one hell of a hurry."

"Going where?"

"Going . . . not too far away, J.Q. Because if he was the one who shot her, he had to be near enough to see us headed out later that day. Near enough to know where we were going riding. Near enough to see which way we went and lie in wait for us when we returned."

"Why would they come here in the first place?"

"Because it's remote. Because they'd be very unlikely to

see anyone they knew. Sarah said lots of their guests come here for that reason.''

He said nothing for a long time, thinking. "I find a flaw," he said at last.

"What flaw?"

"They reserved the place in advance. How would they have known when Emelia was going to have her baby?"

"How do you know they reserved in advance?"

"You told me. You quoted Sarah's conversation. She said they'd reserved for several days and had left without asking for their deposit back.''

"Right. So I did. Of course, we're building a lot out of nothing! It's possible the people here weren't the people April saw at the hospital. Maybe they only looked like the same people. Person. A blond woman and a Chicano man. Which is what Sarah meant when she said, 'not an odd couple for New Mexico.' "

"You know that for sure?"

"No, J.Q. Of course I don't. I'll have to ask Sarah. Tactfully. So she doesn't catch on."

"There may be a better way."

"What?"

"All the records are in the kitchen. I'll see who was in that house last. Home address. All that."

" 'All that' won't tell you what they looked like!"

He sighed. "Right."

"Maybe Xanthy knows."

"How would she know?"

"She said April made excuses for her morning's activities. Xanthy didn't sound as though she was really listening, but she might remember something."

"You go ask Xanthy. I'll see if the records are left unattended."

Their departure brought a protest from the sow pig, who got up and stuck her head through the fence to watch them as they crossed the pasture. At the gate, they went their separate ways, Shirley to the room occupied by Allison and Xanthippe, where she found Xanthippe lying on her bed, deeply immersed in a novel.

"Slugabed," challenged Shirley.

"It's an Anne Tyler novel I've been longing for time to read."

Shirley seated herself. "Xanthy, when you tackled April about spying on the people here at the ranch, what did she say about it?"

Xanthy put the book down, carefully inserting a fancy needlework bookmark. "Let me think. She said she'd seen them before, and they were 'up to something.' "

"Seen them before where?"

"I'm trying to remember. She said 'yesterday.' She'd seen them before, 'yesterday.' "

"Where had she been the day before?" Shirley asked rhetorically.

"Here, with all of us. With Allison, by the pool. And off on her jaunt. And at the hospital."

"And the restaurant where we stopped for pizza. There were other people there."

"None she showed any interest in."

"True. She was too busy being angry at us. Are there any other possibilities?" She scratched her head, thinking. "After we got back from the hospital, but before we went to bed. While we were putting groceries away, Allison and April were in the living room, roasting marshmallows. Could April have left the house at that time?"

Xanthippe shook her head. "Allison would know. But if she'd left, Allison would have joined us, wouldn't she? It seems to me I heard April's voice whining at Allison all the time we were together in the kitchen."

"That's what I thought, too. Where is Allison?"

"Sarah asked her if she wanted to go to the post office with her. They went about half an hour ago."

"Horseback?"

Xanthy nodded.

"If you see her before I do, ask her if April left the house that night, before she left with you. I suppose once you took her over to the other house, she didn't leave?"

Xanthippe shook her head. "When we got over there, I gave her the maximum allowable dose of the pain pills the doctor had provided, in the sincere hope they would knock her out, which they did. I was annoyed with her and with myself. But she was sound asleep, snoring little cat snores by ten o'clock." She fingered her book. "Anything else?"

Shirley shook her head and stood up to go.

"I'm glad you're thrashing around," said Xanthippe, her eyes fixed on the open book once more. "It's nice to see you busy."

Shirley restrained her snort until she was in the hallway. Xanthippe's voice summoned her back.

"I forgot," she said. "You had a phone call. Gerri Olivarez." She handed Shirley a scrap of paper with a phone number written on it. "She'll be there for the next half hour."

Back in her room, Shirley dragged the long phone cord across to one of the couches, where she could enjoy the view. The number she punched was the gallery number, answered by Gerri herself.

Shirley asked, "How's Clara?"

"Oh, about like you'd suppose. She spends a lot of time just sitting."

"Might be a good idea to put her and her little brothers together. She's used to looking after them. It would take her mind off things."

"I thought of that. We're having a conference about the kids this afternoon, and she'll be with them at least while that's going on. Reason I called, I spoke to Ray Apodaca early this morning. He rode out to Blue Mesa last evening. There's no pots out there."

"Well, well," said Shirley, musingly.

"Truck tracks, but no pots. Are you thinking what I'm thinking?"

"The pots were white with black designs. I have some shards here I'd like you to see, Gerri. They were in that little bag I mentioned to you."

"I'll come out when I have time. I'll call first."

Shirley had just hung up the phone when J.Q. came in.

"Would you believe Mr. and Mrs. Bill Jones?" he asked. "That's who the reservation was made by."

"I'd believe almost anything. When was their reservation made?"

"There's a line on the form where the date's supposed to go, but no date was filled in. There's no home address filled in. The dates they're staying are filled in, both on the form, and on the calendar in the kitchen. I checked. There's a credit card number written, and where it asks for deposit, there's an amount written in as received, but no date as to when received."

"Credit card," she mused.

"It doesn't say which credit card," he muttered. "Just the number, five-oh-five-six—"

"MasterCard," she said. "Or American Express. No, I tried to use my American Express, and Sarah said they don't take it. It must be MasterCard."

"Why?"

"All MasterCard numbers start with five. All Visa numbers start with four."

He stared at her. "First Scythians and now banking. Where did you learn that fact?"

"I really don't remember. Having the number doesn't help much. Tell you what. Sarah and Allison went to the post office. When they get back, I'll talk to Sarah. Tactfully."

"What do you want me to do?"

She stared at her feet. "It's too early to tell Chalmers anything. Everything is still guesswork."

"I could look for the couple," he offered.

"What?"

"We're guessing a dark man, a blond woman. You said they'd be nearby. Near enough to have seen us when we went riding. We're not exactly in a metropolis! The number of rental dwellings in the neighborhood must be very limited."

"That business about their staying close is pure hypothesis. He could just as well have been sitting in a car watching the place. However. It's something we can eliminate. You could pretend you're looking for someplace to rent."

"Something like that."

"Be careful, J.Q. This guy has killed twice and tried once that we know of."

Allison brought in Shirley's mail, cards from friends in Colorado who had heard about the accident. A note from friends in D.C. While she opened envelopes, Shirley casually asked if April had left the house the night they'd been roasting marshmallows. No, said Allison, not until she left with Xanthy.

That eliminated that.

"Honey, tell Sarah I'd like to see her, would you?"

Allison departed.

Sarah came in bearing a fresh pot of coffee. "How you feeling?" she asked. "Better, I hope."

"Less weak and woozy, certainly. Yesterday wasn't a good day."

"It wasn't good for me either. I cried all night over Emelia. All night long. Harry got really peeved with me because he had to get up early and go to Albuquerque." She wiped a vagrant tear. "I moved out onto the living room couch so he could sleep."

Shirley was surprised into comment. "That doesn't sound very sympathetic of him!"

"Well, he didn't want me getting mixed up with Emelia over this whole business. He told me what you did, that her business was her business and I should stay out of it. And the Albuquerque business is important for us. He bought some cheap vacant land in Albuquerque about ten years ago. It's gone up in value, he's had an offer, and he wants to sell it before we move. There may be enough money to buy a house near the kids.'' She wiped her eyes again. ''I didn't mind him being angry. He didn't mean anything by it. It's just I couldn't stop thinking about her, wishing we hadn't come to a parting of the ways, you know. Why did anybody do that to her, Shirley?''

Shirley shrugged, carefully noncommittal. ''I didn't know her, Sarah.''

''Harry says Tonio probably did it. I wouldn't have thought so, but Harry knows Tonio better than I ever did. J.Q. says you don't think so.''

''Well, from what the little girl said, her daddy left for somewhere, probably Mexico, a long time before her mother was killed. I'm sure someone is checking up on that.''

Sarah sighed. ''Did you want to see me about something special?''

''I wanted to talk about the place. I might just possibly be interested in buying it from Winston Kingsolver.''

Her face lit up. ''Really! Oh, that would be great. I really love the place. It would be wonderful to think of it belonging to someone nice.''

''Thank you, ma'am,'' Shirley said, with a modest bow. ''I wanted to talk about how you manage the guests. Can you give me a little overview?''

''Well, let's see. We sort of invented our own systems. It's nothing very complicated. We don't do double-entry book-keeping or any of that. Just enough to keep track of taxes.'' She frowned, settled herself. ''We advertise in the tourist magazines, so people can call us for reservations.''

''Most people stay awhile?''

''Well, yes, like you did. From a few days up to a few weeks. We're not a motel! I wouldn't run a motel, not for anything! Most everybody reserves a long time ahead, and our fifty percent deposit weeds out the people who really haven't made up their minds.''

''That's logical. So you write down the date of the reservation, and . . .''

''And all the other information we need, including the credit card number for the deposit. We send them their copy of the credit card charge with a confirmation letter, and we staple the other copy to the back of their reservation.''

''You always write down the date you make the reservation?'' Shirley asked in her most innocent voice.

''Unless I forget. Or if it's the same day, I don't bother.''

''Same day. So some people do make spur-of-the-moment reservations?''

''Well, not often. Same-day people usually don't call until around four, and that doesn't give Alberta time to get a house ready. We don't make up a house until we know someone's coming. Same-day people often want just one night, and we don't do single nights. But once in a while, like for an old customer, we'll do a same-day, if they call early enough. . . .''

''I see. When guests arrive, do you meet them?''

Sarah made a helpless gesture. ''When we started, we met everybody, stayed up half the night sometimes, waiting. Now just send them a map and tell them whenever they get here, their house will be open and the key will be inside.''

''So people might come and go without your ever seeing them.''

Sarah laughed. ''I told you, remember? Like when men bring their girlfriends. If we've got a valid credit card number, they might come and go and we'd never see them.''

This was getting where Shirley wanted to go. ''Let's see, the couple that April was spying on arrived late.''

Sarah shook her head. ''No, it wasn't all that late. If it's same-day people, we tell them they have to be here before nine o'clock.''

''So you can show them where they're to stay?''

"Partly that. Partly just to look them over, since we may not have a good home address or phone number."

Shirley wrote on her pad, saying casually, "What was it you told me about the people who came last Saturday and didn't get their deposit back? That they weren't an odd couple or something?"

"Harry made that reservation. First I knew about it was when I saw Alberta cleaning the house that morning. What did I say about an odd couple? He was Hispanic and she was blond, and she was a lot older than him. That would have been odd, back in Iowa."

"I must have seen her early the next morning. Fortyish? Thin. Kind of pale-looking? Hair in braids."

"I didn't see them that well. I was out turning off the hose when they came. I just saw the car when they drove in, one of those low cars, and then I saw their backs when Harry took them into the house to get the deposit."

"Just the two of them?"

Sarah's eyebrows went up and her voice sharpened. "Why are you so interested in them?"

Shirley shrugged, keeping her voice casual. "Still trying to figure out why April was hanging around them."

Sarah snorted. "Her. I don't think she needed a reason. I think she was just nosy." She flushed. "Poor child, I shouldn't talk about her that way. . . ."

"You're probably right, Sarah, and thinking about her doesn't help me find out about this place!" She turned up a clean page on her notebook and began a lengthy list of unrelated questions, muddying her conversational footprints with requests for detailed information about how the place was cleaned and kept up, what hours Alberta and Vincente worked, what was involved in maintaining the swimming pool, who did the gardening, where they bought and kept consumable supplies—mostly purchased, said Sarah, by Harry at the military commissary in Albuquerque, because in Santa Fe even wholesale prices were ridiculous.

"All the cases of stuff are in the storage room next to the laundry," said Sarah. "Toilet paper and paper towels and cleaning products and everything except food for the farm animals. That's stored down in the hay shed. You know."

By this time, Shirley did know. She had a very clear picture of what managing the place amounted to.

"Do you want to know anything else?" Sarah asked. "Ask now, because this afternoon I'm going to my hair appointment. Three o'clock every Tuesday, I get done."

Shirley thanked her and let her go, contenting herself for the next half hour by making marginal notes and a new list of questions: things she would need to know about the wells and ditch rights, things Sarah either hadn't known or Shirley hadn't asked.

J.Q. returned shortly thereafter. "Find anything out?"

Shirley tallied up the score. "The two people in that house match the two people I saw at the hospital, but the vehicle doesn't. It wasn't a pickup truck. Still no proof, either way. It seems Harry made the reservation, evidently what Sarah calls a same-day reservation, which is why there's no detail on the reservation form. Evidently he collected the deposit from them after they arrived, and it must have been by cash or check, because if it was credit card, there should have been a credit card receipt stapled to the back of the reservation form. Did you find anything?"

"There's another rental place down half a mile toward the Durans' place. Small. Not as nice as this. Did you find out what they're driving?"

"Just that it's not a pickup." She shook her head, frustrated. "Sarah said they were in one of those 'low cars.' "

"Does she mean a low-rider?"

"A what?"

"We saw them. In Española. One of those chrome jobs that sits practically on the ground."

"Of course!" She remembered now. Mostly big, older cars, modified so they sat almost on the pavement, but with hydraulic lifts that could raise them up and let them down again. Bright velour upholstery. Huge stereo systems. There'd been a procession of them going down Main Street, lurching and bouncing, back and forth, round and round. A paseo!

"The reason I ask, there's a low-rider at this place down the valley. I couldn't help but notice it, it looks so out of place among all the Jeeps and Troopers and Broncos and pee-cups."

"Pee-cups?"

"Local jargon for truck."

"Pickups." She shook her head at him reprovingly. "Did you hear a baby crying?"

"Dear old love, I did not, repeat not, go that close. When I was there, I didn't know we were looking for a low-rider, and in any case, I thought we were agreed upon discretion."

"I'm afraid our time for discretion is up. I need to think about it awhile longer, but we should call Chalmers. Do that, will you, J.Q.? I wouldn't bother him with this pure guess-work if there weren't lives at stake. It's too soon."

"You think what . . . ? The couple driving the low-rider have two babies?"

She shook her head slowly. "Probably only the Franklin baby. If they're involved at all. If this isn't total hogwash. Emelia's baby has probably been passed on to its adoptive parents by now. Probably the same day she left the hospital. That's something we could check on by calling Gerri and asking her to find out from Clara if Mommy ever brought the baby home. . . ."

She stopped talking and held up a hand, listening. Footsteps in the hallway. That echo-chamber effect she'd noticed before.

Xanthippe came to the door, leaning in to say softly, "I heard you talking about Emelia's baby as I was coming down the hall. If you want to keep any secrets, you'll need to remember to shut the doors."

"Not secrets, exactly. Just we promised Mr. Chalmers we'd be discreet about the kidnapping case," Shirley replied.

"Are you two interested in lunch?"

"What did you have in mind?" asked J.Q.

"We never did get to the folk museum," she replied. "Allison and I thought perhaps it might be fun to have lunch in Santa Fe, then go to the museum—we'll take your wheelchair, Shirley, so you don't wear your leg out."

Shirley shared a glance with J.Q. "You know what I'd really like? I'd like you three to go do something you'd enjoy, and let me lie here like a vegetable with something good to read. The past two days have been . . . exhausting. I'd love a pot of hot tea and a sandwich, and a chance to lie down and do nothing."

Xanthy wouldn't hear of it. J.Q. wouldn't hear of it. Shirley persisted.

"I've got J.Q.'s handgun under my pillow," she told Xanthy. "I'll be fine. Honestly."

"Are you sure?"

She was sure. Allison came in and argued with her.

"I don't like leaving you alone," Allison said. "Even if you've got a . . . a cannon in here.

"I'm not alone, for heaven's sake, child. Sarah's here. Harry will be home from Albuquerque pretty soon. There are guests here."

"I think all the guests are gone. Even Mr. Kingsolver. All their cars are gone."

"Don't worry about it. Go on to the folk museum and enjoy yourself."

J.Q. brought her a sandwich and asked if they should bring something interesting for supper. Pizza, maybe? Chinese?

"Whatever," she said. "Mexican, Chinese, Italian, but not pizza." They'd had pizza on the way home from the hospital, before April was killed. She didn't want to be reminded.

She ate her sandwich and drank her tea, then stretched out

on the bed with a sigh almost of contentment. Nice, for the moment, not to have anyone being solicitous. Nice, for the moment, not to be conscious of being a burden. Xanthy had selected an armload of books from the library and had piled them on Shirley's bedside table, books Shirley hadn't had a chance even to look at until now. In order to read the titles, she moved the accumulated clutter to one side. Her brush and comb. The little skin bag Dennison had returned last night. The carafe and glass Allison and Xanthy had bought as one of their "surprises." Tissues, pain pills, hand lotion. One of the books looked interesting: a survey of the culture and history of the native peoples of the Southwest. Maybe if she'd read this earlier, she wouldn't have needed to bother Gerri Olivarez.

After twenty minutes of impenetrable prose she decided if she'd read this earlier, she would have given up on the entire subject. She couldn't keep her mind on it. She put the heavy volume back on the table and lay back to stare at the ceiling. Would it be a good idea to buy the place from Winston? What kind of value would he place on it? Was it something she wanted to do? How did J.Q. really feel about it, and how in hell, given his stubborn tendency toward obfuscation, was she going to find out how he felt about it?

Movement outside caught her eye. Cat stalking peacock. Peahen. With chicks! Four . . . no, five of them! They must have hatched today! Shirley sat up on the bed to watch the drama play itself out. Cat crouching. Cat stalking. Peahen turning on cat, wings out, tail fully fanned. Peahen pecking, hard! Like a snake striking. Cat fleeing for life! The chicks were tiny. Much smaller than she'd assumed they would be. Like baby chickens, fluffy little things that looked nothing like Mama. They didn't even have long necks yet, and they were stripy, like pheasant babies.

She returned to her former musing. If she and J.Q. ran the place—always assuming J.Q. would want to do so—what changes would it make in their lives? What new problems?

Shopping would be a pain. A place this size used a lot of consumables.

Abruptly she decided to have a look at the storeroom and laundry. It was only a little way down the hall, past the room J.Q. had been occupying. It was too much trouble to put on shoes. She'd go barefoot.

Her feet made no sound as she went slowly down the hall. Even the door swung silently as she pulled its leather latch-string, sagging almost closed behind her once she was inside. The room was large and badly lighted by one small window, shelves taking up the rest of three walls, the fourth occupied by piled cardboard cartons and a narrow door leading into the adjacent laundry. The center of the room held a folding table, an ironing board.

Two walls of shelves were stacked with linens: bedsheets, comforters, blankets, bedspreads, pillowcases, towels, neatly folded and piled according to size and type. One wall was full of cleaning stuff: floor oil, furniture polish, oil soap in gallon plastic bottles. The fourth wall was hidden behind floor-to-ceiling cartons, light bulbs and detachable mop heads, Super-Soft toilet tissue, Super-Sponge paper towels. It wasn't a brand Shirley had seen in the stores; perhaps it was something carried only by commissaries.

Footsteps went by in the hallway outside as Shirley checked off supplies in her head: Vacuum cleaner bags by the dozens. Cat food by the carton. Sacks of fish food, too, for the koi in the patio pool. Cleaning sponges. Half a dozen new brooms leaning in the corner. For sweeping clean, no doubt.

As she was about to leave, the footsteps went by in the other direction. She heard the door at the end of the hallway swing on its hinges. Sarah, probably.

She looked toward the Fieldings' quarters when she left the storeroom, seeing the door slightly ajar. Back in her room, she settled herself on the bed and picked up the discarded book. Prehistory: the western Anasazi. She couldn't focus on it. Too many other things on her mind!

She poured herself a glass of water and sipped at it, staring blindly over the rim, moving the things around on the bedside table with one hand, puzzling over their arrangement. They weren't as she'd left them. Brush and comb. Medications.

The little leather sack was gone.

Had she knocked it off? She looked at the side of the table. Nothing. Perhaps under the bed? No. It couldn't have fallen under the bed, and she'd have known if she'd kicked it there. Baron Valter, perhaps? She got up and went to the patio door, to find the screen door securely latched. Baron Valter couldn't have come in.

Someone had come by her room and had taken the little leather sack. Someone . . . presumably . . . to whom it belonged?

Well, April didn't need to have found it out at Blue Mesa. They had simply assumed she had found it there, because that's where she'd been last. Actually, she could have found it anywhere.

Shirley filled her glass and picked it up, seeing the surface of the water tremble in her hand. She set it down, firmly. Of course, the two ideas were not mutually exclusive. April could have found it there, where the pots were. And it could still belong to someone here.

She looked at her watch. Three o'clock. It couldn't have been Sarah in the hall. Sarah would have left some time ago for her hair appointment. Someone else had come into the house. Anyone could have come into the house. J.Q. and Xanthy hadn't locked it before they left. Not that she knew of.

Without realizing she was doing it, she slipped her right hand under the pillow, looking for J.Q.'s pistol.

Which was also gone.

The phone was beside the bed. She picked it up and listened. No dial tone. It was out of order. Or someone had cut the line.

* * *

At the folk art museum, J.Q. interrupted Allison and Xan-thy's delight in a case of brightly painted wood carvings to say he was going to find a phone.

"Checking in with Shirley?" Xanthy asked.

"As a matter of fact, I told her I'd call the FBI man, and I forgot to do it before we left. I thought I'd do it now, but it's not a bad idea to check in with her, too."

"We'll come with you," said Xanthy. "I don't know about Allison, but I need to find a ladies' room."

J.Q. was unable to reach Chalmers, but someone took a message. He shrugged at Xanthy, fished out another quarter, and called the Rancho del Valle number.

"This'll ring by her bed, won't it?" he asked Xanthy.

"That's the main house number," she replied. "The Fieldings have their own private phone."

He took the receiver away from his ear, looking puzzled. "Recording. Says the phone's out of order."

Xanthy fished her notebook out of her pocket and found a list of numbers. "The Fieldings' number, and one for each of the houses. Call the Fieldings." She pointed to the num-ber.

J.Q. dialed it. Out of order. Quickly he retrieved his quar-ter and dialed the house they had stayed in earlier. Out of order.

"I think we'd better get back there," he said in a tightly controlled voice. "I don't believe all those phones went on the fritz all at once."

They left the museum at a fast walk. By the time they approached the car, they were all running.

7

SHIRLEY ALLOWED HERSELF thirty seconds more of silent thought. Presumably whoever had taken the gun had come by here looking for her and had not found her. The person wouldn't have thought to look in the storeroom, but would be looking elsewhere. Down in the pasture, perhaps, where she had been this morning. In the living room, or in the kitchen, and eventually, back here again.

It would be wise to be somewhere else, somewhere unexpected. She went out, moving quickly but carefully, not letting the crutches rattle against anything, down the hall past the library, into the huge living room, where she paused to listen carefully for any sound at all. The doors were open into the patio, but the brightness out there would prevent anyone from seeing into the dimness of the room. There were no footsteps in the corridor behind her. And no place to hide as she crossed the room. Which meant it should be done quickly, all at once. She took a deep breath and went, watching her feet, careful not to trip, not to become distracted. All her life she had moved easily. In recent years there'd been a share of aches and pains, true, but she'd moved easily nonetheless. This crabbed and laborious progress was foreign to her, and hateful. She went as quickly as she could, listening all the time.

Nothing. At the far side, she eased the door to the portal open and bent over as far as she could to look out the floor-to-ceiling screens that made up one side of the room during warm weather. No one outside looking in. No one in the portal itself. She climbed the three steps into the portal, gently closed the door behind her, dropped the latch softly into place, and then made a careful survey of what she could see outside.

No one visible. Across the valley, sun glinted from the windows of homes, cars moved down a side road, small as beetles, but there was no one near. No threat visible, and no help, either. She crossed the portal and listened at the open dining room door, peeking through the slit at the hinge side. No one behind it. No one in the dining room. No one visible through the window.

She went around the dining room corner into the back hallway that led to the kitchen and, presumably, to the room Shirley herself had never seen which Winston had referred to as the butler's pantry. And there, blessedly, it was, to the right, just this side of the kitchen: a little branch hallway with three doors; one at the end giving access to the outside service area with its garbage cans and woodpile; the other two across from each other. Of these, the one nearest the kitchen opened on a tall, wide broom closet, its bottom eighteen inches above the hall floor. The other opened upon total darkness.

She felt along the doorframe, one side, then the other, finding a light switch as last, flicking it on. The room was small, windowless, shelves on all four walls, cupboards below, every inch stacked with odds and ends of canned and dry foodstuffs, seldom-used roasters and stockpots, extra glasses and mugs, all the accumulated kitchen stuff of decades of occupancy, tucked away in here to be occasionally sought out or totally forgotten. The room differed from the rest of the house in having a wooden floor, mostly covered by a threadbare Oriental rug. Carefully she shut the door behind her before attacking the rug with her crutches, clumsily rolling it, first one end, then the other, to disclose the tightly bolted trapdoor beneath. It looked stout and immovable, two feet by four feet, the hinges at her right recessed into the floor, as was the bolt to her left. When the rug was down, no one would know it was there. There were no telltale protuberances. Perhaps whoever had taken the gun did not know about the cellar under this room. Perhaps whoever had the gun would not look here, would not find her if she could get down inside and close the trapdoor behind her.

She leaned one crutch against the wall, crouched over, bad leg behind her, all her weight on her good leg, grasped the stout steel bolt, and drew it out of its housing. It came back with a shriek of protest and she bit her lip, head tilted, wondering if someone had heard. Nothing. She grasped the ring handle and heaved. The trapdoor came up readily; when fully opened, it leaned against the shelves at her right. Steep wooden steps began at her toes. No headroom down there. And no lights. She found another light switch inside the pantry door and flicked it half a dozen times. Nothing. She listened, checking that the door behind her was securely closed, then went down the steps as quickly as possible. The clearance was six feet, maybe, from concrete floor to ceiling. A pale wash of light leaked through a six-inch-square screened ventilator at the top of the outside wall, between two beams. She reached out with her crutches, feeling for the walls, encountering instead something that thumped, drumlike. She went down the last two or three steps and craned into the darkness, her eyes gradually adjusting until she could make out the dusty Super-Soft toilet tissue cartons piled in one corner, just as they had been piled, her recalcitrant memory told her, in Emelia's carport. These same cartons, without doubt. Not others, not similar ones, but these.

Winston had said there was nothing down here but half a dozen bottles of wine. If he had seen these, he would have phrased it differently. But he hadn't seen these. He had fetched up the half dozen bottles of wine before the cartons were put here. Winston had not been down here since. Which put a final end to her hope that no one knew of this place but those who had heard Winston mention it on Sunday.

Though every fiber of herself screamed it was unwise to take the time, she could not keep herself from making sure. She stooped forward and pulled at one of the top cartons, tipping it toward her. Something large inside, not heavy, but well wrapped in crumpled newspaper. She felt of it. Rounded. Hollow. She tore a hole in the paper. A pot, black on white.

Which meant the person who took the leather bag, the person with her gun, knew all about a lot of things. Hastily she pulled the cartons toward her in tottering piles, making a hiding place behind them. As she did so, a sound came clearly through the screened ventilator. Someone calling her name outside. A familiar voice, not far away, calling her name over and over again.

The person with the gun circled the house and entered the patio door of the room Shirley had been using, looked around it quickly, explored the bathroom and closet, then went out into the hallway to begin a quick but thorough search of each room opening off the hall. There were no real hidey-holes in this house. Thick adobe walls did not lend themselves to secret closets or intricate spaces. Even in the furnace room or the storeroom, all was very plain and visible, with no cubbies where persons could hide. There were no heavy draperies to secrete oneself behind, no little closets, no heavy chests or armoires to huddle in. The closets were capacious but shallow, mostly rebuilt when the Kingsolvers moved in, nicely equipped with plastic-coated steel racks and drawers and hanging rods, so that everything could be seen and reached easily.

The library and the living room were unoccupied; likewise the portal and the dining room. Nobody home. The person with the gun had already looked in the pastures and the hay shed and the woodshed and each of the guest houses. There had been only a slight chance she had hidden herself in one of the guest houses, but the person with the gun had made sure. Just in case any one of them had been left open. Guests tended to be careless here in the country.

But she had not been in a guest house and she could not drive a car. Nor had she hidden in a car, for they had been searched as well. Which left only two possibilities. She had left the place on foot, going down through the bosque, or she was hiding in the only place that remained to be searched. Calling her name had evoked no response, and that in itself told the person with the gun something. If she had not been suspicious, she would have answered. If she was suspicious, she was dangerous.

Well. McClintock had always been dangerous. From the first day, she had been dangerous. From the first day, she had been on the list to be disposed of. And now was the time to do it. The gun belonged to J.Q. She had had it under her pillow. So she would fall, or slip—crutches were clumsy devices—shooting herself accidentally in the process.

The person with the gun stepped into the kitchen and gave it a quick look-over. The four bottles of wine lying unopened on the kitchen shelf attested to the fact that Shirley probably knew about the remaining hiding place. It had undoubtedly been mentioned. She would remember that. The damned woman remembered too damned much.

The person with the gun returned to the door of the butler's pantry, which was ever so slightly ajar. It hadn't been that way an hour ago, so someone had been here in the interim. The door opened at the touch of a hand. The light was on inside. The light hadn't been on an hour ago, either. But if Shirley McClintock had wanted to go down those dark cellar stairs without breaking her neck, she'd have let the light on. There was a light down below, but she wouldn't have known that. She wasn't familiar with the place. She wouldn't know that the switch for the cellar light was hidden under a shelf on the right-hand wall of the pantry, where it couldn't possibly be found unless one already knew it was there. The switch was an afterthought, as were so many things at the Rancho de Valle. Afterthoughts. Things tacked on later, channels broken into mud walls and wires run in them, wires that frayed and started fires, or pipes laid in them, pipes that leaked and melted mud walls like sugar! Slovenly construction done by slovenly people. Endless maintenance that never was done with!

The rug was slightly askew, not quite hiding the trapdoor. And the trapdoor itself was unbolted. Of course, it couldn't be bolted from inside. Not even someone as tall as Ms. McClintock could manage that. Not even someone as irritating as Ms. McClintock. She had had to leave the door unbolted when she went below, gambling that her pursuer didn't know about the place.

A bad gamble.

The door came up easily. Dark down there, but even dim as it was, the disarranged cartons were visible. They'd been pulled closer to the steps, away from the cellar wall. Someone was down there behind them. Someone had found a hiding place. Unfortunately, it was a hiding place that bullets could not reach without doing a great deal of damage to what was in the cartons themselves.

Damn the woman.

Fingers found the switch under the shelf to the right and flicked it back and forth, but no light came on below. It had burned out. Or she had put it out. Which meant actually going down there to get a clear shot at her. Which meant blood on the cellar floor and walls, where it might be noticed, where it would be hard to explain. Though perhaps not. Provided there was only one shot. People did not accidentally shoot themselves more than once. . . .

Never mind. First things first. Worry about the blood later.

One foot on the top step. The other foot down, the person with the gun bending, peering. Another step down, and another.

"Come out of there! Or I'll shoot you through the boxes!"

No reply. Well, she knew it was an idle threat.

"Damn it, come out of there!" Down the last few steps with a rush.

Then a crash, a slamming, a smell of dust, and sudden darkness. Total darkness except for a thin gray light from the ventilator. And above, the butler's pantry, the sound of the bolt on the trapdoor being firmly driven home.

Gerri Olivarez arrived at the Rancho del Valle driveway coincident with a Wagoneer being driven at a highly unsafe speed coming from the opposite direction. The two cars narrowly avoided disaster, as one pursued the other down the drive toward the parking area. A third car turned in immediately after Gerri's. Simultaneously five persons erupted from vehicles in the parking area: J.Q., Xanthy, Allison, Gerri, and George Chalmers, who was possibly the only calm one among them.

Angry words were aborted when they heard Shirley yelling through the open back door.

"Help!" she was screaming. "Will you get in here and help!"

They found her standing on the trapdoor in the middle of the butler's pantry, one leg or one crutch at each corner, all her weight bearing down as she watched dust clouds rising. The trapdoor was being repeatedly hammered and heaved at from below.

"In a minute there'll be bullets coming through the floor!" she cried in a penetrating whisper. "Your gun's down there,

J.Q. It's fully loaded, and the hinges on the door are starting to give."

"Who's down there?" asked Chalmers.

"Your kidnapper. Among other things," she snarled. "Can you find something heavy to put on this door? Please!"

J.Q. and Chalmers scrambled outside and returned with the heavy woodbox that normally sat by the back door. Shirley moved over with a grunt of thanks as they shoved it over the trapdoor and set about filling it with armloads of the wood they had dumped from it. While they finished this bulletproof barrier, Shirley staggered into the kitchen and dropped into a chair. After a time, the thudding from below subsided, and while J.Q. kept his eyes on the trapdoor, George Chalmers joined the others who were gathered around Shirley in the kitchen.

She looked up at them with a white face. "God," she said reverently. "I have never been so scared."

"What's been going on?" demanded Chalmers.

"George, please get on the phone and get a search warrant or whatever you have to have to search a rental unit down the road a piece. J.Q. knows where it is. Get some people there right now, before somebody gets suspicious and runs for it."

"What am I looking for?"

"The Franklin baby. Maybe the other baby, too, but I doubt it."

"What's happening?" Gerri breathed.

"Everything sort of came together all at once," Shirley said. "Allison, honey, put on some water, will you? I need something hot and sugary. I actually feel faint. Never fainted in my life, but I guess this is what it feels like. I'm shaking. I feel sick to my stomach. I'm sweating. . . ."

George held up the phone. "No dial tone."

"Damn," she said. "I don't think he would have cut it. Probably just disconnected it. Don't you have a phone in your car?"

He left. J.Q. came to the kitchen door, where he gestured

over his shoulder and demanded angrily, "Can you explain all this?"

"Yes, please," begged Xanthy, taking Shirley's trembling hand in her own. "Tell us, Shirley."

For a moment, she couldn't get the words out. Then they came in a rush.

"One or two people have been stealing pots from a grave site or ancient settlement here in New Mexico, or maybe even over in Arizona, and they've been stashing them in a nice weather-tight cave over on Blue Mesa. The people who steal them are paid off by another person, the chief thief. Chief thief sells the pots a few at a time to galleries here and there and everywhere, and chief thief gets a lot of money for them.

"Now, it happens, one of the persons doing the actual stealing was Tonio Grant. He works in construction, sometimes, but when there's no work, he's at loose ends. He has no compunction about stealing from the pueblo people. He stashes the stuff at Blue Mesa, which he can see from his own front window, and he fetches and carries to and from in his pickup truck as needed by chief thief.

"Recently, however, things have been getting a little hot for pot stealers and sellers, and the chief thief has decided to sell out his stock and move on before he is caught at it. Just about this time, however, the chief thief sees a chance to make an additional twenty or thirty thousand when he hears Tonio griping about his wife, Emelia, having another baby. Her people aren't going to take care of any more babies. Another baby is going to be more trouble and expense. It's fine keeping a woman pregnant, Tonio believes, but it's tough to provide for all the resultant children!"

"Bastard," muttered Gerri Olivares.

Shirley nodded weakly. "I'm extrapolating, of course. Probably oversimplifying. Anyhow, this may be idle chitchat so far as Tonio is concerned, but the chief thief sees it as opportunity knocking. He says he can get maybe ten thousand dollars for Tonio if he'll let the baby be adopted by some nice people. Tonio broaches this to Emelia, and when Emelia worries about what her people will think, Tonio arranges to have it taken from the hospital by someone he knows, a man named Max Benez, who steals the baby with the help of a cleaning woman whose name, bet you anything, is Helga something or other.''

"How in hell would you know that?'' J.Q. demanded.

She shrugged. "Someone named Helga something or other didn't clean my room while I was hospitalized, and the supervisory person made quite a point of it. If I had seen Helga before, under suspicious circumstances, Helga might well have not wanted to come into my room. Anyhow, the baby stealing goes off as planned, except for two little problems. The first one is that both April Shaour and I saw something we shouldn't. What I saw was the woman. At the time I saw the woman, she may have had the baby in the laundry basket. Though I neither saw it nor heard it, she may think I did.

"What do you think April saw?'' whispered Allison.

"I think probably Helga went in the ladies' room, Max went there to help her, and April walked in on them. So she saw them together with the baby, first at the hospital, then here. And they, meantime, had made a serious mistake. Helga was so rattled and inexperienced, she hadn't bothered to check the baby's identity, she'd just grabbed the only boy baby available. So when they got here is probably the first anybody knew they had the wrong baby. They tell the chief thief, hey, we've got the wrong kid.''

"So your chief thief decides to hold the baby for ransom,'' said Xanthy.

"Right. Chief thief has Tonio get the right baby, and he pays him off. Tonio goes out and buys a new truck and a color TV. Chief thief takes Emelia's baby to Albuquerque or Santa Fe or wherever, and sells him, probably to some lawyer who makes a business of providing babies to childless couples. Meantime Max and Helga are told to hold on to the wrong baby, and a ransom note is written. There's some delay there, because chief thief has to figure out some fool-proof way of getting the money without being caught. Chalmers will no doubt enlighten us. So. The chief thief delivers the ransom note and, in passing, has a try at killing me because Helga is hysterically sure that I saw or heard the baby when I saw her. Chief thief still needs Helga, and he doesn't want anybody talking about her because Helga and Max are taking care of the baby turnabout, so they can both show up for work, at least part of the time, and they can both be at their homes part of the time. All this to avert suspicion.''

Xanthy wordlessly handed Shirley a steaming cup of well-sugared tea, which she gulped greedily, despite its heat, before going on.

''Meantime, however, there is a hellacious rain which brings down a rockfall out at Blue Mesa, requiring that the pots stored there be moved, at least temporarily. Tonio and a helper see J.Q. and Shaour out there, which only serves to increase fear and suspicion on the chief thief's part. Tonio puts the pots in Super-Soft toilet paper cartons and takes them to his place, where he stacks them in the carport. J.Q. and I saw them there when we went out there Monday. Meantime Emelia was getting to be a liability. She's been talking too much and making threatening noises, and the chief thief is worried about her keeping her mouth shut, so either chief thief gives Tonio some reason to take off for Mexico and stay there, or chief thief plans to kill them both but only finds Emelia at home. Chief thief, I believe, was probably taught to slit throats at one time or another. Chief thief probably meant to pick up the pots at the time of the murder, but for some reason didn't. That part I cannot figure out.''

Chalmers returned. ''Everything's in hand. I need the address where you think these people are.''

J.Q. took out his notebook, tore off a sheet, and handed it to Chalmers. ''Address, license number of the car I saw, which may be theirs, and the individual unit the car was parked outside of. If I were you, I'd make the warrant fairly broad. There are six or seven units at this place, and they may actually be in any one of them. Or they could be going somewhere else in the car.''

"Or," said Shirley wearily, "they may not be there at all, but I'm pretty sure who's involved, so we can find them one way or another.''

Chalmers left again.

Allison asked in a fretful voice, "I'm being dumb, probably, but who is it down there under the box?''

"Harry Fielding," said Xanthy, as J.Q. nodded seriously from the sidelines. "Who else?''

"I can't figure out why it took me so long," Shirley said, setting the cup down with a shaking hand. "I knew he had a varmint gun. Sarah told me he shot coyotes and raccoons. He's ex-military, possibly a sharpshooter. He knew where we were going that Sunday afternoon. He had every reason to get rid of April, and his second shot may have been his first effort to get rid of me.''

"I told you," said Gerri. "I told you Emelia would not sell her baby. I told you our women do not do that.''

Shirley didn't contradict her. Emelia might not have done that on her own, but she had gone along with it. Of course, Tonio may have given her no choice.

"Does Sarah know?" asked Xanthy, softly.

Shirley shook her head. "My best guess is she knows nothing about it at all. Nothing about any of it. She doesn't know about Tonio and Harry working together after Tonio left here. She doesn't know about the pots. She doesn't know that it was Harry that set up the sale of Emelia's baby—and she's not suspicious of the fact he didn't want her talking to Emelia about it in public. She believes Harry suggested moving because he wanted to be closer to their children. And he told her a tale to make her think the money was coming from his sale of some land in Albuquerque. I'll bet there never was any land.''

"How are you going to get him out of there?" Allison asked.

"I imagine Mr. Chalmers will have help arriving pretty soon now. If I were doing it, I'd have Harry put the gun out through the ventilator, then I'd open the door and let him out. And take him away."

Everyone sighed, all at once. Gerri stood up, getting ready to leave. Xanthy shook her head. Allison put her arms around Shirley and hugged her.

"I'm so glad nothing happened to you," she said. "Oh, Shirley, we thought . . . we thought maybe you were dead."

"How did you get him down there in the first place?" J.Q. asked.

"I unscrewed the bulb in the cellar and moved the cartons out, so he'd think I was hiding behind them. I left the trap-door unbolted, of course, and the rug askew. If he'd looked in the broom closet first, I was dead, because that's where I was, shaking like a leaf. It wasn't easy getting up inside that broom closet on crutches. I was counting on his thinking I couldn't do it, and I damn near didn't! I was praying he'd go down the steps by himself; I couldn't hit him with anything. There was no room in there to swing a crutch, and there was nothing else around except a frying pan. I had it with me as a last resort."

"He might have shot you!"

"He wouldn't shoot through cartons containing a hundred thousand dollars worth of pots."

"Even though he had half a million dollars worth of baby down the road!" said J.Q.

"Sarah told me he was money-hungry," Shirley sighed. "She also told me they'd been doing better lately. I wonder what she attributed that to."

"I feel so sorry for her," Allison said, wiping tears. "I feel so sorry for her. Finding out about him."

Allison had more reason than most to know how that felt. They all fell silent, feeling sorry for Sarah, except perhaps for Gerri, who was feeling sorrier for Clara and the little boys.

The phone rang. Shirley picked it up without thinking, listened, said, "This is she," listened again, then hung up.

"What!" demanded J.Q.

"Dr. Humphrey doesn't have HIV," she said in an expressionless voice. "Nor does his friend. It seems rather an anticlimax."

Xanthy and Allison looked a question at each other. J.Q. started to chuckle. Shirley looked at her hands, refusing to let him see her smile. Her effort was interrupted by the voice of Winston Kingsolver, approaching from the dining room.

"And this is the kitchen," he cried, smiling broadly and shepherding two stumpy men before him. "Hello, all! May I introduce the Bellows brothers, Theo and Bartimus, real estate appraisers. Shirley McClintock. John Quentin. Hello, Gerri, how nice to see you! By the way, what's all that mess of firewood doing in the pantry?"

Shirley went back to her room before Harry Fielding was extricated from the cellar. Only J.Q. watched his removal. Shirley had no taste for it, and Xanthy was trying to figure out what she was going to tell Sarah, who hadn't yet returned from having her hair done. The pots, in their dusty cartons, were removed and taken away as evidence.

When Sarah came home, Xanthy gritted her teeth and went to the Fieldings' quarters to tell her what had happened. Shortly thereafter, George Chalmers returned to say the quasi motel down the road had yielded Helga Stomfort and the Franklin baby, but no Max Benez. Max, Helga had weepingly told her interrogators, had followed his half-brother, Tonio Grant, back to Mexico even though he had promised to marry her and set up a little business with the proceeds of their joint venture. The car belonged to Max's cousin from Española. Max had borrowed it because the almost accident as they were leaving the hospital had scared him. The driver of the other car had yelled at him and given him the finger, making Max afraid that someone might be looking for the truck.

The FBI took jurisdiction over the search for Emelia's baby boy. Though Helga protested that she would never have taken any baby if the parents hadn't agreed to let him go, the theft of any baby was kidnapping so far as George A. Chalmers and George A. Chalmers's boss were concerned.

The Franklins were said to be grateful.

Shirley curled up and slept for twenty hours straight.

She was wakened at noon on Wednesday by J.Q. marching in behind a huge bouquet of flowers and stumbling over the high threshold.

"Where did those come from?" she asked sleepily.

"George Z. Chalmers," he replied. "He brought them himself. The card says thank you for his getting a good night's sleep last night, in more ways than one. Also, he says the boxes out at Emelia's contain other pots, so you were probably right. Harry had moved some of them, probably all he had room for in whatever he was driving, and he was just waiting for the opportunity to get the others. Chalmers also says the Franklins want to call upon us to thank you personally."

"Isn't that nice." She yawned, rubbed her eyes, and looked at her watch. "Though I think I can do without any personal thanks. Good Lord, look at the time."

"There's no reason whatsoever to look at the time. If you're hungry, Xanthy says she'll fix something for you. If you want to stay in bed all day, that's fine with everyone."

"I don't think I do," she said doubtfully. "Though that sleep felt good. I must have been worn-out."

"Worried, mostly," he said. "Winston said to tell you good-bye. He went back to Chicago this morning. He says he'll call you tomorrow to talk a possible deal."

"Only if you're interested," she said firmly. "Only if you and Allison would like it."

He seated himself across from her bed, giving her a level look. "Who am I to fight fate?"

She shifted uncomfortably. "I don't know what you mean, fate."

"We have in the past commented upon your being an excess finder of dead bodies."

She snorted. They had indeed commented upon that fact. J.Q. quoted probability theory at her to explain it. Shirley herself thought fate had it in for her.

"Since you are fated to be an excess finder of dead bodies, and since that fated activity has either followed or led you here, and since your finding of dead bodies was instrumental in facilitating this change in our lives, I consider it fated."

"How long have you been practicing that speech?" she asked.

"Since shaving this morning. Or partially shaving, I should say. I have decided to grow a beard."

She peered at him. "You do look a little scruffy. Are you going for a goatee?"

"It's the local look. Buffalo Bill et al."

She sighed. "How's Sarah?"

"About as one would imagine. She doesn't believe Harry's guilty of anything. She's lived with this man most of her life, and she doesn't believe it."

"Did he shoot April?"

"He's got the right kind of gun and the right kind of ammunition. They may not be able to prove it. They've gone back up the trail with metal detectors, trying again to find the bullet."

"Poor April. Shaour seemed so careless of her that Xanthy and I wondered if she was really Shaour's daughter. Not that it was any of our business, and not that we could ever have found out, but it seems a pity that he didn't mourn her, a pity they may never prove who killed her."

"You and I are morally certain Harry killed her, whether they can prove it or not, and they do think they can prove he killed Emelia."

"How?"

"He was so sure he was above suspicion, he kept the knife he did it with. It's got traces of her blood on it and his fingerprints all over it."

"Were his fingerprints out at Emelia's?"

"Not in the blood, if that's what you mean. That smear in the kitchen was from his clothes. No, he left no prints there, but they were all over the knife."

"Was I right? Had he been taught to slit throats?"

"I don't know. But Xanthy says their quarters have stacks of magazines. *Soldier of Fortune. Mercenary Monthly.* Lots of military hardware, too. He had a different image of himself than other people had of him."

"I know. I thought he was just a cheery guy, rather gregarious, not too sensitive to nuance. Beer-drinking buddy type. Better if Sarah goes to be with her children."

"She's going to. She can't or won't tell the police anything about anything, and they can't force her to. They're letting her go to her daughter's today."

"Poor Sarah. What's Winston going to do without a manager?"

"He says he'll talk to you about that tomorrow. I think he hopes you're going to stay."

"Stay. Now? Not go home at all?"

"If you stay here, I can see to moving, Shirley. Or vice versa."

"Will Kingsolver want his furniture?"

"He says not. Except for a few keepsakes, the places goes as is."

"What would we do with our furniture?"

"Bring it down. Some of it is better than some of the stuff here. The bedroom Allison and Xanthy have been staying in is . . . fluffy. Allison would rather have her own furniture,

229

I'm sure. We can use ours where we want it. Sell whatever's left over."

"The ranch machines. The tractor. The—"

"Some of it would be useful here. Sell the rest."

"You've got an answer for everything."

He shrugged. "It's the same answer for everything. Keep what you want, sell the rest. You've got a buyer for the place in Colorado. You'll probably want to work out some kind of a trade for this place. You know that, I know it, Winston knows it."

"My books. And you've got a lot of books."

"A lot of what's in the shelves here is junk. Stacks of old magazines. Old textbooks. I looked in the cupboards. They've got twenty years of junk in them. Clear out the junk, there's room for our books." He leaned forward to take her hands in his own. "Shirley, there's room for everything you treasure here, everything but the cows, and you've told me yourself, you'd already almost decided to let the cows go. There are places to ride here. There's scenery that can leave you speechless. The culture is fascinating. I've seen you be fascinated by it. Maybe it's time, for both of us, all three of us."

"You're saying you're willing to move."

"I'm willing. Allison is willing. Allison, as a matter of fact, thinks it would be fun."

"I don't know. . . ." she murmured.

"I told you before, some morning you'll wake up with your mind made up. All we want you to know, Allison and I, is that you have our blessing."

"Thank you, J.Q.," she said softly. "I've been . . . very hopeless lately."

"We know that. That's one reason that makes us think change is a good idea. It presents challenges. It demands new answers. It won't let you sit on your behind and mutter old truths."

"Do I do that?"

He shrugged. "About average."

"How disgustingly dull!"

"Another thing. Xanthy wants you to think about letting her rent the Fieldings' quarters on a year-round basis."

"She wants to move! I don't believe it."

"No, I think she wants to visit, ad lib. I think she's been having the same problem you've had."

"Sadness? Well, we're both . . . ah, older women, J.Q. We remember too much. When things change a lot during your lifetime, it leaves you . . . feeling sad. Feeling loss. You can crawl in a hole somewhere and hide from life. Or spend energy fruitlessly, frustratingly, trying to force things to change back! Like whoever it was, screaming at the tide! Or you can change with things . . . go with it, as they say."

"That's my McClintock," he said, patting her again. He got up and went to the door. "You make up your mind."

When he had gone, she went to the window and looked out. Canyons and mesas, pillars and buttes, dramatic in any light, changeable as cloud. Changeable. A very different view. A very different perspective. Something everyone needed. From time to time.

Maybe it had been fated. In which case . . . who was she to fight it?

About the Author

B.J. Oliphant, who is also A.J. Orde and bestselling science-fiction writer Sheri Tepper, lives on a ranch in Santa Fe, New Mexico. This is her fourth Shirley McClintock mystery for Gold Medal.